Vampires Don't

A. C. Wright

To the Betallion,

(There's no taking the name back now! It's in print!)

Thank you for your constant support. Thank you for keeping me company until the wee hours of the morning and thank you for your endless patience. My life and my work would be so much harder and duller without you!

To my readers,

As usual, it's not my fault. Fairytales, folklore and stories in general are really like that.

And thank you very much for your support too! Know that whether I saw you in person or you bought this online, whether you love it or even if you hate it, I appreciate that you gave me a chance and made the effort to read my work.

Once upon a time, the universe was naught but the chaos of raw magic. But where there is magic there is life. Born from the chaos was the Goddess Gaia, the First One. The goddess rejoiced in the chaos. In her joy, she danced, and the chaos was whipped up into balls and stars and ribbons. This made her smile, and laughing, she continued to dance, but eventually, she grew tired, and slept.

When she awoke, she found the chaos had died down, but in its place were new delights. Things burned, things shone, things grew... and she was no longer alone. Everywhere she looked, there were creatures that frolicked and played, as she did. But as she watched, she saw that they were not like her, after all. They were formed from clay and earth, not the pure energy that had spawned her. These clay creatures were weak and prone to destruction.

"I can do better."

Chapter 1:

The Stolen Pendant

Fairies didn't mess about when it came to naming things. They were the sort of people who called a spade a spade, although admittedly some of them called it a shovel. But when they named something, they named it well. The country was full of places called 'The Cave of Doom' or 'The Fountain of Death'. The Dark Forest was just such an aptly named place. Largely coniferous, the towering pine trees blocked out most of the sunlight. The persistent drizzle was adding to the murk. All kinds of nasty beasties lived in here, and like the majority of the populace, they were magical. Fairyland had a mana spring beneath it, which caused the evolution of all kinds of unusual flora and fauna, most of it dangerous. Fairies could handle such things easily as long as they kept their wits about them. The most dangerous thing a fairy could encounter was another fairy . . .

The young king made his way through the forest, using the dripping, shrieking canopy for cover. The dark leaves of the conifer-like trees and the general gloom of the place hid him from view and the racket its denizens were making masked any noise he made. His night blue, silk shirt stuck to his skin thanks to the moisture-laden air but suitable clothing had not been a priority when he'd left the palace. There'd been no time to get a weather forecast. He'd just grabbed the sword and got out.

He darted from tree to tree. Just because he couldn't be seen from the air didn't mean there weren't enemies already inside the forest. He'd hidden the sword. That was the important thing. If he got caught, he could do something about it. But if that woman got hold of the sword too . . . If only the Light Guard had held out a little longer, he could have done this better. But then, that was how these things worked. You were handed a mysterious artefact and instructed not to hand it over to anyone and it wasn't until later that you found out it was the key to destroying the universe or whatever. Usually right after you'd handed it over to someone. Mysterious objects weren't supposed to come with a manual or an explanation, that would spoil all the fun. He *had* cheated a bit by handing it to a family member, but that didn't count. His cousin didn't know anything about the sword or what it meant. The problem was that with both the pendant and the staff being in enemy hands, it wouldn't stay hidden for long. He could see the edge of the forest now; the moonlight pierced through the shadows like a spear, outlining the exit. He couldn't hear anything other than the squawking and whistling noises of the forest. That wasn't good. He had expected to hear battle. One of his platoons should have been here guarding the forest perimeter and he knew that the Wild Troopers were on his trail. Something was wrong. He sighed, attempted to unstick his clothing to no avail, and walked right out of the forest. There was a yell and he was seized by three enemy soldiers. Two of them grabbed his arms, the third grabbed his hair.

"All that skulking around for nothing," came a female voice. "Hold him up, I want to see the expression on his face." The soldier yanked his head back.

"Good afternoon Lady Lir," he greeted her pleasantly, ignoring his treatment. He gave her a toothy grin. She wrinkled her nose in disgust. Obviously that was not the expression she'd wanted to see. Good. An annoyed enemy was a careless enemy.

"Smug as ever," the woman said, narrowing her dark, grey eyes and sweeping her long, black hair over her shoulder. She was wearing the traditional attire for a fairy queen; a long, green dress, embroidered around the hems with silver and gold. "That's 'Your Majesty' to you, Tyrian." So she was trying to annoy him too. How dare she address him by his name alone! He ignored the slight;

"Ever aiming for higher titles, aren't we Lady Lir?"

"Where is the sword?" she demanded.

"It would be a bit pointless to have gone through all that trouble just to tell you, now wouldn't it?" he replied. The woman made an indignant noise.

"I changed my mind," she told the fairy soldiers. "I do not wish to look upon your insufferable visage any longer." She turned away.

"Come now Lady, where's the fun in winning if you don't play the game?" he continued. "You wouldn't be satisfied to pluck the crowns from our heads just like that, now would you?"

"This is no game," the queen hissed, spinning back around. She bent down so that her face was almost level with his. "If you and the others only understood that, I wouldn't be doing this. The people need to see how unworthy you all are. You don't deserve the three treasures, any of you."

"Are you saying *you* do?" Tyrian asked her. She bit her lip and her eyes flicked downwards, but then her sneer returned.

"I have the staff already," she said. "It was pathetic how easily I crushed the Light Guard. It's only a matter of time, now. Your resistance is pointless." Villain dialogue? When had she started doing that? He wondered if she even knew she was doing it. At least his tactics were working.

"Ah, so many things in life are pointless, are they not?" Tyrian replied, still smiling. The queen slapped him across the face with all her might. Ow. Villain actions, too. They were working all right. A bird screamed in the distance.

"We'll see how long you can keep up that attitude," Lir hissed. "It was foolish of you to come alone. It's exactly this kind of stupidity that pushed me this far."

"We must disagree on the definition of foolishness, Lir," he replied. He attempted to shrug, and winced as the soldiers tightened their grip. "It would have been amazingly stupid to hide something and tell an entire platoon where it is. Do have some sense."

"So you risked capture to hide it from me? How *noble* of you," she spat the word. "But it's too bad," -she pulled out a large green stone in the shape of a tear drop and brandished it at him-"as long as I have this, I will find it." The stone was attached to a golden chain from which it dangled tantalizingly in front of his face. "I will drag you all through this wretched forest until I find the door you sneaked it through and when I do-" There was another eagle-like scream, but now it was closer, and accompanied by others, rising over even the din of the nearby forest.

There was a flurry of feathers, and a harpy hit one of the guards straight in the back, causing him to let go. He unbalanced the other two guards as he turned round to fight the slashing, flapping thing off. Woman-shaped and sized, covered in thick, brown feathers with the wings and claws of an eagle, she was a good match for any fairy soldier. And she wasn't alone. Harpy after harpy plummeted down upon the Wild Realm soldiers, like a feathery, talon-filled rain. Tyrian wrenched himself free and snatched at the pendant in the queen's hand, ripping it from its delicate chain. He plunged forward, through the mass of warring fairy soldiers and harpies.

'So that's where my battalion went,' he thought to himself as he ran. 'Good old Aurelia, setting up a double ambush.' Nevertheless, he felt a twinge of annoyance. 'Whatever took her so long?'

"Seize him!" the queen screamed behind him. Several of her soldiers tried to obey, but the harpies made sure they regretted it, catching them in their backs and shoulders as they turned. But there were more fairies than harpies, and just as he thought he'd broken away from the scuffle, some of the fairies broke free and he was surrounded by enemy troops once more. There were five of them, too many for him to take on alone, and there would be more any minute-

"Hand over Her Majesty's pendant and you won't have to suffer," one of them commanded. Tyrian tutted.

"Confident, aren't you?" They had reason to be, of course. He tried to keep them all in his sight, but it was impossible. He knew the two he couldn't see were advancing on him, but there wasn't anything he could do about it. Now the guards he *could* see started to move forward-

"You're the one who's going to suffer!" a female voice yelled. Seconds later a yokai woman with brown and gold striped hair landed in the shrinking circle. Her fringe was long, partly covering her face, framing her malevolent, green eyes as she flexed long, silvery war-claws at the fairy soldiers. She was followed immediately by a black griffin, which landed on the other side of the king and screamed in the enemy's faces, driving them back.

"Aurelia, that was terribly cliché dialogue," Tyrian scolded her.

"Sorry Master Tyrian." She flashed him a grin, revealing a mouth full of pointed teeth. "I wanted to make a better entrance, but I was too busy trying to stop you getting your head chopped off." She hissed like a cat at the advancing guards, who were still deciding what to do about this turn of events, and unwilling to tackle the huge griffin that was pacing back and forth and threatening to pounce.

"What took you so long?" Tyrian complained, determined to get the subject off his chest.

"The thing about a great, big flock of harpies Master Tyrian," the woman began with a hint of impatience, "is that they're very easy to see. Not much of an ambush, right? So we had to go up *really* high. Took us a while to come down again, you know." The woman shrugged. "So what now?"

"Now, you will hand over my pendant," Lir commanded, pushing her way through the soldiers at Tyrian's back. She had several guards fending off the attacking harpies and a few more came forward to tackle the griffin.

"Now we run," Tyrian commanded, motioning for her to follow. They turned and sprinted, crashing through the guards in the front, leaving an enraged Lir to deal with the still battling harpies and the griffin.

"You got the pendant?!" Aurelia yelled as they ran. She slashed the face of a soldier that tried to bar their way and he fell aside, screaming.

"Yes, but I need to hide *it* too!" he yelled back. They finally shook off the straggling soldiers and continued to run, determined to put some distance between themselves and the enemy. He'd had a hard enough time deciding where to hide the sword, now he had to think up somewhere to put this blasted thing. Somewhere out of Lir's reach entirely would be best, but where? He glanced behind at the battlefield and swore. Lir's troops weren't as far away as he'd like. There was no time. He'd just have to go. Anywhere would do.

"I don't suppose you can look after the kingdom for a while?" he said. "Looks like I have to make another little trip."

"Right you are, Master Tyrian!" She looked behind her, skidded to a halt and spun round.

"What are you doing?" He almost fell as he forced himself to stop, turning and eyeing the pursuing troops.

"Oh, you know!" she shouted back. "The traditional 'faithful servant hangs back while their master gets away' thing. I'd say you need a distraction right now." She pulled off a salute. "Go! I'll see you later! Hide that thing good! I can't wait to see the look on Lir's face when she sees you've got away!"

"I'll be sad to miss it," Tyrian laughed. "See you later!" He gave her a nod, turned around and dashed off.

He ran on until he was sure he'd be out of sight. He could still hear faint screams in the distance, but his troops must be beating them back or they'd have been here by now. He found himself by a clear, placid lake. It was a desolate place, surrounded by sand, dust and thorn-covered trees. But the aesthetics of the scenery were unimportant. He had to find a door. It was impossible to go back to the one he'd used before, it was too far away, he'd have to double back around the Wild Troopers and in any case, hiding them both in the same place was just plain stupid. What was that saying humans had about putting all your eggs in one basket? Which was a stupid phrase, when he came to think about it. If you were collecting eggs, which was presumably the reason you had a basket, you wouldn't want to go messing about with lots of them. That would just make things more difficult.
It seemed to be safe enough to stop here and look.

"Now if I were a door, where would I be?" he wondered aloud. A raven perched on the nearest tree cawed;

"In a door frame!"

"Not helping!" he complained back at it. That was the problem with Otherworld doors. Normal doors were found in a door frame, certainly. But unless they were made specially, doors to other worlds were not. They were in trees, or on the reflection of a lake at sunset or in some really unforgiving cases, at the end of the rainbow. He'd almost missed a wedding thanks to *that* one. Blasted leprechauns, always making things difficult to find. You'd think if *they* invited you to *their* wedding it would be different, but oh no, everything had to be *traditional*. Looking down, he saw the pendant was glowing, ever so faintly. He lifted it up and it glowed a little brighter. He turned around to look at it without the sun in his eyes and the glow dimmed again.

"Hmm." Tyrian swung the pendant about in a circle, noting the degree of luminescence. "So that's how it works. I always wondered." He walked in the direction where the pendant glowed most fiercely and came to the tree the raven was perched on. Studying the trunk, he found a not so innocent-looking knot on it. It glowed in resonance with the pendant. He pushed it, and the door concealed there opened. He walked through it and immediately stepped on something cylindrical and metallic. He stumbled and planted his face on a brick wall. He swore and rubbed his nose. Hiding the pendant in his shirt, he looked around to get his bearings. The door had vanished. He poked the air where it had been. Nothing. Clearly the return door was not here, if indeed there was a return door at all. That was rather inconvenient, but it was generally how Otherworld doors worked and at least it meant that he couldn't be easily traced. Otherworld doors could usually only be used if you knew they were there, and he doubted that Lir would risk sending her troops somewhere they'd get stuck when she had the Dark Army and the remains of the Light Guard to fight.

He was stood in an alleyway, between what he assumed were two houses. The bricks were red, or at least they were supposed to be; sun and smoke had turned them a dirty orange. He kicked aside the can he had tripped on. The alley was strewn with rubbish; there were a few black bags piled on one side, and one had burst, sending cans, banana peel, used teabags and brightly-coloured wrappers everywhere.

He jumped when someone walked right past the mouth of the alleyway. He breathed a sigh of relief when he realised they'd walked right by, but then there was another, and another . . . Pressing himself against the brickwork in the shadow of a tall, plastic box, he peered out and watched. After a few minutes, it became clear that the people – the *humans*, he realised with delight– passing by were paying the alleyway no mind at all. He had a sneaking suspicion that he knew where he was. He walked confidently out of the alleyway and blinked in the sunlight, which flashed off the cars as they sped past. He grinned to himself. He was right.

This was Earth.

This was *perfect*.

* * * * *

Lucinda walked along her usual route to school for the first time in nearly seven weeks. School. Ugh. She supposed the summer holidays had to end eventually. Too bad this was no day to be in school. The sun was shining, a cool breeze was blowing, birds were singing. It was a day for picnicking by a gurgling stream, a day for skipping through the woods, a day for
rescuing damsels in distress or fighting dragons even, probably at the same time. Granted, those last two options were not what your average schoolgirl would consider a good activity for sunny weather, but Lucinda Martin did not exactly have the hobbies of an average schoolgirl. And that was true even *before* she'd got a part-time job as a prince and started to spend all her free time fighting monsters and bringing down evil tyrants. Lucinda went out of her way to avoid being 'normal'. That was another reason she hated school. Everyone and everything there was so normal and boring. The upside, she thought as she plodded along staring into the middle distance, was that this would be her last year of high school. At least that was something. She'd be sixteen soon. College would probably be a lot more interesting.
With a jolt, Lucinda realised that she'd been going the wrong way. The whole of the summer holidays,

except for the few weeks she had stayed in America, her daily routine had been to head to work. Whether she'd been needed at work or not had been of no consequence. When you can take a walk in an enchanted forest, learn how to make an instant freezing potion or spend the night in an eldritch castle why would you bother spending summer at home on dull, old Earth? Her feet had automatically taken her the way she took to work, and she was almost the whole way there. That wasn't good. She'd been understandably loathe to set out and wasn't doing great for time. She turned around and headed the right way.

Then she heard the argument.

There were two voices; a grown man, who had what she thought of as a 'posh voice' and a girl, who sounded like a typical teenager, considerably less posh, and about her age. It was coming from the park, which she was currently walking parallel to, along the road. Lucinda considered her next move. It sounded serious. The girl didn't want to do something or other, and the man was being quite insistent. It might be a misunderstanding; maybe it was just a father and a daughter, having more or less the same argument she'd had with her parents this morning about school? Lucinda sighed. She was going to be late, but she couldn't call herself a prince if she wasn't going to act like one in this world too. She hurried along the road towards the park entrance and went through the gate.

She hadn't gone very far in before she spotted them, a man in a blue shirt and dark trousers with black hair, and a girl with short brown hair, wearing the same blue and gold school uniform that Lucinda was wearing. The man's shirt looked like the night sky; it was decorated with silver stars.

"Look, this isn't how this is supposed to go!" the man complained, sounding half way between annoyed and desperate.

"I don't care how it's *supposed* to go," the girl retorted, "I'm not taking that thing and you can't make me! It's probably full of drugs, I should report you to the police right now!"

"This is no way to behave at all," the man complained, frowning. "You're supposed to accept mysterious objects without pause and then worry about them later. Please, I don't have much time and this is important!" Lucinda, having realised that wading into a fight in a deserted park on Earth, where stories don't work properly, was a bad idea, nevertheless took a deep breath and strode towards the couple as boldly as she dared. She called out, feeling a lot less confident than she sounded;

"What's going on here? Is there a problem?" The girl gave her a contemptuous look before glaring at the man again. He pushed the hair out his eyes;

"Yes, there's a problem!" he replied, sounding more huffed than angry. "It's of the utmost importance that I hand this pendant over to someone for safekeeping, but this lady here refuses to take it! This is *not* the proper behaviour for this situation." Lucinda blinked. This *was* Earth, wasn't it? She stared at the man. There was something off about him, but she couldn't quite put her finger on it. He looked like he was from the Far East, but his accent was British. That was nothing unusual. What *did* strike her were his violet eyes. They were possible, or so she'd read somewhere, but very rare. It wasn't that, though. There was something strangely familiar about his behaviour.

"I'll take it," she replied, holding out her hand. The man breathed a sigh of relief. He handed over a heavy, green stone, about half the size of her hand.

"Thank goodness *somebody* knows the proper protocol." His face fell and his voice took on a serious edge. "You mustn't hand it over to anyone and you should keep it a secret. Understood? It's very important."

"What's so important and secret about it?" the brown-haired girl asked him, folding her arms. "Is it valuable? Why are you giving it away?"

"Don't ask such silly questions, I can't go telling you, can I?" the man replied. To Lucinda he said, "You'll do as I ask?" Lucinda nodded, but she couldn't help herself;

"It really doesn't have drugs in it though, right?"

"There's no medicine in it whatsoever," he confirmed, sounding slightly baffled. "Now I really must be off." He flashed her a toothy grin and disappeared. It was a bit *too* toothy. Lucinda jumped. *That* wasn't the species she'd thought he was *at all*.

"Freaking weirdo, now I'm lost *and* late," the girl complained, striding off down the path. Lucinda stashed the mysterious green thing in her bag and looked at her watch. She swore. They were both late.

"This way!" she said, hoisting up her school bag. "We might make it if we run!"

Lucinda was certain the girl had followed her, but she disappeared as soon as they were through the school gates. She slipped into the assembly hall and sat on the end of the front row. It was full of first years, who looked terrified enough as it was, without a fifth year looming over them. The nearest two glanced over at her before looking back at the front hurriedly as the headmaster coughed and gave Lucinda a meaningful look. She hadn't missed too much, just the messing about before the real speech began. It was the usual stuff. First years, high school is going to be wonderful, second years welcome back, third years, ooh this is a terribly important year, and so on. Lucinda got bored somewhere around 'New students, we welcome you to this school-' and her mind wandered to the strange man from the park. She could have *sworn* he was a fairy. He hadn't had pointy ears and he hadn't been a small twinkly thing, but Lucinda was wise to that. Her best friend Erlina was a fairy. A fairy princess in fact - the most fairy-like kind of fairy you could get, story-wise. She too had often expressed distaste and even outright anger that people and events on Earth just didn't behave like they did in Fairyland and the rest of the Otherworlds. But . . . his teeth were *not* fairy teeth. She knew someone else with teeth like that, and 'fairy' would be the last description they called to mind. Perhaps that was part of the disguise. She wondered what the green stone was. It hadn't looked particularly special, but magical objects often didn't. It was always the unobtrusive wooden spoon that granted eternal life, whereas any bejewelled masterpiece was probably a trap or at the very least a highly impractical waste of rubies. Oh well. She'd find out soon enough. That was how stories *worked*. Of course, that did mean that something bad was going to happen. Whenever you were handed a mysterious object with an unfathomable purpose all manner of nasty things came out of the woodwork, mostly intent on stealing said object and quite likely also intent on leaving your corpse   in a ditch. But that was okay. Sort of. She had friends who knew how to deal with that stuff.

The assembly had dragged on forever, but it was finally over. The students were called out of the assembly hall class by class. Lucinda had to scoot out of the way, as the classes were being called in order and she was in one of the last ones. Eventually, her form was called and she followed her classmates out.

"Hi Lucinda," came a voice from behind her. She turned to see Shu smiling at her.

"Hi Shu," she responded. "How are you? Did you have a good summer?" Shu had made her acquaintance last year, shortly after she arrived. They didn't have that much in common and they didn't hang out outside of school, but they sat together in some classes and they got along well enough.

"Not bad, not bad," Shu replied. "I spent the summer with my grandparents in China. It was a lot of fun. I only get to see them twice a year, and at New Year's the time is so short, so seeing them for a few weeks in summer is great." She laughed. "I got put to work though! I spent a lot of the last few weeks feeding chickens."

"Oh, they live on a farm, don't they?" Lucinda asked.

"Yeah, Grandma Zhou does, anyway," Shu confirmed. "My other grandparents live elsewhere."

"Sounds like you had a nice summer." Lucinda smiled.

"How was yours?" Shu asked. She tilted her head to one side.

"Oh, not bad," Lucinda answered. "I was put to work too, only in my case, by my boss. She's kind of allowed!" Both girls laughed.

"What sort of work do you do, anyway?" Shu asked curiously. "I'm sure I've seen you around town in a red suit . . ?" Lucinda gave a nervous laugh this time.

"Oh, yeah," she responded. "That's a work thing. I have to dress up a lot. That's er, that's mostly what work is about. Dressing up."

"I see," Shu mused. "Sounds interesting. Maybe I should come visit you there, sometime?"

"Oh, er," Lucinda faltered. "Maybe. I don't know if my boss would be happy about it, though-"

"All right, all right," the teacher boomed, quelling the students' chatter. He was a new teacher, young, with short black hair and a crisp white shirt. "Sit down. I'm sure you can all catch up during break. Now, we have a new student this year, Rina Walker." He indicated a girl sat towards the back of the class. Lucinda turned to look. It was the girl from this morning. "Would you like to introduce yourself, Rina?"

"No," the girl shook her head and hunched up a little. "I moved here in the summer, that's about it."

"Oh. Well," the teacher hesitated, caught off guard. "I suppose it's not great to get so much attention on your first day." He chose to ignore Rina's obstinacy and plunged on, "Right then. Here are your timetables, come and get them as I call your names-"

Lucinda's first class was maths. It was her most hated subject and a terrible way to start a new school year. The class was even more boring than the assembly and she couldn't focus on the problems at all. Why did they expect people to be able to do something like maths first thing on a Monday morning? By the end of the lesson she would have quite liked to see whoever drew up her timetable and give them a good talking to.

Finally it was over and time for the morning break. Her classmates had been equally as bored, and they rushed to the door. As she stood up to pack her things, she was knocked hard by a careless student; her bag fell from the table and her books and pencils went everywhere. She cursed and knelt to pick them up, hindered by the students who were in too much of a hurry to stop and help. Shu stopped though; she started to gather up Lucinda's books and made a rude gesture at a girl who stepped on one. Lucinda tutted as she chased a pencil right across the floor. She banged her head on another table as she tried to stand up and it was then she noticed that Rina was helping too.

"Is that everything?" she asked, handing Lucinda a few errant pens.

"I think so," Lucinda replied, taking them. "Thanks."

"Right then." Rina picked up her bag without another word and left. She hadn't said anything before she'd left this morning, either. Lucinda stared after her.

"Is it just me, or she a bit weird?" she wondered aloud. Shu snorted.

"Because you're totally not," she retorted.

"Fair point," Lucinda conceded, rifling around in

her bag. She opened it to take a closer look inside. Then she glanced at the floor.

"Right, what have you got next then?" Shu asked.

"German . . . I think," Lucinda replied, distracted.

"Oh, me too. I guess we have the same schedule?" Lucinda tipped her bag out onto the desk.

"Something wrong?" Shu asked.

"It's gone," Lucinda muttered. She got down on her hands and knees and scanned the floor, looking under the cupboards and the teacher's desk. But it was no use. The green pendant had vanished.

From her own magic Gaia birthed three children. Unlike the clay things they were strong and vibrant.

The first child was dark as the chaos from which she had come. She called him Night. The second child was radiant as the brightest star. She called her Day. The third child was all the colours of the earth. She called her Nature.

Gaia found that birthing the children had weakened her, and she could not see everything as she had before. So she took her eyes and threw them into the sky, as the sun and moon. Now she could see all again. Concerned for the clay things, she bade the children watch over them and keep order. She had Day and Night regulate the darkness and light and bade Nature manage the earth. But it was to no avail. Despite their care, the weak clay still crumbled easily.

"I can do better."

Chapter 2:

Not Another One!

Tyrian found a quiet spot and plonked himself down on a bench in the park. There were a few humans out walking their dogs, but they paid him no mind. The concealment spell he'd cast made sure of that. Fairies were used to sneaking about on Earth and other human-dominated places, although it was much more difficult than in his grandfather's time, or even his father's time. The research passed onto him by his grandmother had said that it was the magic level here that was the problem. Magical beings like fairies, unicorns and dragons couldn't survive in a magicless environment like this. They'd sicken and die. Fairies simply couldn't live anywhere other than Fairyland because of the high concentration of magic there, but what made the magic level so low? Fairies had always associated the uncomfortable feelings they got away from home with homesickness, the proximity of any iron or dreadful human technology. Humans on Earth had been using more and more iron in the past two hundred years. Surely the two were connected?

The witch's research hadn't said so, but it did say the more unnatural a place the less magic it produced. Useful to know, especially for fairies like him, but he wished he'd never told anyone else. He ought to have made a proper proclamation. Then again, some people would have misunderstood anyway. The anti-foreigner feeling had been growing since the mass immigrations started decades ago. Earth's magical races had mostly departed, thanks to an ever expanding human population and unexplained-but-now-explained sicknesses. Knowing the reasons for the immigrations should have made everyone more understanding, but it had only made things worse. The witch's research had been why he'd headed for the park. He felt better here amongst the trees and pond, but the air was still terribly dry, an indication of the low mana level. For once, he had an advantage over other fairies. He could top up his magic if he needed to. He grinned to himself. Lady Lir wouldn't be able to hunt for her pendant here indefinitely, but *he* could. Still, he couldn't keep using magic like this. He dropped the spell. As long as he avoided busy places and didn't smile too broadly at anyone, he should be fine. The pendant was safe, at least, safe from Lir. But he couldn't stay here. He had to find a door, as soon as possible.

It wasn't until a few hours later that he realised his mistake. He knew what sort of things to look for and he'd waited patiently for any likely Otherworlders to come past so he could follow them, but there had been nothing. Otherworld activity in this area appeared to be frustratingly low. It occurred to him that finding a door using the pendant *before* he handed it over to a random stranger would have been a better idea. There was no hope for it. He was going to have to find that girl again. But how? He wandered back into town, near the place he'd met the two human girls this morning. Having no luck there, he wandered into a busier area. It was a street lined with shops and it wasn't long before he spotted what he was looking for.

"Come on, we're going to get in trouble if we don't hurry," a blonde girl chided her friend, as they came out of a nearby bakery. "I don't see why you can't just eat in the cafeteria like a normal person." Her friend, a girl with mid-length black hair, followed her out holding a bread roll and a white cup. The two of them were wearing the same uniform as the girls from this morning.

"Go on ahead if you're that worried," the black-haired girl shrugged, turning towards the park. "We've got loads of time. I'm not wasting all dinner waiting in the stupid, long cafeteria line." The blonde girl snorted;

"God Shu, you've got no patience at all!" she complained. "Come *on*, we're not supposed to leave school grounds during dinner in the first place! If we ever get caught getting through the fence-"

"Excuse me!" Tyrian called to the girls, holding up his hand. "I'm looking for someone, she goes to your school I believe. Perhaps you can help me?" The blonde girl was watching him warily.

"This is *exactly* why we're not supposed to leave school during break," she mumbled. The girl addressed as Shu gave him a crooked smile;

"Oh?" she said. "Depends on who you're looking for."

"A red-haired girl, blue eyes, about the same height as you. Her hair is quite short," Tyrian described, holding his hand an inch or two below his ear.

"Hmm." Shu considered the description. "That could be anybody. I don't think we can help you. Sorry." Tyrian sighed. He thanked the girls and headed away towards a nearby railway bridge. Once hidden in its shadow, he cast an invisibility spell again. He would have to follow these girls back to their school, but it wouldn't do to have them notice. Stalking girls wasn't particularly acceptable behaviour even back home, and whilst a lot of human behaviour mystified him somewhat, he wasn't completely ignorant.

"What the heck was that about? There's so many creepers around these days." Shu's friend shuddered. "What was with that costume? I bet he thinks he's Mr. Spock or something."

"Huh?" Shu looked away from the bridge, much to Tyrian's relief. "Oh, he probably just has a job at the same place as Lucinda. It's some acting job. I guess there are no changing rooms there if their employees keep having to walk around town in costume," Shu laughed. "I'm going to go eat my lunch in the park," she finished abruptly. Her friend pulled a face.

"You're going to the park even after everything I said?" She scowled. "Please yourself, I'm going back to school. I'm weirded out, I don't want to hang around." Shu merely shrugged and turned towards the park. The blonde girl made a final protest before turning round and heading back down the road. Watching from the bridge, Tyrian realised with a jolt that he'd approached the two of them without any kind   of disguise. It had upset one girl, but the other seemed nonplussed. He found the disparity between the reactions odd, but this was no time to wonder about it. He headed after the blonde girl, leaving the other one to enjoy her lunch.

* * * * *

By the end of the day, Lucinda was distraught. She'd been thoroughly distracted in all her lessons, spent lunch frantically searching the room from first period and asking at the office if anyone had handed the pendant in and to top everything off, earned herself a detention. All in all, it had not been a good first day back at school. And it wasn't quite over yet. As is traditional in these situations, once you think it can't get any worse, it immediately does, preferably in a comical fashion. Lucinda spotted the strange man waiting just outside the school gate. He was leaning against a tree on the opposite side of the road. She hung back until the other stragglers from detention had gone. The Otherworlds weren't exactly a secret, but they weren't something you could reveal to just anyone. She'd never been *told* as such . . . but this was another story thing. You couldn't discover a magical world and then go blabbing, even if you could prove you *weren't* crazy. It just wasn't done. She groaned inwardly. This wasn't going to be pretty. She crossed the road to go and meet him.

"Ah, there you are!" he exclaimed, his face breaking into a smile. "And you remember me, good. I'm afraid I made a bit of an error in judgement-" Lucinda steeled herself mentally. It was as she feared. He was going to ask for it *back*.

"Um, listen," she began nervously, "about that green stone thing-"

"Don't tell me you refuse to return it?" the man said. "It doesn't do that sort of thing, you should have no compulsion to own it whatsoever. Unless you're Lir, of course," he added.

"Um, it's not that I refuse to," Lucinda explained. "I *can't* give it back. I'm afraid that, well, I sort of . . . lost it," she confessed. "I'm really, really sorry. Someone knocked all my stuff all over the floor this morning and when I got everything back together it was gone."

"Oh." The man fell silent. "Oh well," he said with a shrug. "It'll turn up. You lost it amongst other humans, right? Can't imagine it'll go far." Lucinda made a mental note of the word 'humans'. It didn't surprise her, but his reaction did.

"Aren't you mad?" she asked. "Not that I *want* you to be mad or anything," she added quickly.

"No, not really." The man shook his head. "It was bound to happen. I suppose Earth isn't entirely a dead loss." Then he added, "I'll just have to tag along with you for a bit."

"Oh goo-, wait, tag along?" Lucinda repeated.

"I can't hang around here," he said. "I have things to ask you that I can't ask out in the open like this." Lucinda sighed and resigned herself to the inevitable.

"Why do fairies always insist on following me home?" she complained. "Am I fairy-bait or something?" The man raised his eyebrows. So she'd guessed right after all.

"We do love humans." He cracked a smile. "But mostly I'm going to follow you home because you happen to be the human that lost my pendant."

"Can't argue," she replied, setting off. For a normal teenage girl, bringing home what looked to be an eccentrically-dressed man in his twenties would not be a good idea. But whilst Lucinda's parents didn't know what it was that she actually did, they did know it was a bit strange and involved dressing up like you had no shame whatsoever, which she didn't. She had hoped her parents would be out altogether, but it was her mother's day off, and she walked right across the hall just as Lucinda opened the door.

"Who's this, Lulu?" she asked, looking the fairy up and down. Her mother had short, dark hair and was currently sporting some baggy trousers and a loose t-shirt, a sure sign that she was in the middle of her exercise routine.

"He's from work," Lucinda replied quickly. "We need to discuss some work stuff, so I said we may as well do it now, since we met on the street and everything."

"Tyrian," he said, offering her mother his hand to shake, which she took.

"All the people at your work have unusual names, don't they?" her mother observed.

"Ha ha, I'm sure we do," Tyrian said. "Mine happens to be a shade of purple."

"I'll let you get on then, I'm sure you don't want to be late." Lucinda's mother gave their visitor a smile and then disappeared back into the living room.

Once the two of them were safely in her room, she made absolutely sure her mother wasn't going to follow them and shut the door.

"Look, bringing home a girl my age is not a problem as such, but I can't have an older guy stay in my room, fairy or not," she said, wagging a finger at him. "Okay? Besides, fairies can't live on Earth for long. Um. They turn into vampires."

"It's a bit late for that." He flashed her a grin. "As you can see."

"I noticed," Lucinda admitted. "I thought I might be seeing things. But seriously, you can't stay here."

"Why not?" he argued. "I won't have a problem if I conserve my magic and even if I don't, I just have to get some blood in me." Lucinda suppressed a shudder. One of Lucinda's friends was a vampire, and indeed one of her enemies, but neither had shown the slightest interest in biting her. The thought that they might was not a pleasant one.

"I'm not having you going around biting people," Lucinda ordered. Tyrian stifled a laugh.

"Who are you to give me orders?" he asked in a jovial tone. "Which reminds me, I never did get your name. What was it your mother called you . . . Lulu?" Lucinda wrinkled her nose.

"Call me that and I'll throw you out right now," she threatened. "My name's Lucinda."

"Lucy then," he said. Lucinda made a face, but Tyrian ignored her. "Well, aren't you a mysterious young lady-"

"-says the fairy-vampire with a special green rock?" Lucinda interrupted him, giving him a look. "What was that thing anyway? Why do you need it? And if you need it so badly, why the heck did you give it to *me*?" Tyrian paused, before answering,

"Legend has it that the Goddess Gaia gave to the rulers of Fairyland three magical treasures, that they might rule wisely. These were the Staff of Light, the

Sword of Shadow and the Wild Pendant. There are three Realms in Fairyland, each has their own royal family and each royal family has one of the three treasures. Should all three come together, they are said to unlock a terrible power. I'm sure you can figure out what the green stone was." Lucinda nodded. Her friend Erlina was the crown princess of the Light Realm; she'd always known there was more than one - Erlina had run away from home because she didn't want to marry the prince from a neighbouring Realm. There were still a few things missing from his story, though. He'd deliberately not told her everything, and she couldn't exactly blame him, but she still wasn't sure if she could trust this man. She didn't have anything against vampires per se, but they were a mixed bunch. She certainly didn't have anything against fairies, but the fairies of the Otherworlds were not the twinkly kind, and the reactions to Erlina in various worlds had been less than positive.

"I suppose you're going to tell me this pendant belongs to you?" Lucinda said.

"I most certainly am not," the fairy replied, sounding a little offended, "it belongs to Queen Titania of the Wild Realm. She's currently missing, and I'm trying to keep it out of the wrong hands. I'd like to say I chose Earth because it's difficult for fairies to get about here, but I can't. I was fleeing a battle and I stumbled upon a door. Now I'm stuck. You know how tricky doors are."

"Do I *ever*," Lucinda replied without thinking. "Took me forever to find that return door to the office last month." The doors led not only to other worlds, but to different places on Earth. Lucinda had used one to visit her friends in America, but finding one that would get her back to the UK had been trying. "It's no fun trying to search for something without letting your friends know what you're doing, especially when it's invisible. I had to pretend I needed to find a bathroom *so* many times. It was getting embarrassing." Lucinda froze when she realised what she'd said. She looked up to see a triumphant expression on Tyrian's face.

"So you *can* help me find a door then," he said. Lucinda was reluctant. The only door she knew about in the area was the one leading to Rent-A-Legend, and the problem with that was Sara. Sara was not co-operative at the best of times. And that was with a normal person.

"I don't know about that," she began doubtfully. "My boss hates vampires. The last time I brought one back to the office she threatened him with a dagger."

"Ah well." Tyrian shrugged, throwing his legs onto the bed and taking up a relaxed position. "This bed is rather comfy. I'm sure I'll settle right in." Lucinda scowled at him.

"Oh all right," she gave in. "But I'm warning you, this is not going to end well."

"Get that vampire out of my office," demanded Sara, receptionist of Rent-A-Legend and Lucinda's boss. She was a tall woman, with dark skin, brown eyes and black hair. It was thick and wavy, and it fell down to the middle of her back. She was wearing a red sari; it was embroidered with golden birds and it had gold strips along the edges. She also had a red veil over her head, decorated in a similar fashion to the sari. Lucinda thought it all looked very pretty; it was too bad Sara's expression was anything but.

"Um. This is Tyrian. I ran into him on Earth and he's kind of stuck," Lucinda explained regardless. "He's a fairy," she added, hoping Sara would take the hint. Sara stopped looking daggers at the newcomer and looked back at her paperwork.

"Is he indeed," Sara replied. "I'm sure he knows where he should get back to, then."

"That's kind of the problem," Lucinda plunged on. "If you'll just point me to the Fairyland door, I'll escort him there myself."

"We don't *have* a Fairyland door." Sara told them.

"I do apologise for the trouble," Tyrian said, clearly feeling he owed an explanation. Sara's glares tended to have that effect on people. "There's a bit of a situation and I had to leave in a hurry, now I'm trying to hurry back." Sara peered at him for a moment. Then she leaned over and tapped a bell on the left side of the desk. The desk itself was huge and round and made of mahogany. Above it were a collection of horns, shells and other odd objects that functioned like phones. One began to make a whirring noise. Sara answered it and jabbered away in a foreign language as two women appeared from a corridor to the left. One was a large, blonde woman in armour, the other was dressed in fur. She was wearing an enormous, white, fur coat, a fluffy hat and furry boots, plus a scarf, so that only her black fringe and blue eyes peeked out.

"You rang?" said Gerda. Sara pointed to Lucinda, indicating that she would explain.

"I found this fairy on Earth and he needs to get home," Lucinda explained, moving away from the desk. "I don't suppose either of you know where there's a door to Fairyland?"

"I think the only one who knows that is Lina, and she's not in today," Freya said. There was a sudden, almost violent cough from Sara. Gerda's eyes flicked to the counter and back, before she continued;

"I reckon Freya's right. I certainly never been there. It's no place for humans to go wanderin' into. There's a lot of yokai there, though. You sure you don't know any doors there?" Freya shook her head.

"There's no snow women there," she replied. "There's no snow. So I've never been."

"You sure you don't know any doors Mr . . ?" Gerda asked.

"Of course, how rude of me. I never properly introduced myself." Tyrian made a flamboyant bow. "Tyrian von Stollenheim, pleased to make your acquaintance, ladies." The room fell silent. Sara narrowed her eyes, and the other three stared. Lucinda was the first to speak.

"Did you just say *Stollenheim*? You're not *really*, are you?" The fairy looked understandably confused.

"Should I not be?" he asked cautiously.

"That explains a lot, then," Lucinda said, scratching her head. "Sort of." The name Stollenheim was well known but certainly not well liked to the Rent-A-Legend employees, Lucinda included. You tend to get negative feelings towards the name of people who've tried to kill you.

"Get that *Stollenheim* out of my office," Sara said, pointing to the corridors. "I don't care which door you take, just pick one please. Honestly, you really must stop picking them up, Cinders." Tyrian looked genuinely lost, and Lucinda actually felt sorry for him.

"I'll handle it." She tugged on his shirt sleeve to get his attention.

"Look, I'm terribly sorry if I offended you somehow-" he began.

"You didn't," Sara explained matter-of-factly. "I'm just a completely unreasonable person. Now kindly get out." Without another word, Lucinda led him up the corridor. She took him through a door engraved with leaves and a pair of unicorns, rearing up and crossing horns.

The door led out into a lush green forest, full of flowering trees, bushes and plants. By far the most common flowers were the bluebells; they covered the floor on both sides, so thickly that when the wind blew through them they looked like the blue waves of the sea. For this reason, it was called the Blue Forest. The excessive and magical plant life was the result of the magical spring beneath it.

"What was all that about?" Tyrian asked, hurt. "What do you have against the Stollenheims?" Lucinda sighed.

"It's a long story," she replied.

"Well, what's the short version?" he persisted. "I can't do anything about her animosity if I don't know what caused it." He folded his arms. Lucinda thought for a moment about how to sum up almost a year of her life in a sentence or two.

"Until about six months ago, Rent-A-Legend was a cover for a rebellion against Alucard von Stollenheim. He stole the throne of Sara's country, basically. But mostly she hates both Stollenheims and vampires because she blamed him for the death of her mother. It's kind of complicated." Tyrian ran a hand through his hair.

"I see . . ." He looked around the colourful forest, as if searching for something to say. "Why did you bring me here? I take it it wasn't a random choice?"

"It wasn't," Lucinda replied. "There's a few reasons I brought you here."

"I can feel one of them," the fairy replied. "This place doesn't itch my throat like Earth does. It's the same sort of place as Fairyland. Well done."

"That's not the only reason," Lucinda said. "This is where my fairy friend lives right now. Plus there's a door here, somewhere." Tyrian frowned.

"I thought you said you didn't know any doors to Fairyland?" he asked.

"I don't," Lucinda explained. "It's a door *from* Fairyland." Tyrian smiled, without showing his teeth for once. He didn't seem to have any inclination to hide his fangs at all. It was a little disconcerting.

"Yes, there might be a return door here somewhere too," he mused. "Let's find this friend of yours, I'm very curious to meet them."

So. His cousin had gone off the deep end. He wasn't surprised, but he was saddened. Story karma did terrible things to people. Tyrian had first met Alucard as a little boy, at a family reunion. Family reunions were usually the only time the scattered Stollenheims saw one another, with a few exceptions. He'd found him in a hallway, bawling like a baby because he'd got lost on the way to the bathroom. Tyrian had calmed him down and walked him back to the ballroom, where he kept him company for an hour or two until some Stollenheim children his own age turned up. The next reunion he almost didn't recognise him, humans ageing as fast as they did, but Alucard said hello and introduced his wife and son, only a tiny thing at the time. The next reunion however . . . It was about nine, perhaps ten years ago now. Though in appearance Alucard had merely greyed around the temples, this time his temperament was unrecognisable. He was sullen, distant and alone. After the reunion ended, he asked if he might stay at the palace a while longer. They obliged, as he was clearly in quite the state, though he declined to talk about it. He went home eventually, but he visited often over the course of the next year, his visits getting longer and longer . . .

It was on one such visit that another painful reminder of what story karma might have in store for him happened. Aunt Maia, Queen of the neighbouring Light Realm, had brought over her daughter to play with Tyrian, as she so often did. They were in one of the drawing rooms, where they always entertained family. Tyrian's mother and his cousin were sat on the chaise longue, and Maia was sat on a chair nearby. He suspected that Maia had really come to offer moral support for some sort of intervention, rather than her usual play date.

"Your wife will be worried about you, Alucard," his mother said. "You should return to her."

"I . . . I *can't* Nareena," his cousin replied, staring into his brandy. "I just . . . I can't be around humans any more. When I look at humans, all I see is a mob. E-even Marissa. If it weren't for my visits here, I'd have gone mad."

"You need to stop that," his mother warned, pursing her lips.

"Stop *what* exactly?" Alucard asked.

"You persist in referring to humans as if they're a different species," Nareena said. "I'm a vampire too, you know. It doesn't stop me being a fairy."

"I expect it doesn't," Alucard replied tartly. "What's your point?"

"You *are* human," his mother said. "Whether you like it or not."

"Yes well, tell *them* that," he snapped. "It's *different* for you. You're not being fair."

"We fairies are feared by humans too, but by opening the borders and letting them in, we've started to change that," Maia put in. "Running away and shutting them out won't help you."

"That's easy for you to say, here amongst your own kind," Alucard argued. "Every day I'm surrounded, surrounded by enemies-" There was a knock at the door. A guard poked her head through;

"Please, excuse the interruption Your Majesties-" she began, before a dark-skinned elf woman dressed in a green and gold sari squeezed under her arm and stumbled towards Maia.

"Oh Maia, I c-came through our door, but you weren't home, th-they said you were here, so I had your guards escort me," she said, her voice hoarse. He'd been stunned to see the Queen of Sheva like that. Unannounced and unguarded, her face was wet with tears.

"Khalira, whatever's the matter?" Maia said, standing up and rushing over to her. She dismissed the guard with a nod.

"He's dead, Maia, Alvas is *dead!*" the elf sobbed, falling into Maia's arms. "He was killed on the way home, his ship sank!"

"I'm so sorry, Khalira," Maia said, hugging her friend tight. "I'm so sorry."

"Sara has locked herself in her room, she won't come out, she won't eat, she says it's all her fault for being a princess!" Khalira continued. "I don't know what to do! I told her to be strong, but here I am in tears! What am I going to do without him?"

"We all have trouble following our own advice," Maia soothed. "I'm here for you, Khalira."

"It's just . . . it's just so *unfair!*" Khalira burst out, weeping into Maia's shoulder. "He was wise, he was kind, I loved him so much! Why did he have to die? Did we do something wrong?"

"Of course not," Maia said.

"We defy story karma and it kills us, we obey it and it kills us," Alucard spoke up. "You did nothing wrong. It is the story at fault." The elf woman looked up sharply.

"I-I'm sorry," Khalira apologised. "I did not see you." She pushed herself away from Maia and took out a handkerchief, turning away to wipe her eyes. "I am ashamed to lose myself so in front of a stranger. Forgive me. Allow me to compose myself."

"It is quite all right," Alucard replied. "I too know the sting of losing someone unfairly. I recently lost my cousin, Heinrich. He behaved as the humans wanted him to, so they murdered him."

"I'm so sorry," Khalira apologised, fighting off a fresh wave of tears. "It seems stories are cruel to us all."

"Stories and their karma," Alucard muttered. "We would be so much better off without them."

Many people would have gasped and said that would be terrible, but there in that drawing room, he'd silently agreed. Perhaps if Lir had been there, she would feel differently. She had never had to live with the ticking time bomb that was the title of 'princess'. She was jumping straight to queen, an unfairness all of its own. It really was too bad he couldn't live on Earth, where story karma didn't work properly. If only there was more magic there. Perhaps the lack of magic and the lack of story karma were connected. If there were a way to keep magic and change story karma, he would do it gladly. But that was something he'd have to worry about later. He had more immediate concerns.

As the two of them walked through the forest, Tyrian quizzed Lucinda about where she'd lost the pendant. After she'd explained what happened, and when she noticed it was gone, he made a guess;

"So you were talking to your friend after the other lady from this morning had gone . . . and that's when you noticed?" he said. "Could it be that this Rina was interested in the pendant after all? She had the opportunity to take it and she knew you had it."

"Yeah, she started acting all interested once I had it," Lucinda said. "It must have been her, she must have taken it! That little-" Tyrian held up a hand to stop her.

"Let's not jump to conclusions." He rubbed his chin thoughtfully. "Is there any other time your bag was open at all?" Lucinda shook her head furiously.

"No," she replied. "I went to assembly and only had one class. I would have noticed if someone had tried to mess with my bag. Not to mention they would have had to do it in the middle of class. Unless there was a fairy in my classroom, it had to be her."

"Well, it's clear that fairies don't last long on Earth, and I'm certain no-one followed me here, so that's extremely unlikely. Hmm." Tyrian stopped dead while he considered the situation.

"I'll just have to ask her about it," Lucinda tutted. "I hope I'm wrong. I know what it's like to be the new girl. It's bad enough without being accused of theft on your second day . . . ugh." She was *not* looking forward to tomorrow. If she was wrong, it would give Rina a bad reputation before she even got to know anyone, and it wouldn't reflect well on Lucinda either. They walked along in silence for a while, Lucinda thinking of how best to broach the subject tomorrow without sounding like she was accusing Rina outright. After all, maybe it *was* a misunderstanding. Rina may have picked up the pendant by mistake or maybe it really was still on the floor or in the lost property locker . . .

She was jolted out of her thoughts by the glaring shine of a unicorn walking across their path. She raised a hand to greet the unicorn, but it took one look at the fairy accompanying her and left in a haughty manner. Puzzled as she was, it didn't matter, because the answer to most, if not all, of her problems was right in front of her. They had arrived at a clearing, in the middle of which was a witch's cottage. It was easy to tell it was a witch's cottage, because it looked perfectly normal and it was surrounded by flowers and butterflies. Granted, some of the flowers were pretty unusual-looking, even more so than the usual flora of the forest, but there's something about a normal house in the middle of an abnormal forest that should set alarm bells ringing in one's head. It was thatched and the gravel path leading to the front door was brightly coloured and it did have the traditional twisty chimney. It belonged to Rosalind Fisher, also known as the Silver Witch, and a good friend and mentor of Lucinda's.

However, Rosie was not the reason Lucinda was here.

"We're here," she told Tyrian. "I just hope she's in." Lucinda knocked on the door. After a few moments it was answered by a petite, blonde girl with pointed ears and a streak of white through her fringe. She was wearing a white dress and a semi-translucent, golden cloak, decorated with feathers.

"Lucinda!" The girl practically threw herself at Lucinda, hugging her tight. She was a full head shorter than Lucinda, but for someone so dainty she could hug like a boa constrictor. "You aren't wearing your prince clothes. I thought you were working today?"

"I am," Lucinda replied, extracting herself from Erlina's vice-like embrace. "I brought someone to see you." Lucinda stood aside so that the two of them could see each other properly. There was an intake of breath before they chorused;

"What are *you* doing here?" The two fairies stared at each other from either end of the garden path. Lucinda looked from one to the other. Erlina had gone white; she looked like she might faint. Or explode.

"What are you *doing* here?" she demanded, her face screwed up as if she were sucking a lemon. "I do *not* want to see you!" Tyrian drew himself up to his full height and brandished a finger;

"I might ask you the same question!" he said. "We've been searching *everywhere* for you! Do you have any idea how worried we all were, and what-" Erlina stamped her foot.

"I don't *care!*" she yelled. "I know why you're here and I'm not coming home, I don't care what you say! *And* I am *not* speaking to you, just, just *leave me alone!*" Erlina turned on her heel and strode back into the house.

"Don't you take that tone with me, you've no idea why I'm here or you'd have come home already!"

Tyrian scolded, striding after her. "Get back here this minute!"

"I'm not listening!" Erlina yelled back.

"Hey!" Lucinda tried to bar Tyrian's way, but he pushed her firmly aside. Lucinda turned and rushed after the pair of them into the house in time to hear the back door slam.

She ran right through the house after them and caught up with Tyrian in the back garden. Erlina was nowhere to be seen and he appeared to be shouting at the sky;

"Erlina! *Erlina!*" he called after her to no avail. Erlina's feathered cloak was no decoration; it was essentially a pair of wings in disguise. Tyrian let out a string of curse words.

"What was all that about?" she demanded, when he'd stopped swearing. He shook his head in dismay.

"I was hoping *you* could tell *me,*" he groaned, and massaged his forehead. "I have no idea what I'm supposed to have done. This is terrible."

" . . . How do you know Erlina?" Lucinda asked, narrowing her eyes. Erlina wasn't just anybody, and despite the fact that Lucinda personally knew three princesses, a queen, a king, a prince and a lady, which is an awful lot of nobility for one common girl to know, she still found it odd that the only other fairy she had ever met should know the Crown Princess. True, the Otherworlds ran on stories and had a habit of having more royalty than you could fit into the very special sort of police box, but they weren't completely devoid of logic. Tyrian didn't appear to be listening.

"If there was anyone above me to get angry with me, they would be very, *very* angry," he lamented, pacing about the garden. "As there isn't, I have no choice but to be angry with myself." Lucinda frowned. If there was anyone above him?

"Who *are* you?" she asked. He stopped pacing and looked at her as if seeing her for the first time.

"I thought I told you. I'm Tyrian Von Stollenheim," he replied irritably. "You were familiar with the name, as I recall."

"That doesn't explain how you know Erlina," Lucinda pointed out. "In fact, it only raises further questions. The Stollenheims might be vampires, but they're *human* vampires. It's about time you explained yourself." She crossed her arms in what she hoped was a business-like manner. Tyrian stopped pacing and gave her a brief, lopsided smile.

"Who are you to demand that I explain myself, young lady?" His tone was not unkind, he just didn't seem to believe what he was hearing. That was another puzzling thing. Resistance was not the usual reaction she got from people. Then the words 'young lady' sunk in. She looked down and realised that she was still wearing her school uniform. People here did not address her as 'young lady'; they usually said 'my lord'. This was because Lucinda was employed by Rent-A-Legend as a *prince*, and princes could demand a lot of things. But Tyrian had met a *schoolgirl*-

"I don't know about Miss Prince here, but *I* certainly demand an explanation," came a stern voice from behind them. "What in the blue blazes is the King of the Dark Realm doing in my back garden, and what is he doing having a blazing row with my assistant?" The two of them turned to see a woman in a grey robe leaning on the door frame, holding a basket of cut plants. She had long, white hair that shone in the sun. Her eyes were rose pink. She was also wearing a flowery apron, which rather ruined her mystique.

"Isn't the Dark Realm . . ?" Lucinda began hesitantly, as realisation dawned.

"One of the three Realms of Fairyland?" the woman finished for her. "Yes it is, and I have no idea what the King of the Fairies wants with me, but he'd better make it quick, because I'm a busy woman."

"The world is lamentably full of busy women today it seems." Tyrian shook his head, but he was smiling. "Fancy meeting you here. Miss Rosie, wasn't it? It's been quite a while."

"Well remembered," Rosie replied curtly. "Now what are you doing on my lawn and why on Earth were you having a shouting match with Erlina?"

"We've been looking for Erlina for over a year now," Tyrian explained. His smile was gone, his expression had darkened. "I take it from your question that you don't know she's the Crown

Princess of the Light Realm." Rosie stayed quiet as he continued. "I came here by chance, but now that I've found her I have to take her home. If you'll excuse me-" He went to leave.

"You're the prince she ran away from!" Lucinda accused him, flinging out her arm to point at him "When I first met her, she said she ran away from home because she was being forced to marry the prince from the next Realm! That's *you*, isn't it?" Lucinda drew herself up and looked as defiant as possible. "Well tough, because she doesn't want to and I won't let you." Prince uniform or not, Lucinda wasn't about to let this guy walk off with her best friend if she didn't want to go. And this was a story place; story causality was often on the side of people who don't want to get married. She glared at Tyrian. She'd expected him to glare back, but his expression was merely grim.

"That's got nothing to do with it," he said. "I'm taking her home because the Light Realm is under enemy control and her mother Queen Maia has been captured. Fairyland is in a state of civil war."

Gaia gathered up the clay that had so sprung life and mixed with it her own blood. From this blood clay she made more children. They were stronger and they lived longer. These were the first fairies. So pleased was she, she made more and more... but again she grew weak, and she called her children to her.

"I must sleep again, but I fear for the creatures of the clay. I cut open my veins, but there is a better way to make children. I leave them to you. Mix your blood with the clay, so they might grow stronger. Rule them, so they do not go astray. Teach them to love the world."

Chapter 3:

Warning

Back in Rosie's kitchen the three of them sat sipping some of Rosie's herbal concoctions. Lucinda had a cup of tea, but the other two were drinking some steaming, pinkish-purple liquid. Tyrian eyed his suspiciously;

"I don't suppose you're trying to poison me since you're drinking this too, but what on Gaia is it?"

"It's medicine," Rosie explained.

"I didn't know I was sick?" There was the merest hint of worry in his voice.

"All vampires are sick," she replied patiently. "Didn't Lady Contessa spread my research?" Lady Contessa Von Stollenheim was the head of the prolific Stollenheim family. She'd been a human sorceress once upon a time, but overuse of magic had turned her into a vampire. She'd been trying to cast a spell to give herself eternal youth at the time, so she hadn't been particularly distressed about it. Vampires were essentially sick people; the more a person used magic, the more damaged their body became, until they needed magic itself to survive. The way to do this was to drain it from other people, via their blood. True vampires were extremely rare and easy to spot – Rosie herself was sporting the tell-tale white hair, but her eyes were still pink and not the red of the truly turned.

"Yes, actually. Grandma Connie sent us all some pills and a letter explaining how our blood intake is related to our magic use and so on . . . and about different magic levels." Tyrian replied, taking an experimental sip. "Some of it went over my head, but I think I got the gist of it."

"So what's this about a war?" Rosie asked, sipping her own medicine. "It's been three years since I was there, but it all seemed fine back then. There was the usual speciesism and stuff about immigrants, but you find that everywhere," she complained. "No matter the planet or country. It's depressing."

"I'm afraid it's taken a bit of a step up from that..." Tyrian began hesitantly. "You see, the reason everyone - by which I mean mostly Earth's magical races - have been moving to Fairyland has become apparent, and given that we fairies can't live elsewhere, the anti-foreigner types have been getting up in arms, saying it's not fair and we should kick them all out." Rosie looked up sharply.

"Are you saying *my research* is why you're at war?" she asked, glaring at him.

"I wish I could lie and say no, but it's definitely a factor," he explained.

"Oh for goodness sake!" Rosie slammed her cup down. "What have . . . Oh, why are people so *stupid?*"

"I never said it was your fault," Tyrian cut in quickly.

"Damn right it isn't!" Rosie replied, stabbing the table with a finger. "But I bet you know whose it *is*."

"Indeed. It's the new Wild Realm queen, Lir." Tyrian wrinkled his nose. "I say 'queen'. She's just meant to be standing in for the real queen, Titania. Aunt Titania has been missing for several years. Nothing unusual there, of course," he said. "The Wild Queens always vanish from time to time. It's traditional."

"I sense a 'but' on the horizon," Rosie said.

"But my own parents have been missing for about five years now as well," he continued. "At first we thought it was just a standard story they'd got caught up in, but there's been no news of them at all, we can't find them anywhere. I thought Erlina had gone missing thanks to a convenient story too. You have no idea how relieved I am to find her."

"And how does my research fit into this exactly?" Rosie asked.

"She's been discontent with how the country is being run for years, she doesn't like the borders being open. She's a traditionalist, and she seems to think that the apparent decay of story karma is something to do with it," he said. "All the royalty going missing has the people spooked, and then this. She's got

everyone thinking humans and other immigrants are responsible for the breakdown of karma and magic level drop elsewhere. It's been the final nail in the coffin of peace. Whether it's a genuine misunderstanding or a trouble-stirring ploy, I don't know.
Either way, she's using it as an excuse to seize power."

"Using my research for her own ends when it was meant to help people," Rosie muttered. "If I could still use magic . . ." she trailed off.

"So what about Erlina?" Lucinda asked. "If the country is at war, wouldn't it be safer for her to stay here?"

"Her mother Queen Maia has been captured," he explained. "The people of the Light Realm need to know they have hope. If they won't rally around me, I certainly don't want them rallying around *Lir*. I need her help." He turned to Lucinda. "And it looks like I'll need yours. Lir *can't* get that pendant back. She already has the staff. I left the sword with my cousin."

"How can we help?" Lucinda asked.

"Are you sure helping is wise, Lucinda?" Rosie cut in before the fairy king could answer. "I don't think you know what fairies are really like. And now they're at war." She shuddered.

"It is my fault that the pendant is lost," Lucinda pointed out. "I have to at least take responsibility for that. Plus Erlina is my friend. And it *is* kind of my job."

"This isn't your run of the mill damsel in distress situation," Rosie said. "This would be a million times worse than Sara's rebellion-"

"Please don't worry, Miss Rosie," Tyrian stopped her. To Lucinda he said, "I don't want you to do anything dangerous. Firstly, I'd like you to talk to Erlina for me. If she won't listen to me, perhaps she'll listen to you. Secondly, talk to this girl you think took the pendant. The humans on Earth didn't respond to me very well. If you can at least find out if she has the pendant or not and what she did with it, that would be useful." Rosie visibly relaxed.

"I see. Very clever," Rosie answered. "Lucinda can get where you can't. So long as you don't ask her to do anything too difficult. We're not fairies. A lot of what you take for granted is difficult or impossible for us. And outside help won't be welcome given the circumstances."

"I'm well aware of that," he replied. "But there are things you can do that I cannot. Thus my requests." He blew out his cheeks. "I'm afraid I must ask you to take me back to the Princess of Sheva, as well. The elf lady in the office, that is. She must be warned." The two girls stared at him.

"Do you know all the princesses we do, or what?" Lucinda asked him in an accusatory tone.

"I'm sure you know Sheva is the neighbouring nation to Fairyland. It's only natural I should have visited there. Not to mention I'm invited to the coronation tomorrow." There was a pause.

"I'll explain about the war to Erlina, but I'm not going to talk her into going back if it means she has to marry you," Lucinda told him, folding her arms. "She doesn't want to and I'm not going to let it happen." Tyrian stared at her before practically collapsing onto the table.

"Is that all she was so angry about?" he mumbled into the wood. "Yes, it all makes sense now . . . her disappearance, her refusal to speak to me-"

"What do you mean 'is that all'?" Lucinda challenged him. "Don't trivialise her feelings like that! You-"

"Please stop." Tyrian held up a hand. "You don't understand. I've no intentions of getting married to *anyone,* least of all my surrogate little sister." Lucinda faltered. Surrogate little sister? "I've been resisting my mother's attempts to marry me off for *decades*, I'm disappointed that she'd take the whole thing seriously." He sighed and lifted his head back up. "But she is just a child, after all. She had no idea there was a war brewing."

"*Ah,*" Rosie said. "So the betrothal was just a ploy by the Light and Dark Realms to unite against this new queen? A warning, as it were?" Tyrian nodded glumly.

"Yes. To send the message that we were united, should she start any trouble." He sighed. "It didn't work, obviously. It seems to have made things worse." Lucinda couldn't agree *less;*

"If she hadn't run away from home, me and a whole townsworth of people would have been dead, and I guess she would have been captured too," she said. "Personally, I'm glad she misunderstood." Tyrian smiled at this. He gave her an oddly amused look again, as if she'd done something funny and he wasn't going to share the joke.

"You make a good if mysterious point," he replied. "I'd ask you what exactly you've been getting up to, but I suspect it would take more time than I've got to recount. If you could please take me back to these offices of yours whilst Erlina cools off?" Lucinda agreed and they stood up to leave.

The two of them made their way back to the Rent-A-Legend offices. Tyrian was quiet the whole way. It seemed to Lucinda that he had something on his mind. She didn't blame him. If she had to talk to an angry Sara, she'd be preoccupied too.

Sara looked up from her endless paperwork as they walked in.

"Persistent, aren't we?" she remarked, before the two of them could explain. "It must be a family trait."

"Please Princess Saharaleia, before you kick me out again, I must warn you about something." Tyrian pleaded. This earned Lucinda a sharp look.

"Don't look at me, *I* didn't tell him," Lucinda protested. "He already knew. He's the king of-"

"I'm well aware of who he is," Sara interrupted her. "Which is why I want him out of here as soon as possible. Sadly, I'm still unable to locate a door."

"I must thank you for your co-operation-" Tyrian began.

"Don't bother," Sara replied. "I don't intend to be particularly co-operative. I just want to get you out of here before you drag any of my employees off to Fairyland." Her eyes flickered to Lucinda, who frowned.

"I haven't the slightest intention of dragging any of your employees off to Fairyland," Tyrian replied, baffled. "It's not the bad old days any more, you know." Sara blinked. She looked back down at her work and continued;

"Very well then, what's this warning you need to give me?"

"Fairyland is in a state of civil war. Given that your Sheva is the neighbouring country, I thought it only fair to warn you."

"I heard the situation was getting unstable some time ago. So it's finally gone critical." Sara looked troubled. "Can you elaborate on the situation?"

"Queen Titania went missing some time ago, and Lady Morgana Lir is standing in as queen regent until she gets back." He paused meaningfully. "*If* she gets back. The unrest grew and there were protests and rallies, spouting nonsense about foreigners being to blame and 'returning Fairyland to its former glory'." He made a disgusted noise. "It finally came to a head a few days ago, when Lady Lir invaded the Light Realm."

"That is indeed grave news," she replied. "You're telling me the only people in charge are you and this woman? I take it she's not going to be reigning over a splendid new utopia if she wins?"

"It's exceedingly unlikely," Tyrian confirmed. "Whatever she's told her followers. I suspect that she won't stop at ruling Fairyland. She's out to fix the world, out for foreign blood, and Sheva, our nearest neighbour, is a prime target." Sara steepled her fingers and gazed unseeing at the desk.

"The desert has always protected us from invasion from Fairyland," she answered vaguely. "But it doesn't do to be careless. . . . Is that really all you wanted?"

"I'm still having some trouble with a few other matters and I still haven't been able to locate a return door," he said. "I can fix these problems shortly, I think."

"There's *really* nothing else?" Sara asked him.

"No. Nothing," he replied.

"You aren't seeking any unions?" she continued. "Like *marriage* for example?" Tyrian gripped the edge of the desk, his face a picture of seriousness.

"Though in a desperate situation it may seem a good strategy to gain Sheva as an ally that way, I'm sure you're well aware it would be political suicide to marry an elf, and that's if we *weren't* in a civil war driven by nationalist pride and speciesism!"

"I'm pretty sure it would be more than *political* suicide . . ." Lucinda mumbled.

"Besides which, I don't intend to marry *anybody!*" he finished, taking his hands off the desk and folding his arms. "Honestly, you people are worse than my mother!"

"If you aren't intending to marry Erlina, what *are* you planning to do about her?" Sara asked him. The two of them looked at her in shock.

"She works here for you?" he asked. Sara nodded. Lucinda mentally slapped herself. Sara had been trying since the moment Tyrian had walked into the office to keep him from Erlina, and Lucinda had led him right to her.

"You need to tell her about her mother," Sara told him.

"I tried, but she wouldn't listen. She made the same mistake you did." He tutted. "Honestly, if you all wouldn't act like it would be dreadful to marry me this could have been sorted out by now. I have to say much as I don't want to get married, it is rather hurtful."

"I have issues with Stollenheims marrying people," Sara replied darkly.

"So do I, if the Stollenheim is me," Tyrian said, pouting. There was an awkward silence before he suddenly announced, "I need to find somewhere to stay and I suspect that isn't something you can help me with either." He paused. "I think I have no choice but to ask Miss Rosie. I shall take my leave." He turned and walked back towards the corridor they had come from.

"Your Majesty, wait a moment," Sara called. He turned;

"Yes?"

"I believe I had invitations sent out to the Fairyland royalty for my coronation," she told him. "It's tomorrow."

"Indeed you did," he said. "I intended to be there, but I had started to think I wouldn't make it, for obvious reasons."

"I suggest you attend," Sara replied. "We may not have a door to Fairyland, but it's elementary that we have one to Sheva. You can get home from there. I presume you had some plan to get there and back?" Tyrian stopped.

"I did, but it involved being in Fairyland," he responded. "If I'd known I was going to get stuck, I would have just stepped right through the door . . ." Sara's brow wrinkled. He smiled and continued, "In any case, that is a very helpful suggestion. I shall see you tomorrow then." He disappeared down the corridor and there was a bang as the door to the Blue Forest closed. Sara tilted her head towards the corridor. Lucinda looked at the corridor, and back at Sara. Sara now made a shooing gesture towards the corridor. Lucinda got the message and went to look down the corridor, making sure to walk the whole way and check everything. She was wise to both pretending to go through a door and fairy invisibility.

"He's gone," Lucinda confirmed for Sara as she re-entered the office. "That really was helpful of you. I'm surprised."

"If I didn't suggest it he might have been stuck here for days. Weeks even," Sara complained. "Honestly Cinders, where do you keep finding these damn Stollenheims?"

"You say that," Lucinda replied, "but I don't think you hate them as much as you did."

"What makes you say that?" Sara asked. Lucinda shrugged;

"You didn't threaten this one with a dagger."

* * * * *

The fairy king headed back towards the witch's cottage. He wasn't in a hurry; Erlina might not be back yet. He inspected some of the magical flora of the forest. This might not be a bad place for humans to live if they knew what they were doing. On the other hand, he speculated, humans seemed to be poison to magical landscapes. Them and their iron. On that account at least, he knew where Lir was coming from. How did Earthlings live like that? No magic! It didn't bear thinking about.

He pondered how best to tell the witch that he would be staying at her cottage until he could talk some sense into Erlina. He didn't seem to do very well talking to foreign women. Fairies had something of a unique culture and they were open and honest about certain things. Like eating people. Tyrian had never had to worry about being a vampire. Earthlings may have forgotten, but it wasn't unheard of for fairies to drink blood or even eat people. A lot of the other Fairyland residents had fangs. And there were far worse species in Fairyland than vampires. Lamias drank blood *and* ate children. Harpies ate whatever they could catch. Sirens drowned people for fun. Fairyland was full of all the species that had been pushed out of other places when their habitats had been destroyed or they'd been driven out by scared humans. Centaurs, sphinxes, yokai . . . the place had more magical creatures than you could shake a whole bunch of sticks at. It had proved impossible to stop them from being, well, themselves, so the official stance was that you can't deny your nature but you can be a reasonable person. Fairyland had a reputation to keep up, after all. Residents were to be left alone but travellers were fair game. Anyone suffering from incurable stupidity deserved what they got

however. If you were dumb enough to approach a siren or a huldra then they were probably doing the gene pool a favour.

He came to the flower-covered cottage once more and knocked at the door. The problem with humans was, they were hard to judge. There was only one Fairyland, but humans had lots of countries, all with their own cultures. Thanks to Otherworld doors, a human could be from anywhere. Elves were easier, in a way. Fairies and elves had hated one another for centuries, so it didn't matter where they were from.

"Yes?" Rosie answered the door holding an alchemic flask.

"I'm going to need to stay here until I can talk to Erlina," he told her. She pursed her lips together.

"You know your grandmother lives not too far from this forest?" she suggested. "I don't really appreciate people commandeering my house."

"I see the young lady isn't the only one immune to royalty," he remarked.

"When you live with royalty for long enough, it loses its shine," the witch replied. "I don't suppose it was Sara that sent you here? Because if it was, I shall need to have words with that woman." Tyrian sighed inwardly. No-one had any trouble putting up a cute, blonde, fairy girl but for some reason a fully grown, vampire male was a *problem*.

"You know I could be adorable too," he complained out loud, pouting.

"What?" Rosie said.

"I thought about it, but if I stay at my grandmother's then Erlina can avoid me forever," he explained. "I don't have time for that. I only need to stay until she comes back. I won't get in your way." The witch considered this.

"I guess you're right," she conceded. "Very well then. Just don't bother me. I'm busy making a potions order."

Tyrian waited as patiently as he could manage in the front room. The place was full of potted plants and brightly coloured potions. But what really caught his eye was the bookshelf. It was mostly full of Earth literature. He had to watch out for Erlina, but the bookshelf was too tempting to pass up. Fairies didn't write much themselves. They still used vellum for books, made of cured and dried animal skin, and that was the way it was going to stay. Fairies revered nature, and had always believed that chopping down great swathes of trees was one of the reasons Earth was so dry and horrible. On the other hand, they reasoned that since Earth was a lost cause anyway, they had no problem whatsoever with Earthlings doing it and they got their hands on all the Earth books they could find. Books were valuable and a good laugh. It was funny how Earthlings had quickly forgotten what fairies really were. They seemed to be quite confused about a lot of species. They didn't get out and about any more, after all. Tyrian scanned the shelves and found some about vampires. Those would do nicely. He plucked a book from the shelf and settled down to read.

* * * * *

Lucinda headed over to Sheva to help with the coronation preparations. They were having a quick run through of the ceremony today, minus all the pomp. The real thing was tomorrow. Lucinda and the other ex-rebels were all to be there, in their own special section. They were more or less the reason Sara was queen, after all. And of course, Johann Von Stollenheim. He had always held that Sara was the rightful heir, and that he would hand the country over when it was time. It was time now. It hadn't been very long. Lucinda hadn't been able to see him as much the last few months, kinging being serious business, especially after a hostile takeover, but now he was going to start a new life with Rosie, leaving both Sheva and the traditional vampire life behind.

"Johann!" Lucinda greeted him when the practice was finally over.

"Well if it isn't Miss Prince." Johann smiled warmly at her. He was still king for twenty four hours and it looked like he was going to make the most of it. Lucinda thought privately that despite his complaints about the desert weather, he'd secretly liked being king. Johann had once told her he'd rather have her job and be a prince. He didn't much like living alone in a spooky castle surrounded by dismal woods. She suspected he really wanted to hand over the kingdom to please Sara. He seemed to feel some responsibility for his father's actions and was desperate to make amends. And he'd been delighted to find that he had a sister. Despite everything, Sara really did seem to have warmed up to him.

"How are you doing?" Lucinda asked. "Ready for the coronation tomorrow?"

"As ready as I'll ever be." Johann replied. He yawned. He had bags under his eyes and he seemed a little jumpy. "I just hope nothing goes wrong. There was so much stuff to plan. The most complicated thing vampires have ever had to plan is a boat journey and a house purchase. Vampires aren't meant to be kings."

"Um, speaking of . . . I met a relative of yours this morning," Lucinda said. "Tyrian. Have you had much to do with him?"

"Oh dear," he replied. "Did he give you a mysterious object, by any chance?" Ah. No wonder he was looking harassed. Since Tyrian had turned up, Lucinda had felt nothing *but* harassed. And it wasn't even as if he was doing it on purpose.

"How did you know that?" she asked, with a sinking feeling.

"He paid me a visit this morning too." Johann pressed his lips together. "Let's just say our experiences were not dissimilar. Although I expect an Otherworld door did not open in your bedroom at 5am."

"So um, you've still got yours then?" she asked him, trying to keep the pleading out of her voice.

"It's locked up safe and disguised to boot," he said. " . . . It's been half a day and you lost yours?"

"It wasn't even an hour," she admitted shamefully. "Um, aren't we not supposed to talk about this?" she added, remembering Tyrian's instructions to tell no-one.

"I'm being as vague as possible, but that's stories for you." He sighed. "Let me know if you need any help."

"Afraid you can't," Lucinda replied. "It's on Earth somewhere. At least you seem to have everything under control."

"If only it were that simple," he sighed.

"You're expecting something bad to happen?" she asked.

"Of course," Johann replied. "We're talking ancient artefacts here. We'll be lucky if we don't let out an ancient evil and destroy a city or two." Lucinda cringed.

"You really think it's going to be that bad?"

"All we can do is wait and see, I'm afraid," he replied. "Anything can happen in a fairytale with actual fairies in it . . ."

* * * * *

Tyrian looked up from his book. He'd nearly finished the whole thing, which was just as well, because the light would fade soon. Should he carry on reading, and pretend to ignore Erlina, or should he just jump up and grab her before she even saw him? He could use a spell, but the problem with fairies using spells against one another was that they knew what was coming; it was like trying use psychology on a psychologist. When fairies fought each other, physical force was usually the best choice. Tyrian decided it was best to go with ignoring her.

The witch had largely ignored him all afternoon, although she'd given him a mug of something red and spicy and a plate of biscuits a little while ago when she'd told him she was off to gather fresh herbs. He bit a chunk off one and took a sip of the now cooled liquid. It was sweet, and tasted of cinnamon. There was a tang to it that he'd detected in the purple stuff earlier. More vampire medicine, then. Was she worried he'd need blood? He was fine for a while yet. It did cross his mind that he might be in trouble without his servants. Traditional vampiring was *so* not his style. Sneaking up on women in their bedrooms was for bad guys. You got into a lot of trouble with story karma for that sort of thing. He heard someone open and close a door very carefully. No witch would enter her own house with such caution. He looked back down at his book. He waited for a moment before theatrically licking a finger and turning the page. Apart from the rustling of the pages, the house was unnaturally silent.

"I've no intention of marrying you whatsoever," he announced to the room at large. "You can drop that invisibility spell at once. I heard you come in." The silence took on a resentful quality. "I'm disappointed. You ought to know I wouldn't chase you down like this just for avoiding a marriage."

"So you say," Erlina appeared at the door. "But I don't see why else you should come and find me."

Tyrian sighed inwardly. He had to admit that searching for relatives was normally done by other people if you were royalty, but it wasn't unheard of. Kings had feelings too.

"Oh, so you going missing in addition to almost everyone else I care about isn't traumatic at all?" he scolded her. "No, I couldn't possibly have any other reason than to drag you home by your ear." Erlina looked down at her feet.

"I'm sorry . . ." she mumbled. "It's just that it's not the right time, and it's not been very long . . . I didn't think anyone would be worried."

"Normally we would have left you alone, it's true," he said. "Erlina, there's something very important I have to tell you-"

It was a good while before Erlina calmed down. The last words she'd had with her mother had been harsh and it had been a fight about the engagement to boot. But regret would have to be put aside for now.

"Erlina, we have to get back to Fairyland," Tyrian said as her sobs finally subsided. "Do you know where there's a door?"

"No," came her muffled reply. She pulled her face away from his shirt long enough to say, "When I ran away how to get back home was not a priority. I was only going to stay away for ten years or so, but I thought I had plenty of time to find a door."

"I suppose we'll just have to go back through Sheva after all," he replied. It was too bad he couldn't use the door he'd used this morning to hand the sword to his cousin. But it was one way as they usually were, and that would mean someone would need to be contacted to open the door from the other side. With Wild Troopers crawling all over the forest trying to find it and the sword, it wasn't worth the risk. He'd have to take the coach road across the desert like the other guests.

"Are you staying here tonight?" Erlina asked him.

"No. I don't think Miss Rosie would appreciate it," he replied. "She made the excellent suggestion that I stay with Grandma Connie. I'll do just that. I have a coronation to attend tomorrow after all."

"Do we not have better things to worry about than the coronation?" Erlina asked him.

"Erlina, we're fairies," he reminded her. "We get very testy when we don't get invited to important royal events, so when we *do* get an invite we really ought to show up. Stay here tonight. I'll come and find you tomorrow." He stayed with her for a short while until Rosie returned. Then he left for his grandmother's.

"Vhy did you not come to me sooner?" his grandmother scolded him. "You turn up on my doorstep and tell me there is a var, vhich by the vay, is none of my business, and then you say 'Oh I'm stuck vith no door home, can I stay for zer night', I mean, vhat, is it okay to leave your country in var

vithout zer king, Johann is never zis irresponsible-"
Tyrian tuned out as his grandmother continued to
lecture him. She wasn't royalty herself, but she'd been
related to quite a bit of it over the centuries. She was
his great great grandmother, related to him by her
daughter Cordelia, who had married into the Dark
royal family four generations ago. She'd gone to
Fairyland to study witchcraft. His great grandfather
had come across her gathering herbs in a forest,
thought she was pretty and asked her to marry him on
the spot, as was traditional. If you were a king or
indeed a prince, and came across a pretty girl you
fancied in a forest, that's just what you did, and
political unions could go to Hel if she actually turned
out to be a commoner, unlikely as it was.

Contessa, like Johann and a few of her other
relatives, walked the shaky tightrope of being a
traditional vampire in a relatively modern world. She
did the accent and she was beautiful and alluring and
she had a great big, spooky mansion, even if the
outside did look more like a giant cottage. The inside
was all red and black and poorly illuminated. Black,
dribbly candles burned in antique sconces, their blue
flames illuminating portraits of relatives long dead.
There was barely an inch of wall without a portrait or
other painting and the floor was carpeted in red too,
embroidered in silver with bats and other dead
giveaway animals. She'd chosen to lecture him in the
drawing room, or indeed, the 'drawink room', where
she met most of her guests. She normally lounged on

the chaise longue, a long couch designed for such things, all delicate carvings and red plush. She was sitting up on it now though, frowning at him across the hearth of the wide fireplace. The fire added little light to the room, but it did highlight her red eyes and long, white hair, and sparkled off her jewellery. She was clothed in a long, black, velvet dress and matching gloves. Her eyes were dark with red eye shadow and her lips rouged. He'd always thought she overdid the make-up a little, but certain things were expected of vampires out here. It wasn't so much of a species as a job description. For some stupid reason, humans complained if their local vampire wasn't putting the bite on them, so to speak, but if they were a little too scary, people came calling with pointy sticks, hammers and determined expressions. Humans were weird like that.

Contessa clipped him around the ear.

"Are you even listening to me?" She stood up and seized his ear, pulling it towards her.

"Ow, yes! Mostly-" he protested. "Let go, that hurts!"

"That is zer point," she replied primly. "So as I vas saying, I know a return door, but it is razer far avay, and I presume you have a coronation to attend tomorrow."

"I do," he replied. "I would have brought Lina, but if *we* couldn't find her where she is, neither will Lir. And I expect she'd like some space." No one had even thought to look for Erlina on Earth and that was where she'd been until about three or four months ago, so she'd said. No-one had been too worried at first, because stories took people away on adventures all the time, and princesses always got rescued, but by then two-thirds of Fairyland's royalty had disappeared, and suddenly it seemed a little too convenient. "You know, if Lina were in my position this would all be so much simpler. Princesses have it easier when it comes to this sort of thing."

"Zis is true," Contessa replied. "If you vere still a prince, perhaps simpler still."

"But I'm not." He flopped back onto his own couch. He gazed glumly up at the shadowy ceiling. "Kings don't rescue people. I have to get someone else to do it for me. I can't even protect my own family because of the damn rules."

"Better zat than how it vorks on Earth, child," Contessa replied darkly. "Zey have no rules zere, the poor things. But I am sure you have karma on your side."

"Oh good. I'm sure if I just sit around karma will rescue everyone for me," he replied, continuing to sulk at the ceiling.

"Zere's no need to take zat tone, I vas just trying to cheer you up," Contessa complained. "Vorrying about it von't help you. You just need to do vhat you can, vhich you are."

"Mmm," he responded. He wondered if it really would be worse if Fairyland were more like Earth. The humans there didn't follow any story rules whatsoever, it seemed. And stories weren't exactly fair.

Say some dragon has been rampaging and demanding sacrifices. Finally the townspeople run short on virgins, and the man at the top has to give up his own daughter. She's willing to do so, terrified as she is, and of course some knight or prince comes by, and rescues the fair maiden, marries her and becomes the next king or whatever. That's all very well and good for him, but it doesn't help the poor townspeople who lost their daughters. They may not have come with a dowry, but they were surely just as loved. Sometimes story karma took a long time to catch up. But his grandmother was right. There was no use sulking about it. Turning his head towards her, he asked;

"I don't suppose you have any spare clothes lying around that are suitable for coronations?"

* * * * *

Lucinda got home and fired up her laptop and opened her messenger. If talking to her Otherworld friends about things she'd specifically been told not to mention was hard, talking to her Earth friends about her day was impossible. She was reduced to talking about school. Luckily, Pens and the others were also in a school-lamenting mood. She talked for a little while before settling down to go to sleep.

What a day that had been. But tomorrow was going to be worse. Tomorrow she was going to have to talk to people. Who didn't want to be talked to. And the fate of a nation might depend on it. Fabulous. Why couldn't Rina be a monster? She knew how to deal with monsters. She'd been building up her experience. She knew how best to fight dragons, hydras, griffins . . . But it seemed like no matter how much experience she got with 'normal' people she never got any better at dealing with them. She drifted off into a troubled sleep.

"Is that her?"

"It must be."

"I've seen her before. That's definitely her."

"She doesn't look like a thief." A jumble of voices. Three, maybe four? It was difficult to make them out. Were they talking about *her*? The discussion continued.

"How exactly does one look like a thief?" There was a pause as the other voices thought about this.

"You know, black and white stripes, or, or a piece of cloth tied round your nose."

"You know, I never did trust zebras."

"A piece of cloth tied round your nose?"

"That's how you can tell in Japan."

"She isn't Japanese. *That* I can tell by looking."

"Isn't it a bit *counterproductive* to look like a thief?"

"I know, right? If you want to steal stuff, you don't want to look like you're going to. People would watch you."

"So you're saying that because she *doesn't* look like a thief, she's more likely to be one?"

"That's stupid. On that basis, everyone looks like a thief."

"How come she doesn't come look at this girl herself, anyway?" Lucinda opened her eyes. At least, she thought she did. She wasn't in her bedroom. She was by a pond, surrounded by all manner of flowers. There were trees and bushes surrounding the pond on all sides, making it impossible to see what lay beyond it. But that wasn't all. A pair of birds, both species she didn't recognise, were watching her from one of the trees. There was a badger peeking out from one of the bushes.

"She can't," the badger spoke, apparently addressing one of the birds. "It might get . . . awkward. You know that. You know the rules."

"Yeah, but she isn't going to know, is she?" the bird replied testily. "It's a dream. Humans dream all sorts of rubbish."

"Still, better to be safe than sorry," the other bird chipped in. Lucinda sat up. All three animals turned to look at her.

"Speaking of which . . ." the badger said. The dream blurred.

Lucinda awoke with a jump. Which was odd. Talking animals were practically standard in real life, never mind dreams. She went back to sleep.

* * * * *

Having picked out an outfit for tomorrow, Tyrian went back downstairs. His grandmother had moved to the dining room, where she was being fussed over by some of her servants. They were laying out dinner.

"Did you find somezing?" she asked him as he entered the room.

"I did," he replied. He'd picked out the most modern-looking of the men's clothes from her wardrobes. It was a simple, green tunic with a pattern of white and gold along the hem and dark brown trousers. He was wearing a long sleeved, white shirt underneath. It wasn't really fancy enough for a coronation, but it would have to do. At least it was green and looked like something you'd traditionally find in Fairyland. There was the *other* traditional fairy 'attire' of course - the ever popular birthday suit - but he didn't think Princess Saharaleia would appreciate it.

"Sit down and eat," Contessa told him. "Are you thirsty?"

"I'm all right," he replied. "What I came in for is, I wanted to use your mirror. Aurelia doesn't know where I am."

"Go ahead, you know vhere it is," she replied. "I'll ask the servants to leave you out somesing that von't spoil." Tyrian thanked her and headed for the magic mirror.

It was right at the top of the house, in a set of rooms only accessible via a combination of a secret passage and a highly localised Otherworld door. She was unlikely to come to blows with any mobs out here, but old habits died hard.

He waited anxiously for someone to answer. What if Lir had invaded already? What if Aurelia hadn't gotten away from the Wild Troopers? What if-

"You better have a good reason for calling the king's-" an angry voice began, as someone whipped the blanket away from the other mirror.

"Aurelia!" he said, flooding with relief.

"Master Tyrian!" Aurelia responded, a smile spreading across her face. She dropped her voice to a whisper, "I knew you'd get away! Where are you?"

"At Grandma Connie's," he replied. "I'm so glad you're safe!"

"It'll take more than Lir and her cronies to finish me off," Aurelia replied, grinning. "Now listen," she continued, still in hushed tones "The nobles are demanding you call Parliament immediately. We've stalled them by telling them you had to flee the country to hide the treasures, but we won't keep them quiet much longer, not with the Wild Troopers gathering at the borders. You have to get back here as soon as you can."

"I'm working on it," he replied. "I'll be coming home tomorrow after the coronation in Sheva."

"That should work great!" She gave him a thumbs up. "The coronation party just left an hour ago, they'll arrive tomorrow afternoon. I thought I'd better send someone just in case you didn't make it. Don't want to look like we're giving Sheva the finger on top of everything else."

"Indeed," he replied. He could have persuaded Sheva's queen to be very understanding under the circumstances, but her nobles might take a different view. Ugh. Nobles. Speaking of which. "*Must* I call Parliament? I can't stand dealing with those people. That's why I dismissed them in the first place."

"You must," she replied. "Half of them are baying for blood. Foreign blood, for preference. You need to deal with it."

"But I'm so *bad* at dealing with it . . ." he muttered.

"Don't you *want* to be king?" the yokai asked, folding her arms.

"No," he replied, without thinking. Aurelia glared at him. He might have tried to deny it if it were someone else, to bite back his words, but not to Aurelia. There was no point. He could back pedal like a champion, though. "I mean, not like this! I thought I had a few decades left to learn how to be a king! Dad wasn't even born to it, and he's a thousand times the king I'll ever be-"

"I've told you a hundred times, you'll never get anywhere if you keep comparing yourself to Connall!" she stopped him. "You're not him, and he's not here! It's like you expect him to come striding in and rescue you. It's not going to happen! You're not a prince any more, you're king, and you need to start acting like it!"

"But I'm no good with all this politics stuff . . ." he sulked.

"Let me put it another way, then," Aurelia said, "Do you want *Lir* to be queen?"

"Oh *Hel* no." Tyrian shook his head.

"There you are, then," she replied, matter-of-factly. "Now get your butt back here and *call Parliament!*" She dropped the cover back over the mirror, ending the call.

She was right of course. He ought to be ashamed... Aurelia knew what he was going through more than anyone. He would always remember how she'd come to the palace . . .

"Tyrian, come here," came his father's voice from down the hall. Tyrian poked his head out of his bedroom doorway. It was early, almost breakfast time. The maids hadn't come to get him up yet. His father, being a commoner, never waited for the maids. He stood in the hallway, ready and dressed, staring intently out of the window.

"What is it, Daddy?" Tyrian asked, joining him by the window. He rubbed sleep out of his eyes as his father opened the window a crack. Fresh air streamed through, along with the panicky tones of one of the maids. He stood on tiptoe to peer over the window ledge. One of them was looking every which way in the garden.

"Not again!" she wailed. "If it keeps happening they'll fire me or worse!"

"What now?" came another woman's voice.

"That wretched little thief again!" the first woman sobbed. "I'm going to get in so much trouble if the king and queen find out! Wh-what if they decide to eat *me* because I let something get away with their breakfast?"

"There, there," the other woman soothed. "They probably won't. Come on, we have to start serving soon."

"I s-suppose so," the first maid sniffled.

"Now then Tyr," his father said. "We have a damsel in distress. So what shall we do, hmm?"

"Rescue her!" Tyrian replied excitedly, all sleepiness forgotten.

"That's right," his father replied, ruffling his hair. "Come on then, quickly." His father set off down the corridor at a brisk pace.

"But I'm not dressed!" he protested. He was wearing his silk pajamas still.

"It's a poor hero who worries about how he's dressed when there's folk in trouble, Tyr," the king replied. Tyrian knew he was going to get a scolding from his mother later, but this was a hero lesson and he would much rather brave a telling off than miss it. Tyrian trotted along the corridor after his father.

They went down the stairs into the kitchens and out the back door. His father scanned the gardens and then nudged his son. He leant down ever so slightly and whispered;

"In the corner there, where the bushes are," he said, barely audible. "Go on." The 'garden' was small and walled. It was really just somewhere to throw out kitchen scraps and let the servants have somewhere nice to sit on their breaks. There were bushes along the edge closest to the palace wall, a little bit of lawn and a bed of flowers on the opposite side, with a few benches. The whole thing was surrounded by walls, cutting it off from the royal pleasure gardens beyond.

Tyrian crept along the dew-laden grass, his feet still bare. He didn't know what his father thought he would find in the bushes; they were too short for anyone to hide under, even a child. But obviously he expected Tyrian to find *something*, and he didn't want whatever it was to get away. Crouching down, he peered into the undergrowth. He couldn't see anything, so he had no choice but to kneel down and crawl under. His knee squished something. He looked at the dark, purple stain on his pajama bottoms. It was a berry. It hadn't come from the bush though, that was in flower. He crawled a little further and got as low as he could. Cowering against the wall, eyes wide as saucers with all its fur on end, was a tabby kitten. There was a little pile of berries beside it, as well as trio of freshly made pastries. He could smell them from here. He looked from the pastries to the kitten and back.

"So you're the thief," he said. He reached out and the kitten hissed, swiping at him. He couldn't quite reach, so he crawled a little closer. The kitten scratched his finger and he yelled. It bolted and he exploded out of the bush in pursuit, hurling a spell at it. There was a yelp as it hit, pinning the kitten in mid air. It struggled and spat, but to no avail. Covered in leaves and petals, Tyrian approached it cautiously. His father joined him.

"That's no way to treat a damsel in distress, Tyrian," he chided.

"But that's the thief," Tyrian protested. "I thought the maid was the damsel in distress?"

"She was certainly distressed, but she wasn't *in* distress," his father replied. Crouching down, he addressed the kitten in gentle tones;

"You don't need to hide, I'm not angry." The kitten's form shifted. It became a little girl. Green eyed with shoulder length, brown hair and dressed in rags, she shouted at them in a foreign tongue, still struggling against the spell. "It's all right, we won't hurt you," the king tried to reassure her. "Calm down. Tyr, drop that spell." Tyrian did as he was told. The girl dropped to the ground. She practically slammed into the wall in her haste to back away where she hissed at them.

"Tell her it's all right, Tyr," his father said. "She's frightened."

"She looks angry to me," Tyrian replied doubtfully.

"When people are frightened they often cover it up by getting angry," his father said. "Say something reassuring." Tyrian thought for a moment as the girl continued to snarl, baring her fangs at them.

"I've got fangs too, see?" Tyrian told her, opening his mouth and tapping one of his. She stared at him.

"Tyr, I don't think-" his father started.

"Yokai?" the girl asked, settling down a little. "You yokai?"

"So you are a yokai," the king said. "There's more and more of them about lately. Did your parents abandon you, little girl? How did you get here? There's no need to steal, you know. There's plenty of food out there, just growing on the trees." Hunger was not a problem in Fairyland. The magical atmosphere kept the whole country in a state of eternal spring and autumn. The magical plants bloomed and bore fruit in a continuous cycle, never losing their leaves. This in turn, supported plenty of animals, so the hunting was good if you needed meat. There was one problem;

"'Never eat the food in Fairyland'," she quoted. "Fruit here bad. Stone fruit. Poison fruit. Can't eat." Of course. Tyrian knew many foreigners were scared to eat any 'fairy food' because it was magical and dangerous. Magical flora was like that. One magical apple might give you eternal youth, another might make you so full you never ate again and starved to death. That explained the pile of berries. "I watch people. See what people eating. But tired, fall down wall. Can't go. Tried, go kitchen, kitchen people shout, run here again."

"That was clever of you, watching people to see what was safe," his father praised her. "I'm sorry the kitchen people shouted at you," he said, imitating her limited English. "They should have known you couldn't get out here, the walls are too high, aren't they?" The little girl nodded. "You want some breakfast?" he asked her, holding out his hand for her to take. She took a hesitant step forward.

"Kitchen people no shout?" she asked.

"No, the kitchen people won't shout," he reassured her. She didn't take his hand, but she stepped forward to show she would follow him.

The two of them led the yokai girl into the dining room, where his mother was waiting, a sour look on her face. Tyrian clung to his father's hand.

"Connall, this is not proper," she complained, giving his father a stern look. "Wearing such dirty things at the dinner table. I take it this waif is what you disappeared to take care of?"

"Now dear," the king began, "it's traditional to take in orphans you find stealing your food. The dirty clothes can't be helped."

"Very well, dear," she said, settling down. "I married you for your compassion, I shan't scold you for it." Sighing in relief, Tyrian seated himself next to his father and helped himself to the various dishes set out on the table. There were fruits, various pastries, cooked meats, plenty of fresh baked bread and an assortment of juices and herbal concoctions. The three of them could never eat it all, but what there was left was free for the maids and other servants to eat or take home. "They feed us, we have to feed them," his parents said.

The yokai girl was eyeing the table with apprehension.

"Sit with her and talk to her," Connall instructed Tyrian. "You're supposed to be rescuing her, yes? She isn't rescued yet, and she's still very nervous." Tyrian didn't quite understand, but he would do as he was told. He patted the chair next to him.

"Sit here," he said. "You can eat whatever you like, it isn't poison." The girl sat with him and looked at the selection, making furtive glances at the queen. "Mama won't shout at you," Tyrian told her.

"Go ahead dear, it's all right," the queen said. The girl took a few slices of dried meat, then a piece of fruit. Her movements were slow and uncertain.

"Where are your parents?" Tyrian asked her. She shook her head. "Your Mama and Papa?" he tried.

"Mama and Papa move," she said. "Move home. People shout, make go. Not like yokai. Move again, same. We move again, people run us, shout, I run in door. Mama and Papa no run in door. I wait, door no open, I wait again . . . again door no open . . ." she trailed off. She looked around at the table and the high ceiling. The Dark Palace was mostly made of dark, blue-black marble, inlaid with silver swirls and patterns. She froze.

"What's wrong?" Tyrian asked. The girl pushed herself back from the table, shaking from head to toe. She cried something in her own language. "What is it, what's wrong?" Tyrian tried again.

"No!" she shouted. "No want! No want story!" She jumped off the chair and ran, hauling open the huge doors and slipping through them.

"I'm going to find some yokai, dear," Connall said, standing up. "I think we need a translator." Tyrian was already halfway across the room. This time, he didn't need a nudge from his father. The distress was apparent. He followed her through the palace as she frantically searched for the way out, heading down the stairs and dodging startled servants. She made it all the way outside, only to run into the portcullis. She collapsed in front of it, sobbing.

"It's all right," Tyrian said, kneeling beside her. "What's wrong?" She replied in her own language, but all he understood were the words 'Mama' and 'Papa'. "We'll find them," he tried. "Don't worry, we'll help you." She let herself be led back into the palace.

His father arrived with several yokai, one of whom was able to speak to her.

"She says her family was moving again after being driven out of their homes," the yokai man explained. "Her family was travelling when they were attacked and she ran through a door by accident. She thought her parents would come through, but they didn't and although she has waited by the door many times, it has not opened. She doesn't know where they were when they were attacked or where they were headed."

"Could you ask her what frightened her so in the dining room?" Connall asked him. The man asked her and she started to cry again. He made some consoling noises before answering the king.

"She is frightened that she is stuck in a story and that she will never see her parents again," the man answered. "She says she doesn't want to be an orphan." The girl pointed at the portcullis, tugging at the yokai man's trousers and pleading for something. "She asks if you can open the gate, she badly wants to find the door she came through, in case her parents come by."

"Very well," Connall replied. To Tyrian he said, "Tyrian, you look after her. She doesn't need to ask the guards to open the gate, does she?" He winked. Young royals always knew a way to give their own guards the slip. "She'll stay with us for now, so you show her."

"Yes Papa," he said.

"That's a good boy," Connall replied, ruffling his hair.

"Do they need an escort, Your Majesty?" asked one of the guards. Connall shook his head.

"No," he replied. "If a story wants to take them, no amount of guards will help. Besides, Tyrian is with her. She won't come to any harm."

Tyrian kept up with her as she walked briskly through the town and out into the forests. He couldn't tell where she was heading, but she seemed to know her way. At what seemed like an entirely random spot she stopped and stared at a patch of air. He knew that it was a closed door. There was no way to open it from this side. All they could do was wait until it opened from the other side. And wait they did. For days, all she did besides grabbing breakfast and supper was stare at the empty air. She wouldn't even leave for dinner, so Tyrian brought her fruit and nuts to eat. After a while, she followed him to help him gather them. The door was in sight of a clearing containing a pool. It was filled with flowers and the water was safe enough to drink, as long as the inhabitants could be avoided. Over time she strayed away from the door, exploring the clearing and making necklaces with the flowers. She started wandering out of sight of the door and began staying longer at the palace after breakfast and going home sooner, even going home for dinner. At night, not wanting to be alone, she curled up as a kitten and slept on the end of Tyrian's bed.

"Aurelia," his father asked her one day. "I need to ask you something."

"Ask me then," she replied. Her visits to the door had become infrequent and her English was much improved.

"I want to offer you a job," he explained. "Do not feel like you have to accept. I do not want you to feel trapped."

"What job?" Aurelia asked.

"I would like to register you as Tyrian's fool," he said. "We'll pay you a wage and we'll buy all your food and clothes for you."

"Fool?" she asked. "What does it mean? What do I do?"

"All you have to do is keep Tyrian company," he explained, "to be his friend. You've been getting along well, haven't you? We may as well pay you for it." Tyrian looked from his father to Aurelia. He hoped she would say yes. He didn't get to play with children his own age very much.

"I can leave if my parents come back?" she asked.

"Of course," Connall replied.

"I'll do it," Aurelia replied. "Then, when Mama and Papa come back, they will be proud of me."

"That is a very grown-up thing to say, Aurelia," Connall praised her. "I'm sure they'll be very proud of you."

Later, when they were alone, Tyrian had to ask his father something. It was something that had been bothering him more and more since she'd run out of the breakfast hall, crying.

"Papa, did we do a bad thing helping Aurelia?" he asked.

"No Tyr, it wasn't a bad thing," his father replied. "It's not bad to be kind."

"Why did story karma take her away from her parents?" he asked. "She's nice, why is the story being mean to her? Stories want us to be nice, don't they?"

"If stories were always kind, we might become cruel," his father said, kissing him on the forehead. "Stories teach us to be kind, precisely because they are not. You remember that."

Aurelia's parents had never come back. They'd looked for them using scrying spells but they'd never been successful. She'd taken solace in the fact that they were at least alive and had decided that staying put was the best way to have them find her, if they managed to figure out where she was. Yokai lived a long time, almost as long as fairies. There was always a chance they would turn up some day. It did happen. One day, the once-orphan would come into the presence of their parents, unrecognised, and something would come up that would identify them to one another. It was different for Tyrian, but he held out hope nevertheless. Most of the kingdom had given up on his parents, but Aurelia had not. He was grateful for it. And he had to do as she had done.

When they came back, he wanted to have done them
proud.

Night and Day were dutiful, and they did as their mother asked. But Nature was wild and wilful. Though she performed her tasks and had many offspring, she felt she had been burdened with these creatures, and with a greater task than her siblings. She grew bitter and angry.

"Why should I protect the weak? Why should they not die? Why should I tame the world?"

Nature abandoned her duties, and there was much suffering and pain. Crops would not grow, the skies would not be calmed and the clay creatures were imperiled.

Day and Night were much troubled and they did what they could, but they were unable to manage everything alone. Day tried to perform Nature's duties, leaving Night to perform hers, but it was to no avail.

Chapter 4:

The Coronation

Today was the big day. Sara's coronation. Lucinda had a bad feeling about it. In story country, with a war going on in the next kingdom and an involved artefact on the premises, there was no way things were going to go smoothly. And she had the joy of school to deal with first.

She'd seen Rina walking through the park yesterday, so maybe that was her route to school. She had time for a little detour. She headed towards the park. But it wasn't Rina she found. It was Shu. She was sat on a bench, looking up at the trees.

"Shu?" Lucinda called out as she approached. "I didn't expect to see you here." Shu looked down as something fluttered away.

"Tch. You scared him away," Shu complained, getting up. "And you should've. I always walk this way to school."

"Sorry," Lucinda apologised. "Having a little nature walk?"

"Trying to." Shu waved an admonishing finger at Lucinda. "Before Ms. Loudmouth turned up."

"Is before school really the best time?"

"If you don't mind what you're looking for, any time is the best time," Shu replied.

"I don't think there's much interesting here, though," Lucinda said, looking around. "Is there?"

"That's your problem, Lucinda," Shu said. "You don't think *anything* here is interesting. But you haven't looked hard enough. You know a guy once discovered like, eight new species just by studying what was in his back garden?" Lucinda scuffed the dirt with her toe.

"Sorry," she said. "I didn't mean anything by it. I guess I'm just not as much of a nature buff as you are."

"I wasn't talking about that . . ." Shu replied. She looked wistfully at the park. "Ah well. I guess I should get going anyway. You too. Speaking of which, you're early, aren't you? You never get to school before me." Lucinda tilted her head to one side;

"Is that so?" she said. "Sounds like a challenge to me." Shu put on an affronted expression;

"Oh does it now?" Shu hoisted her bag onto her shoulder. "Race you to school?"

"Last one there is a generic spoiled food!" Lucinda yelled, taking off towards the school.

Shu won their little contest. Lucinda had never been particularly athletic. Training with Gerda and running away from monsters a lot in the past year seemed to have helped, though. Still. She'd missed her chance to talk to Rina outside of school, but she wouldn't have been able to talk to her properly with Shu there.

"Say, Lucinda," Shu began as they plonked their school bags down on the table. "What were you doing in the park, anyway? I've never seen you go that way before." Lucinda had two options. An out and out lie that she would have to make up on the spot, or the truth, part of it anyway, which would sound just as unlikely, if not more so. She went with the truth.

"This probably sounds dumb," she replied, "but I thought I'd try and talk to Rina. I saw her walking through the park yesterday." She left out the bit about wandering fairy kings. "I thought, you know, she's the new girl and all."

"That's a bit of a detour just for-" Shu was cut off.

"I don't need your pity, thank you." Rina had chosen that moment to appear in the doorway. "I didn't need your help yesterday and I don't need you trying to be my friend just out of some good Samaritan B.S." She glared at the pair of them. "Just leave me alone. I'll talk to people when I want to talk to people." She pushed her way past them and sat at her desk, ignoring them as hard as she could.

"What-" Shu began indignantly, but Lucinda waved her into silence. She'd already screwed up the day royally and this time school hadn't even begun yet.

Lucinda tried to apologise throughout the day, although she wasn't entirely sure what for. Not that she'd expected this to be easy, but it was still terrible. She'd made Rina angry and she hadn't even got to mentioning the theft yet.

Lucinda landed herself another detention for not paying attention in class. The whole time she thought and thought but could come up with nothing to remedy the situation. Plodding dejectedly through the corridors on her way home in a deepening despair, her lack of attention got her hit by a door.

"Oh man, I'm so sorry!" came a girl's voice. Lucinda rubbed her nose and was surprised to see the offending door close to reveal Rina on the other side.

"I know I upset you this morning and all, but I think trying to break my nose is going a bit far," Lucinda protested.

"Sorry," Rina apologised again. "For the door I mean. I didn't know anyone was there."

"What are you doing here anyway?" Said door belonged to the staff room. Students were forbidden to go in there.

"My mum is a teacher," Rina explained, with some reluctance. "She forgot something so she sent me home for it."

"Look, I'm sorry about this morning," Lucinda blurted out before she missed her chance again. "It's just that I was the new girl last year, and . . . well, you know."

"Yeah, well," the girl said begrudgingly. "Sorry, I guess."

"Umm, can I ask you something?" Lucinda was going to have to ask or have a rotten night's sleep. "You know yesterday, when all my stuff went all over the floor . . ." She hesitated. She couldn't accuse Rina of theft. Whether she had taken the pendant or not, being hostile would do no good. "Did you see a big green stone?" Rina narrowed her eyes.

"You mean the one that creepy guy tried to give me?" she replied suspiciously.

"Yeah," Lucinda replied, scratching her nose. "That's the one."

"I thought I saw it on the floor when your stuff went everywhere," she replied. "What was it?"

"Um, it's a family heirloom, sort of thing," Lucinda replied.

"*Sure* it is." The girl rolled her eyes. "Why are you asking, anyway? . . . You've gone and lost it, haven't you?"

"Yeah," Lucinda admitted. "When my stuff went everywhere. I was hoping you'd seen it, since you're the only other person who knows what it looks like. It's important I get it back, so-" Rina snorted.

"That's what you get for taking stuff from grifters," she said, her tone unsympathetic. "I'll keep my eye out, I guess. But you should just call the police, y'know?" Rina shut the door and headed off down the corridor, without so much as a goodbye. Lucinda was almost used to it by now, but it still stung a little. She left the school more riddled with doubt than ever. And that wasn't all she had to worry about. She'd lost an hour and she had a coronation to get to.

* * * * *

Tyrian spent much of his day catching up on missed sleep, difficult as it was. He had a little time before the coronation so he thought he'd visit Erlina. When he got there however, he was frustrated to find the cottage deserted. His plan thwarted, he decided to just head to Sheva a little early. Princess Saharaleia wasn't at her offices of course, so he enquired of the person manning the desk which way he should go and headed right through to Sheva.

When he arrived, he found himself amongst a steady stream of incoming guests, including, to his dismay, Lady Lir. No doubt she was using Titania's invitation as her own. He should have known. This was just the sort of event she could use to flaunt her false queenship. In front of a great deal of foreign dignitaries, no less. No retinue, though. Doubtless she couldn't spare the soldiers, with a newly occupied Realm to keep under control. She only had two guards with her that he could see. Still, she was best avoided for now. Blending into the crowd, he headed for the palace to find Johann.

* * * * *

Lucinda arrived at the Rent-A-Legend offices dressed and ready to go. She'd been instructed to wear her prince outfit. Everyone else was all dressed up, but she was there as a member of Sara's rebels and she was supposed to be a boy. Her prince outfit would just have to do.

Gerda and Freya, Sara's right hand women, were there waiting already. Gerda was wearing gold armour that had been polished to an eye-watering degree of shininess. She was wearing her long, blonde hair down for once, and she had thick leather sandals on under a knee-length white dress and leather bracers. Lucinda half-expected her to break out into opera at any moment.

Freya was wearing her normal array of fur and fluff, with only her blue eyes and the merest wisps of coal black hair showing in the gap between her scarf and hat. The only thing different was the colour. Freya was clothed head to toe in black. Sheva was a desert kingdom and Lucinda would have questioned the sanity of this were it anyone else, but Freya was a snow woman. She wore all those layers to stop *other people* getting cold.

"You took your time, Cinders!" Gerda remarked, giving her sword a little wave. "Couldn't decide what to wear, eh?" Lucinda stuck her tongue out at the valkyrie.

"I got detention," she explained sulkily. "Again."

"No harm is done," Freya soothed, her voice slightly muffled. "The coronation isn't for another hour yet. We have lots of time." Lucinda looked around for a conspicuously absent member of Sara's rebels.

"Isn't Charming coming?" she asked.

"'E's coming from a different door," Gerda replied. "Picking up a lady friend, he said."

"So we're all here then?" Lucinda prompted, eager to get going.

"We are now, yeah," Gerda confirmed. "Sara's gone ahead to set up." The three of them set off down the corridor for the door to Sheva. It was more carving than door. From top to bottom the wood had been carved into a phoenix, each feather lovingly detailed and coated with red, gold and bronze. The eyes were two rubies. It was the symbol of Sheva's royal family and an excellent metaphor. It certainly looked pretty, but there were claws under there somewhere and it was liable to burst into flame at any moment.

"And just where have you three been?" the soon-to-be queen scolded them. "I thought I was going to need some new employees." She gave them an icy look, or tried to, but Lucinda could tell her heart wasn't it. Today was the day she finally succeeded her mother to the throne. There had been a pair of vampires in-between the two of them, but they didn't count. It was the result of years of hard work and sacrifice - she radiated happiness. She was also getting to boss about a lot more people than usual, and she'd be enjoying that, too.

The coronation itself wasn't to be held in the castle, but in a special courtyard a short distance away. She would have to leave before they did, to get ready. There was a purification ritual beforehand, and it wasn't public. There was a priest involved and that was all Sara would say.

"I don't remember Johann going through all this," said Lucinda. She gazed around at the whirlwind of activity consuming the palace. "There wasn't a ceremony or anything."

"Actually there was," came a reply from behind her, making her jump. She turned to see Johann, dressed in full regalia and smiling broadly. He was wearing a voluminous white robe, tied at his waist, with the baggy trousers tied up just below his knees. It was overlaid by brightly coloured cloth; red, decorated with squares and diamonds of yellow, black and orange. He was wearing a matching hat. It was round and flat, almost like a frisbee. "I asked them not to, but they said I couldn't rule without it. So I insisted that I just do the secret bit and leave it at that." He held up a hand as Lucinda went to ask something. "Don't ask me about it, because I shan't tell you," he reprimanded her, pre-empting her question. "The priests were very firm about that. They said if we went about revealing how you make royalty then everyone would be at it."

"Correct me if I'm wrong, but you got to be king because we had a better army than the other guy," Lucinda countered. "I should think it doesn't matter what the priests did."

"Well, yes, but there's more to it than that." Johann shifted uneasily. "The people could have rejected me, but they didn't. The coronation makes it official."

"I suppose so. . . . But they might still have thought rejecting the guy with the best army was a dumb idea."

"Look, are you happy to be part of a grand and historic occasion or not?" Johann said, folding his arms.

"No, no, I am, I really am. Sorry," Lucinda apologised. "I just have a hard time turning my logic off."

"Unfortunately, Lucy has a point," Tyrian appeared at her shoulder. That was twice a vampire had snuck up on her in five minutes. "I'm afraid you need both, but in the absence of national approval I'm sorry to say that having the nastiest army might well suffice," he said. "Lady Lir certainly thinks so, at least I hope to Gaia she doesn't have national approval." Lucinda shuffled sideways to allow him into their circle. As Tyrian joined them, he glanced sideways at Lucinda and his worried expression melted away into puzzlement. But it didn't last long, because he burst out laughing. It took the group a little while to work out what the joke was.

"Um, I can explain. Kind of," Lucinda began. "If you could please not draw attention-"

"Oh, you don't need to!" the fairy laughed. "This explains everything." He shook his head, smiling. "I thought you were a mysterious young lady, but I never thought it was because you were a mysterious young *man*-"

"*Lucian* 'ere," began Gerda, meaningfully, "is a prince in the service of Her Majesty Queen Saharaleia. If you don't mind." Gerda had been persuaded to acquire a scabbard for the purposes of not injuring Sara's fellow nobles and thus inciting any political incidents, but she had her hand on the hilt, and she was fiddling with it.

"Speaking of Her Majesty," Tyrian said, obediently dropping the subject. "Do you have any idea when she's supposed to be so?" Technically Sara wasn't queen until she was crowned.

"It won't be long now," Johann reassured them all.

"Do you have time for a quiet word?" Tyrian asked.

"I expect so," Johann replied. "I've done all my preparations already, there's nothing I can do now but wait." The two of them disappeared back up the corridor leaving the rebels to talk amongst themselves.

* * * * *

"Might I ask what you did with the sword?" Tyrian asked his cousin when they found a suitably private place to talk.

"I've still got it if that's what you're worried about," Johann replied. "I had it disguised and placed in the vault with the Shevan artefacts. It's posing as part of the crown jewels. I had it covered in gold like the Shevan sword so it doesn't stand out. Don't worry though, it'll come right off." Tyrian was unsure about that. It was a good idea of course – the sword was black; legend said it was carved from adamantite, a magical mineral harder than diamond. How they'd made it was a puzzle. Presumably they'd had to carve it with more adamantite. Covering up its tell-tale colour was a good touch, but he hoped it wouldn't be ruined.

"I see," he replied. "That's a relief."

"If that's all you wanted, we should get back," Johann said.

"I suppose we ought to," Tyrian replied. "You'll be needed at the coronation site any time now, I presume?"

"Yes, I had better get a move on," Johann replied. "It's not long now. Rosie is preparing the oils and flowers and so on for the ceremony as we speak. Erlina is helping." Tyrian started.

"Erlina is helping?" he repeated, alarmed. "I don't suppose you've seen . . . Where is she now?"

"Over at the courtyard, doing the final preparations." Johann caught some of Tyrian's anxiety. "Is something wrong?"

"I must find her immediately!" He strode away.

* * * * *

Lucinda saw Tyrian stride right past them followed closely by a worried Johann. Johann stopped as he reached them, but Tyrian disappeared rapidly down the corridor. The group watched him go.

"What was all that about?" Gerda asked. "Who was he again?"

"He's my cousin, and a king of Fairyland," Johann replied. He wanted to ask me about something, and then he took off when I mentioned Erlina." Lucinda was about to ask about the sword, but then another, nastier thought hit her. Despite the desert heat, she felt herself go cold.

"Johann . . ." she began, "besides Tyrian, who else from Fairyland was invited?"

"All the Fairyland royalty were invited," Johann replied. "They're a neighbouring nation. Not to mention what happens when you don't invite fairies to important events and they get huffed about it. I don't think there's a spinning wheel for miles, but I'm sure they could think of something else to curse." Fairyland was in a state of civil war and they'd invited 'all the royalty'. The invitations had been sent out at least a month ago, back when there was no actual war, but that didn't make this any less terrible.

"I'd better help find Erlina," Lucinda blurted out and took off after the king.

* * * * *

Tyrian hurried towards the courtyard where the coronation was to be held. The crowd was slowing his progress, and they would make Erlina harder to spot, so he decided to approach from the air. He was concerned that he might need his magic later, but it wouldn't do him any good if Lir found Erlina first. Turning into a bat or mist wasn't a good idea in heat like this, so he used a simple levitation spell. From the air, the courtyard was easy to see. It was in fact an oasis, enclosed by four walls, with a tiled floor that left the water untouched in a star of sand. Rectangular in shape, the areas where the audience should stand and the participants should stand were clearly marked out; there was an almost plain, yellow and brown tiled area either side for the onlookers, whereas the path that led from the entrance to a carved black throne was a glorious mosaic made up of countless phoenixes. The throne was made of polished granite and was itself carved like a fire bird. There was a definite theme going on here.

He had to find Erlina quickly. He landed just inside the entrance to the courtyard. There were quite a few people here already; the early arrivals had taken refuge in the shade provided by the walls and a few servants were fussing around a priest. He was dressed similar to Johann, a white robe overlaid with strips of bright fabric draping over his shoulders. The only difference was the simpler cut of the robe. There was a feather on each strip, like a crimson peacock feather with a white eye. They worshipped the phoenix here, after all. It seemed odd to him that they should worship a single bird. Fairies revered nature in general, figuring that if you showed any favouritism the rest of nature might get cross. Technically the fairies worshipped their mother goddess Gaia, but legend said that she was asleep, and no-one wanted to bother her with unnecessary prayers. Her temple, situated right in the middle of Fairyland, was well maintained, but only the truly desperate prayed there. Fairies relied quite heavily on magic when it came to problem solving. If magic couldn't fix something, it was generally unfixable.

He spotted Erlina. She was helping Rosie to pull the petals off a large pile of flowers. The pair of them were engrossed in their work, both clad in simple, white dresses. Thankfully, they were alone. Lir hadn't arrived yet, it seemed. Still, he ought to warn her-

"There you are!" a boy's voice cried out from the shade of the wall. "Geez, you could get *here*, but you couldn't send word back? Where have you *been?* We were worried sick!" A figure emerged from the shadow of the wall and sprinted towards him. Tyrian shaded his eyes against the sun as they approached, but he didn't need to see to know who it was.

"Will!" he exclaimed, stepping forward and sweeping the boy up into a hug. "I missed you!" Will was his jester; blonde, blue eyed and curly-haired, he always put people in mind of Cupid.

"It's only been twenty-four hours, Master Tyrian," the boy replied, pushing him away. He was wearing his dress clothes; a baggy cream-coloured shirt with more ruffles than ought to be decent and plain, brown trousers.

"Then why are you scolding me for not contacting you, hmm?" Tyrian replied.

"I don't know if you noticed Your Majesty, but there's a war on," came another male voice. Tyrian looked up to see Louis and Harald approaching, two of his royal guardsmen. Good. Now he was on equal footing with Lir. "We were worried," Louis continued. " Aurelia thought we ought to turn up to this thing in your place, just in case."

"Yes, she told me," Tyrian replied. "I contacted her late last night, but you'd already left."

"Where *were* you?" Will asked.

"I was on Earth, actually," he answered. "I was stuck until a young lady helped me out. Couldn't find a return door, you see. Sheva was the nearest place to Fairyland I could get. I'm just lucky she knew Sheva's princess."

"She just happened to know the neighbouring princess?" Louis remarked. "Are you *sure* it was Earth sire?"

"There were cars and schoolgirls and everything," Tyrian assured them.

"Huh. It's a bit too convenient, don't you think?" Will asked him, his brow furrowing.

"No, definitely not," the king glanced up to look over to the two girls, who had almost finished pulling apart their mound of flowers. "I think it's a story at work. They always make sure that the ring you throw into the ocean returns to you or that you meet the one person in a foreign country that can help you."

"But Earth doesn't work that way," Will said.

"You're sure about that?" Tyrian had always thought that Earth didn't work that way either, but perhaps there were exceptions.

"I lived there for twenty years, I should know," Will replied. "You sure it's not a trap? If Lir-" Tyrian hushed him quickly. He'd spotted Lir and her retinue approaching from the gate.

"Tyrian," the woman nodded curtly. He tried to keep himself from looking around to Erlina.

"Lady Lir," he responded. She leaned down to look Will in the eye and he felt the jester grab his hand.

"So this is the famous Will Winters," she said. "What a charming pet."

"Thank you for the compliment, my lady," Will replied levelly.

"You should teach your fool how to address royalty," she said, straightening up. The king looked around him in a theatrical manner;

"That's very strange," he replied. "I don't see any."

"I'm just as royal as you and the Light Realm brat, you mongrel," Lir responded, dropping all pretence of civility. "How dare you take that tone with me, your father was a commoner too-"

"My father won his kingship fair and square, he didn't bully his way in like a two bit grand vizier," Tyrian snapped. Lir glared at him.

"We shall see who is a two bit grand vizier," she said quietly. "Good day to you." She turned on her heel and headed away, followed by her flunkies. Will breathed out.

"Master Tyrian, it might not do any good to be polite to a tiger, but that doesn't mean you should poke it with a stick," he warned.

"She's just here to play queen, Will," Tyrian said, as much to reassure himself as his jester. There was a pause before he added, "You can let go of my hand now."

"I thought she might try to cast something on me," Will explained. "I thought I could use you as a magical shock absorber or something." Tyrian ruffled his hair.

"Oh, so I'm a magic shield now, am I?" he said in mock disgust. "What a terrible way to think of your patron."

"It's my job to entertain you and it's your job to protect me," Will threw back at him. "Besides, you promised my Mom."

"I *did* promise your Mom," Tyrian acknowledged. Then he added, "Did I mention I missed you?" It was only now that he risked looking around for Erlina. She was nowhere to be seen.

* * * * *

Lucinda pulled Erlina into a little alcove at the far end of the courtyard, out of sight of the surge of coronation guests. Rosie threw her a questioning look and made to follow them, but Lucinda waved her away and she returned to her preparations. It was quite dark in here, bare apart from a little square pool on the far end and golden sconces on the walls where long white candles stood unlit. There was a stained glass window over the entrance, which threw an orange and red bird shape onto the floor.

"Lucinda, we're not done with the ceremony things yet," Erlina reprimanded her, crossing her arms. "And all the guests are arriving!"

"That's kind of the problem," Lucinda explained urgently. "I think you should stay out of sight if you can. I think there might be someone trying to kidnap you." Erlina looked at her as if she was mad.

"Don't be silly, Lucinda," she replied flippantly, and attempted to leave. Lucinda grabbed her by the wrist.

"I'm serious!" she persisted. "Tyrian was over in the palace and Johann said that all the royalty from Fairyland had been invited and when he heard you were here helping, he rushed away to find you. You should have seen his face-" She stopped. Erlina's face was no picture either.

"That Lir woman?" she snapped. "She's here?" She turned her head to glare out of the doorway. She stuck her chin out in a determined manner. "Let me go, Lucinda! I have business with that wretched creature!" The fairy made a spirited attempt to wrench herself away, but Lucinda clung on. It was surprisingly easy. She never would have guessed that fairies were so frail.

"Erlina, no!" Lucinda pulled her a little further away from the entrance. Erlina burst into tears. Not daring to let her go outside just yet, she tried a hug. The fairy tried to push her away.

"She has my *mother!*" Erlina sobbed, trembling with rage and digging her fingers into Lucinda's shoulder. "I'm not just going to hide out of sight! I *can't-*"

"What's going on in here?" The two of them turned sharply to see Sara outlined in the doorway. "There are two guards looking for you outside, Erlina. They say Tyrian sent them. He's out there looking for you himself, they said. I told them I didn't know where you'd gone." She moved away so she was stood out of sight of the door. Lucinda couldn't help but smile. Sara would have known *exactly* where

Erlina was supposed to be, given that she was helping with the ceremony. Sara had been an exiled princess herself for many years, and she'd become very secretive. Erlina wasn't in exile, but she *was* a princess in hiding. It was something Sara had always seemed to understand. "Cinders, go out and ask Rosalind if she's done with those flowers," she instructed loudly, with a meaningful glance towards the door. Lucinda understood.

She walked out of the alcove like there was nothing wrong and made her way over to Rosie, who had indeed finished with the flowers. She was bent over the nearest basket of petals, pretending to inspect it. Lucinda leant down to talk to her.

"What's going on?" Rosie whispered, indicating the basket farthest away from them, as if she were giving some kind of report.

"Sara wants to talk to you," Lucinda replied, nodding as if she were listening to said report. "There's two guards here looking for Erlina, have you seen them?"

"I saw a pair of fairy guards earlier, before the guests arrived," Rosie answered quietly, holding up a hand as if indicating the number of baskets. "They had a human boy with them." She straightened up and said, "I'd better go and tell the queen that everything is ready." Rosie headed for the alcove. Unsure if she should follow her mentor back in or not, Lucinda hung back and looked around the courtyard. It was a reassuring sight to see some of the people she'd fought alongside outside the palace, what now seemed so long ago. They were a motley bunch. There was a giant looming over the wall, clearly trying to resist the urge to lean on it. There were humans, and elves, and a sphinx or two, lazily sunning themselves in the middle of the floor with no regard to the other guests. Freya's Japanese relatives, her aunt and cousin, were here too, resplendent in their kimonos. They were in their own private corner, and Freya was with them. She'd removed her coat. The natives were keeping their distance, but the other less desert-tolerant guests were happily chatting in the cold spot the yuki onna created.

The heat was getting oppressive, and Lucinda considered moving towards them, but it was then that she spotted the guards. There were two of them, wearing what she presumed were uniforms; green tunics edged with yellow. They carried no visible weapons, but they *were* fairies after all. Normally it would be impossible to tell a fairy from an elf just by looking, but their clothes were clearly foreign to Sheva.

They signalled one another. Another man squeezed his way between the guests behind them and said something, before shaking his head. He wasn't a guard, but they were obviously together. She was alarmed when he looked up and headed straight for her. One of the guards went to follow him, but the other stopped him.

"Excuse me," he gave her a little wave in greeting, and now that he was closer she was surprised to see that he was human and looked to be only a few years older than she was. Was it a trick?

"Yes?" she replied stiffly. She didn't have Sara's talent for secrecy. It was hard enough not letting people know she was a girl. The boy touched his forehead in a respectful manner.

"I was told if I couldn't find a certain fairy, you were a close second," he said. "Are they around, do you know?" He was studying her face carefully. Was he trying to see if she was lying? Well, she wasn't going to say anything about Erlina and she wasn't good at lying, so she'd just go ahead and use his vague question against him, then.

"I saw him in the palace last," she replied, referring to Tyrian. "He disappeared somewhere, he seems to be good at that." The two of them waited to see if the other was going to impart anything helpful. The boy appeared to reach a decision.

"That's not the fairy I'm looking for," he said. He smiled at her. "See you later, I expect." He turned and left. She watched him and the two guards disappear into the crowd and then headed back into the alcove with as much nonchalance as she could muster.

* * * * *

Tyrian was in a corner near the snow women when his jester caught up with him again. The three women together were causing quite a chill; it was surprisingly convenient for keeping unwanted eavesdroppers away. The stone wall was still pleasantly warm though, and the both of them stayed pressed up against it.

"Did you find her?" Tyrian asked, keeping an eye out for unwanted guests nevertheless.

"Yes and no," Will replied. "Louis and Harald looked everywhere too, but none of us could spot her. I found that prince you described though."

"And?" Tyrian prompted.

"He refused to tell me anything," the jester replied. "A good sign, I'd say. Means he knows where she is and he isn't telling." He tutted. "I gather you didn't explain what was wrong before you took off? You might have told them, it would have made this easier."

"Shakespeare doesn't have a quote for that one, then?" Tyrian replied, both relieved and amused. Part of a fool's job was to criticise and advise their master, and Will normally did so in a distinctly Shakespearean manner.

"Shakespeare doesn't have a quote for a lot of the stuff I have to tell you off for," Will said.

Now that he more-or-less knew that Erlina was safe and that other people were endeavouring to keep it that way besides himself, Tyrian felt a lot better. It helped that there was a rebel army that Erlina had once been a part of gathered right in front of his eyes. Lucy had had a point, indeed. National approval was nice, but a lot of people with pointy things and the attitude that whatever you said went was far more reassuring. He could afford to relax a little for now. So there was something he was dying to find out.

"Have much trouble with this prince, did you?" he asked innocently.

"He was stubborn right from the word go. I don't think he knew we were on the same side," Will replied, before looking sidelong at the king. "So that's your 'mysterious lady' from yesterday, huh?" Will guessed. "People don't pay attention around here, do they?" He laughed. "I could tell where she was from as soon as she opened her mouth. I'd make some comment about it being a weird profession for an Earthling but I really can't talk, right?"

"Indeed." Tyrian couldn't agree more. Most people came to Fairyland to study magic. In the old days, they found a master and worked as a apprentice or similar and left when they felt they'd learned enough. These days things were more organised. The palace ran an informal home stay program and provided assistance finding tutors. Fairies actually liked humans very much; the problem was that some of them liked them with ketchup. So suitable homes were screened in advance and a list was made of willing volunteers. Little magic schools where students could study in groups were starting to spring up. It was proving to be quite a lucrative business, but the students needed money to pay for tuition, and the palace employed more humans than anywhere else in

Fairyland. People really were starting to lose their fear of fairies. According to Will, it had been like that on Earth for a hundred years or so. Will was a particularly strange case. People risked coming to live somewhere as dangerous as Fairyland because it was the best place in all the known Otherworlds to learn magic. But you needed to be fairly adept at magic in the first place to be able to get settled down. Will had just walked in using a hooded cloak to hide his ears and talked his way into the palace. And he wasn't here to study magic at all. Apparently he thought Fairyland was *interesting*. He just wanted to live there for a while and soak up the culture, whatever that meant. He'd also mentioned something about finding his roots, which most fairies had assumed meant he was related to a tree. In Fairyland, this was entirely possible. He'd asked right out to be employed as the king's fool, since he'd heard Tyrian was easy to work for. Tyrian had been a little taken aback at this, but he'd given him a brief test and he'd passed. That was roughly four months ago now.

"Maybe you should go with her," Tyrian suggested. "To Earth, I mean." His jester looked away from him.

"Not this again," he said, sighing.

"We're at war," Tyrian said. "It's not safe." Will snorted.

"It's not safe anyway," he countered. "Do you know how many times people have tried to eat me?

Besides, I can go where you can't. Being human and all."

"I have plenty of other human servants," Tyrian pointed out. "They can do magic. You can't."

"You're going to need more than magic to sort this out," Will argued. "Look, I'm not going anywhere. I can be just as stubborn as you. I feel like you're trying to win this war all by yourself. It's not going to happen. Besides," he carried on in the face of his master's silence, "if it does look like something really bad is going to happen to me, I'll just bail out through an Otherworld door. I know where loads are. It's not like I haven't had to do that before."

"Hmm," Tyrian didn't want to admit it, but Will had been good at keeping out of danger so far. But it was largely because people liked him, and the enemy wasn't going to be so nice. Will was a minor celebrity in the Dark Realm and fools were a bit of a special case. They were marked out by a pair of yellow stripes on the bottom of their clothing. Anyone stupid enough to attack what was essentially Dark royal family property would be the true fool.

A trumpet sounded. That was the signal for everyone to take up their positions. The snow women put their protective garments back on and the heat returned. The two of them merged into the crowd, making their way to the front.

* * * * *

The priest stood in front of the small pond at the back of the alcove, to the left of a white screen that was currently blocking Sara from view. The image of the phoenix from the stained glass window shone on it exactly. The coronation was to be held at sundown to symbolise the ending of Sara's time as a princess. She was undergoing a special purification ritual that wasn't meant to be observed and the priest had been looking daggers at Lucinda and Erlina, hid from prying eyes in the corners, since the screen had gone up. He and Sara had had quite an argument in their native tongue in which the invisible glasses look had been used to devastating effect. Lucinda, huddled in one corner with her hands around her knees, ignored the priest and kept looking over at Erlina. The fairy was sullen and tear-stained. It had taken all four of them to keep her from striding out and challenging Lir. Johann had given her a stern talking to, reminding her that Tyrian was out there somewhere trying to keep her safe and that waltzing out into the open now would be a terrible way to thank him. She hadn't

spoken to Lucinda at all since she'd plonked herself down in the corner, and she wouldn't look at her either.

"Erlina-" Lucinda tried, but the priest hissed at her to be silent. Erlina didn't look round. Now two members of Fairyland royalty had a problem with her. No wait, three. Whoever this Lir woman was, she'd be no fan of Lucinda's for helping her enemies. Great.

In the space of two days, she'd essentially managed to annoy, disappoint or enrage an entire country. She supposed that was what princes generally did one way or another, but she hadn't meant to.

Sara finished whatever secret things she was doing and called for her handmaidens. Rosie had been waiting just outside the door, and she took the special white robes from the priest and went to help Sara get dressed. Erlina didn't move. Sara moved out from behind the screen, and thanked Rosie. She stole a worried glance at Erlina. Then she motioned for the others to follow her out.

"Stand guard outside and keep an eye on her," Sara instructed quietly before gliding away towards the oasis and the stone throne. Lucinda took up a position just outside the alcove door.

The priest made a speech in Sheva's native language and Sara made a considerably longer one afterwards. Then there was an announcement in English.

"Today we mark the coronation of a new monarch of our great and glorious kingdom of Sheva," the priest boomed. "Today, the old reign dies, and from the ashes will rise our new ruler-" The priest prattled on as Sara began to walk down the path towards the oasis. The petals were scattered thickly before her as she progressed. Rosie sprinkled something on the petals as she walked behind Sara, and they were set aflame, forming a line of fire. Sweet-smelling smoke wafted through the air. When Sara reached the edge of the oasis, she began another speech, first in her native tongue and then in English;

"My people, I was cast out of my native land, and through the fires of war and rebellion, I endured. I was indeed as ashes, but like our noble phoenix, I shall rise up to become the ruler you deserve." She nodded to Rosie. Who set her on fire. She poured some kind of potion over her clothes that ignited immediately. Lucinda gasped. Sara however wasn't in the least bit surprised, and didn't seem to be having any trouble. She walked slowly forward towards the edge of the pool, spread her arms out wide and fell forwards into the water. A few seconds later she emerged, her white robes now charred rags, and made her way over the burnt petals to the granite throne. Johann was stood before it to the left, the priest on the right. All Lucinda could see was Johann's back at an angle, and a little of the priest on the other side of the throne. Johann was wearing a magnificent cloak made of red, gold and orange plumage, and on his head he was wearing a golden crown, adorned with jewels. There was a spray of feathers in the middle, like that of a peacock, only red. The eyes on them glowed like golden embers in the fading light. The sun was setting. Now it was Johann's turn to make a speech;

"The people of Sheva welcomed me and my father before me as their king," he declared nervously. "But I have never felt worthy of the honour. Today I pass the crown back to the true heir of your ancient, royal bloodline. The sun now sets on my time here-" He removed his cloak, placing it around Sara's shoulders as the sun finally sank below the horizon. "-and now it shall rise on the reign of your new queen, Her Majesty Queen Saharaleia Cornelia Phedoria Sarvadaman!" he announced. Sara seated herself on the throne. The priest then stepped forward holding an odd-looking sword and a sceptre. Johann removed his crown and the priest continued;

"I now present you with the royal sceptre, representing knowledge and wisdom, and the Sword of-" The priest faltered. It seemed as though he would stop, but then he continued, "-and the Sword of the Phoenix, forged in the flames of ancient firebirds, and passed down for generations, representing strength and justice." Was something wrong? Whether there was or not, the three of them carried on regardless;

"I relinquish the authority of this crown, which I now pass to you," Johann finished, and placed the crown on Sara's head. The priest unscrewed a little bottle of something and leaned forward to make a mark on Sara's forehead;

"With the authority vested in me by the great and noble phoenix, I crown thee Queen Saharaleia the Second!" The feathers flared up, wreathing Sara's head in flames. With that, both Johann and the priest knelt down on the floor, on one knee, bowing their heads. The audience followed suit, as did Lucinda. Glancing up, she saw the two of them exchange worried looks again, and heard the priest hiss;

"That isn't the right sword!"

Lucinda glanced backwards into the alcove. Her heart nearly stopped. Erlina wasn't there. Perhaps she had just retreated further in? Lucinda would have to wait until they were allowed to get up again.

The audience stood up and Lucinda shuffled backwards and quickly looked into the alcove. Erlina was nowhere to be seen. She looked around the courtyard to see if she could spot her, but there was no sign. She groaned inwardly. She knew better than anyone how good fairies were at avoiding detection by humans . . .

* * * * *

Tyrian hadn't really been paying attention to the coronation. He'd been keeping an eye on Lir. He wasn't sure what precautions the princess had taken out. They hadn't been expecting her, after all. Did Sara's guards know Lir might be a threat? Both he and Lir were stood on the front row, facing the oasis. He kept glancing around the rest of the courtyard in case Erlina showed her face, but nothing yet. Suddenly, something changed. Glancing over at Lir, he saw her stiffen. She was staring straight at the priest, following his actions like a hawk. There was a hunger in her expression, she practically radiated it-

"Oh surely not," he said under his breath. Following Lir's gaze he saw what had so captured her attention. The priest was handing a sword to the new queen. It was oddly shaped; golden, with sweeping notches along the edge, decorated with engravings of ancient fairy runes. His sword had evidently been disguised a little *too* well. Silently cursing it and story convention with every bad word he knew, he kept flicking his gaze between Lir and the priest. She looked like she was ready to leap forward and seize it at any moment, but then whatever the priest and his cousin were prattling on about, they finished and bowed to the new queen. The audience did the same. There was no help for it but to bow and hope that Lir would do the same. The pair of them refusing to bow to the new queen would be a terrible insult.

The crowd got to their feet once more and Johann and the priest bellowed;

"Long live the Queen!" There was an answering roar from the crowd, but as it parted to let the new monarch make her way down the phoenix-decorated pathway, there was a note of discord amongst the cheers;

"*What have you done with my mother?*" came a shrill demand from his left. He snapped his head round in time to see Erlina materialise right in front of Lir. Eyes flashing, she appeared to be ready to hurl a spell right in the woman's face. Lir stepped forward and seized the princess by her wrist, which she wrenched upwards.

"Fancy meeting you here," the woman said, sneering.

"Take your hands off me!" Erlina, only half the size of the queen, tried to pry herself away, kicking out at her captor. The woman stood hard on her unprotected foot. Tyrian strode forward ready with a spell, snapping his fingers to signal his guards to move. He could see Lucinda running towards them too. Lir swung around, pulling the girl against her like a shield. She grabbed a handful of blonde hair and threatened the approaching king;

"Tell them to hand over the sword."

Before he could draw breath to demand she release Erlina, Sara was behind them with the sword in hand. But the elf didn't make the slightest move to hand it over. In a flash, she had the sword held to the woman's throat.

"Let the girl go," Sara demanded. "Whatever arguments are going on in your country are not to be settled in mine." Lir didn't move, so Sara pressed the sword a little closer. "You are at a major royal event right now. Will you really risk the humiliation of your country like this?" Lir considered her position;

"Very well," she conceded, releasing her grip. Erlina turned round and snarled.

"You attack me here, where my comrades-in-arms-" she began. Sara removed the sword from Lir's neck.

"I meant you too, Princess Erlina," Sara interrupted. "If your quarrel concerns Fairyland, then please keep it there. Sheva will *not* be dragged into your war. Gerda, escort the princess somewhere suitable." Gerda came forward and after a few protests, managed to lead the seething Erlina away.

"If you only knew," Lir said. "You have no idea who you're dealing with! If it weren't for that wretched Stollenheim woman *he* wouldn't be here,"-she flung out an arm and pointed an accusatory finger at Tyrian-"and I'd be queen by birthright! I'm *entitled* to my throne!"

"I'm sure that Alucard von Stollenheim laments that he'd still be king if weren't for me" Sara said. "You can't simply claim royal rights on the basis of an alternate time line."

"Oh and what about your little speech just now? Didn't *you* rebel?" Lir laughed. "And why? Because you couldn't stand to see your country suffer so! We are the same, you and I!"

"Don't you *dare* presume to know me." Sara narrowed her eyes.

"I just want to restore everyone to their proper place," Lir continued. "Story karma is breaking down and it's all because of this mixing of races. Humans get everywhere, and they poison *everything*. Even karma and magic! They need to get back where they belong, before it's too late!"

"Story karma is the only poison here," Sara told her. "Don't you see what the title of queen is doing to you?" Sara asked. Lir shook her head.

"Human thinking," she said. "Alucard should have stayed king. He was trying to drive the humans out, it was the right thing to do-"

"*Get out of my country.*" Sara snapped her fingers. "Freya, make sure she leaves immediately. Have your cousins and a few guards help you." Turning towards Tyrian, she thrust the sword at him. "Get this thing out of Sheva and don't bring it back," she commanded. To Lucinda she said, "Escort the fairy king and his people out of here." She inclined her head towards the palace. Lucinda motioned for Tyrian to follow. Both of them took a last look at Erlina, being escorted off in the distance.

Tyrian followed the girl along the path the guests had come, his jester and two guards in tow. She was silent and distracted, staring unseeing at the scenery ahead of them. He looked around to see if there was anyone else following them. There wasn't. The path was practically in the middle of the desert, only the mad would hang about to eavesdrop here.

"Don't worry. I'm sure Erlina is fine," he reassured her. "I appreciate your discretion earlier. It really is too bad she ruined it."

"Oh?" Lucinda glanced behind her at the three men and he saw her expression change. He could see her struggling between honesty and avoiding embarrassment. Honesty won. "Actually, I thought your guards were with that other woman," she admitted sheepishly, "but I guess it worked out all right. Until Erlina ruined it, as you say."

"The important thing is you tried," he replied cheerfully.

"I'm sorry about Sara," she apologised. "She's . . . well, she's Sara." He noted again Lucinda's complete lack of honorific or respectful term when addressing royalty and smiled.

"Are you a fool, Lu-" he faltered. Blast, what had that valkyrie called her? "Uh, Lucian, was it?" She stopped dead.

"*Excuse me*?" she asked.

"Master Tyrian is asking after your profession, mi-" Will paused too, "-Milord." Tyrian tried not to laugh. Will never used the proper royal terminology either.

"Oh. You mean like a jester?" she said, walking onwards again. "Do I look like one?"

"The worst fools are those you can't see, Milord," Will replied. "At least if he be wearing a cap and bells, you expect a man to say something stupid. Or a woman, of course."

"I'm a prince in her service, whatever I look like," Lucinda replied, stiffening up. "And that had better not have been a crack at Sara. I know she's difficult but you just have to get used to her."

"I'm *glad* she's difficult," Tyrian said. "Gaia knows I couldn't have done what she did. I wish I could . . . maybe if I was more like that we wouldn't be in this mess." She hadn't messed about, she hadn't tried to bargain or play a good guy. She'd just set out in simple terms that Lir should obey or die. He had to admire someone with guts like that. "She seems to have rubbed off on Erlina a little . . . but I do wish she'd be more careful."

"I think she's mad at me," Lucinda said in a worried voice. Tyrian waited politely for her to elaborate on this vague statement. "I think she's *really* mad at me."

"I could have sworn she was mad at you yesterday afternoon, when you brought me to her office," Tyrian said. "It was the way she immediately ordered us to get out that tipped me off."

"I mean Erlina," Lucinda clarified in a gloomy tone. "I stopped her confronting that woman and I think she's taken serious offence at it."

"Oh come now," Tyrian reassured her "I'm sure it isn't that bad-"

Day and Night despaired. They had to abandon their children, leaving the eldest to rule in their stead. They sought out Nature's children too, and found the eldest to rule in her place.

To each child they gave a gift.

Night gave to his eldest a sword.

"Use this to protect your people. It represents strength. Rule as I would rule."

Day gave her eldest a staff.

"Use this to guide your people. It represents wisdom. Rule as I would rule."

But to the child of Nature, they did not know what to say.

"How shall I rule?" the child asked.

"You shall have to ask your mother," answered Night.

"I do not know where to find her," the child replied.

Chapter 5:

Search Party

"I'm going home," Erlina declared. "I have to help my people." She crossed her arms, adding, "Since no-one else will."

They had regrouped in the palace with the intention of going their separate ways via the Rent-A-Legend door. Tyrian and his staff had split off to make arrangements for a carriage back to Fairyland.

"Lina, we did our best back there," Gerda tried to explain. "Just wait until Sara gets back. She just has to finish up the ceremony proper and-" Erlina practically exploded;

"You let the woman who's trying to destroy my family and my country walk away free!" she cried. "How could you?! How could *she*? I helped *her* avenge *her* mother!"

"Erlina, I don't think-" Lucinda tried. Erlina rounded on her.

"No, apparently you don't!" She was on the verge of tears again, but they were tears of rage. "I am *not* speaking to you, Lucinda!" Lucinda felt like she'd been stung. "I'm not speaking to *any* of you!"

"Lina, if you'd just let Sara get back, she'll explain-"

"She doesn't need to explain anything!" Erlina turned on her heel and headed for the door. "She has her crown now, so she can turn her back on me and my problems. It's all perfectly clear. I'm going now."

"Erlina-" Lucinda stepped forward to take her arm. The fairy shook her off.

"Goodbye Lucinda," she said with an air of finality. She turned and headed away down the corridor, leaving them dumbstruck. Lucinda stared after her at a loss. As Erlina disappeared out of the doorway, she shook herself and went to run after her, but Gerda held her back.

"Let her cool off," she said. "She'll realise she's bein' silly and come back."

"But-"

"She's obviously not in the mood to listen to reason, so leave her be," Gerda insisted.

"You don't think Sara meant what she said about Sheva not helping, do you?" Lucinda asked, after a pause.

"I expect she did," Gerda replied. "She's queen now. She can't go dragging her people into a war the second she gets crowned. Very bad politics. I expect the fairies wouldn't like it, neither."

"They certainly wouldn't," Sara added, appearing in the doorway. She looked around the room. "Where's Erlina?"

"She got upset and stormed out," Gerda answered. "I told Cinders to give her a minute to cool off. You didn't see her then?"

"No," Sara replied, frowning. "Why did she leave?"

"You said Sheva wouldn't help, and she took offence," Lucinda explained.

"She didn't . . ." Sara's face went pale.

"She seemed to think it was unfair, because she helped you with your rebellion," Lucinda continued.

"That *idiot*," Sara spat. She sat down so hard on a nearby chair that it threatened to fall over. "You'd think she'd try to understand my position. But no." She massaged her temples. "Does she think I don't know what it's like to have your mother in peril? Wasn't she paying the *slightest* bit of attention?"

"She is not thinking," Freya soothed. "Her mother is in trouble, her country is in trouble. And she is only a child." Sara sighed heavily.

"I suppose this is more a matter of childishness," she agreed. "If she would have just listened, I would have explained."

"So, when you said that *Sheva* wouldn't help-" Lucinda began.

"Exactly," Sara confirmed. "I said I wouldn't drag *my country* into the war. I never said *I* wouldn't help. You'd think she'd have realised that's what Rent-A-Legend is *for*. But . . ."

"But what?" Lucinda asked. Sara leaned on the desk, looking thoughtful.

"The thing is . . ." Sara started, "this is a civil war. On the surface, it's a squabble for power between the three royal houses. It's most unusual."

"It is?" Lucinda asked. As far as she knew, fighting over power was what royal houses did. Sara herself was no exception to the rule.

"Yes," Sara continued, "the three royal houses treat each other as family, even though they're very distantly related by now, if they ever were. On top of that, since they live long enough to replace any lost heirs, they tend to only have one child to avoid sibling squabbles over the thrones. It's something to do with an ancient queen of theirs. She unlocked a terrible power and took over the country. 'The Reign of Hel' they call it. They never wanted that to happen again, hence the restrictions."

"Sounds sensible," Lucinda replied. "So why do you think this woman started a fight?"

"I don't know," Sara replied. "This whole thing smacks of Grand Vizier."

"Oh." Grand Viziers. It was a wonder anyone still employed them. "Is that better or worse than a family squabble?" Lucinda asked.

"It really depends *what* they're fighting over," Sara explained. "If the woman was just a Grand Vizier after power, it would be easier to handle. But it looks like she's in line for the throne, somehow. We could be in trouble."

"What sort of trouble?" Lucinda asked, feeling uneasy.

"There's politics afoot here," Sara explained. "We have to be careful, we can't just openly stick our noses in. They might not want outsiders like us to interfere. It's quite the tricky situation. I can't publicly take sides, which is why I ordered everyone and everything out of the country. The faster they get that sword off the premises, the better."

"Tyrian said it's something to do with Rosie's research and foreigners," Lucinda said.

"Then they *definitely* don't want us to openly interfere," Sara replied. "We're going to have to tread very, *very* carefully-"

* * * * *

Tyrian wiped the final traces of gold dust from his sword as he walked back from the palace stables. He and Johann had gone there to arrange a pair of horses for his servants to take back to Fairyland when they were certain that Lir would be long gone.

"I never thought about disguising it like that," Tyrian remarked. "We usually see through spells, but manual methods tend to elude us."

"It still didn't work though," Johann replied. "It might have worked if we hadn't had a coronation today or perhaps someone more competent had been sent to get the Shevan sword."

"The two do look remarkably alike," Tyrian said. The Shevan sword was gold plated, and shaped something like a stylized, outstretched bird's wing.

His own sword was curved in a similar way, and there were several large, triangular notches along the edge that in a bad light could be mistaken for feathers. "I'm not sure you can blame your servant though."

"Oh?" Johann replied.

"The harder you try to lose something magical, the more cunning the ways it uses to get back to you," Tyrian replied, sighing. No doubt the pendant would also find its way back, soon enough. Stupid things. Did they *want* Lir to win?

"At any rate, I'm afraid we can't keep it here," Johann told him. "I'd suggest another relative, but perhaps that woman will be wise to your strategy now."

"I think you may be right," Tyrian replied. There was one strategy she couldn't predict though, and it might kill two birds with one stone . . . or save them.

* * * * *

The room had fallen silent, and no-one seemed to have a solution to the problem of Fairyland politics. Perhaps they would just have to work out something with Tyrian when he got back.

"What's with the silence?" Rosie asked, appearing in the doorway with Tyrian and Johann. She looked around the room. "Where's Erlina?"

"She ain't here," Gerda replied. "There was a bit of a misunderstandin', and she stormed out. I reckon she'll be back once she's 'ad a bit of time to 'erself."

"That's twice she's stormed off without listening to an explanation," Tyrian muttered. "I do apologise. But I'm sure you understand, we're under a lot of stress. Do you know where she went?"

"She said she was going to return to Fairyland. She knows we don't have a door there," Sara said, thinking out loud. "I doubt she would be foolish enough to walk."

"I'm afraid she's far more stubborn than you know," Tyrian told her. "She may well have been serious. Is it possible to walk there?"

"It's *possible*, but it's not wise," Sara replied. "I'm sure you're well aware that there's a desert in the way." The fairy king considered this.

"Surely it's in-between, rather than in the way?" he asked.

"Have you ever tried to cross a desert by yourself with no provisions and no idea what you're doing?" Sara replied. "Trust me, it's in the way. It's nearly a day's journey by carriage using the trade road. And if she starts walking even slightly in the wrong direction she'll end up in the mountains. She ought to realise quickly and come back." There was a thoughtful pause.

"Just how upset was she, again?" Tyrian asked in a concerned tone.

"She thinks we've all turned on her because we wouldn't let her confront Lir and then I stopped her from possibly getting you both killed which she's also taken offence at, and to top it all off, she said she wasn't speaking to Lucinda, who she has been known to say she's going to marry." There was a pause as Sara realised what she'd said, and everyone turned to look at the three servants to see what they'd do. They took one look at the woman who'd nearly cut a fairy's head off in public less than an hour ago, saw her expression, and adjusted theirs accordingly. Clearly they thought Lucinda was a *nice* name for a boy. Something else had caught the king's attention though.

"I'm sorry?" He raised an eyebrow. "Did you say marry?"

"I did," Sara replied simply.

"Pretty upset then?" he said.

"I'd better go and get her," Sara said, standing up, and heading for the door.

"I'll go with you," Tyrian said. "She might try to avoid you, but she won't try to avoid me. We already cleared up *our* misunderstanding, perhaps I can help clear up yours-"

"I'll go too," Lucinda said.

"Oh no you won't," Sara told her sternly.

"But," Lucinda started, "she's my best friend, I can't just sit at home knowing she's wandering in the desert, especially not when she's partly doing it because she's mad at me!"

"It's late and the more spare baggage we take into the desert, the less chance we have of all getting out again," Sara told her. "You need to go home. I *am* aware that you have one to get back to."

"I agree," Tyrian backed her up. "And-" He pushed his jester forward. "Take Will here with you. I believe you live in more or less the same place."

"Oi!" his jester protested, "I told you-"

"Take the sword with you," the king commanded. "I can't leave it here and I don't know what else to do. Do something with it, please."

"Just because we live on the same planet, it doesn't mean we live anywhere near each other!" Will carried on. "Earth doesn't work like here, you can't just turn up at people's houses and say 'What ho good mother, some shelter if you please'!"

"Listen Will, if I have to cross a desert to get home, I'm sure it can't be that difficult for you two when you live on the same island," Tyrian replied crossly. "You're a smart boy, you can figure something out."

"Hey, I haven't agreed to this yet-" Lucinda protested.

"Yes, but you're going to," the king replied firmly. "I just gave you charge of two treasures of mine. Please don't lose either of them this time," he added pointedly. Realising she was beat, Lucinda gave up. But there was still one thing;

"Will you tell Erlina I only stopped her because I didn't want her to get hurt or kidnapped?" she pleaded. "I think she thinks I betrayed her by stopping her going after that woman."

"She's going to get a stern telling off first at the very least, but I'll tell her," he reassured her. "I shall send her back with an apology."

"Don't get your hopes up yet," said Sara. "We have to find her first. Rosalind? I'm going to need some help from you-"

* * * * *

The search party had assembled on the edge of the desert wastes. A large hand mirror had been procured.

"I'm not sure this is going to work too well," Rosie warned. "The desert isn't exactly full of landmarks and it's likely she's using an invisibility spell to boot. Not to mention scrying is a difficult enough business as it is."

"There is still the possibility that she didn't go into the desert. I don't want to cross it if I don't have to," Sara explained. "And if she did, I need a direction. We can't wander in blindly. Now, if you can just guide me through the spell . . ."

"Oh? I didn't know elves knew such magic," Tyrian remarked.

"We can do magic if we want," Sara replied, rolling her eyes.

"I just thought you weren't very magically inclined, is all," he apologised.

"Just because we don't need magic for every little thing," she said, "doesn't mean we can't do it."

"I didn't mean to sound speciesist, you just took me by surprise," he said. "You're going into the desert too, aren't you?" Most royals would send out a search party or delegate it some other way.

"Yes? I lurked around the deserts here a lot when I was rebelling against my father-in-law. I know them very well. Why leave it to someone less competent?"

"Is there anything you can't do, Your Majesty?" he said, smiling at her.

"I suggest if you want to get out of the desert in one piece you stop that immediately," she warned, giving him that look again. She settled down on the sand, with the mirror in her lap. "Now be quiet, I have an invisible princess to find-"

* * * * *

Lucinda and Will made their way back through town. She was going quite slowly. It was late, and her mother wasn't going to appreciate her bringing some strange boy home. She might have hoped that he could catch a train, but Newton-le-Willows train station was tiny, just two platforms, and they'd be lucky if they were still running. Even if they were, what if he lived somewhere obscure?

"So where *do* you live, anyway?" she asked him. "You *are* from Earth I take it?"

"Yeah. From the Midlands. Kinda," he replied. Odd. She wouldn't have thought he was British. He had a strange lilt to his accent. It had an American twang to it. "Y'see, my Mom is from Anima and my Dad is from Stratford," he explained. "I spent a lot of time out of the country so I'm kind of from both places."

"And by out of the country you mean . . ?" Lucinda prompted.

"Oh sorry, I just kinda assumed . . ." he faltered, "Anima is the name of the planet my Mom comes from. I usually just say 'Anima' because no-one has ever heard of the tiny village she's from even in the Otherworlds. As for Earthlings, I just pretend it's some town in America."

"Oh. You know . . . I never thought about that." Lucinda had learned a lot in the Otherworlds, but their *names* had escaped her so far. Speaking of names;

"What's your name again?" she asked.

"Will," he answered. "Remind me of yours?"

"Lucinda," she replied. There was an awkward moment as he thought about his next move. Eventually he hazarded;

"I wasn't gonna say in front of Her Majesty, but that's a funny name for a prince."

"It certainly is," she replied, wondering how best to explain her situation.

"I mean, I asked Master Tyrian back there what an Earthling girl was doing dressed as a prince and he couldn't answer me."

"So, out of professional pride, and to try and avoid this mistake in the future sort of thing, how could you tell I was a girl?" Lucinda asked. It wasn't the first time her disguise hadn't worked. Far from it. But it worked on an incredible amount of people, and any way she could up that ratio was to be seized upon.

"I've got this special technique," Will answered. "It's called 'Not Being Blind'."

"Ah. Well at least there's nothing I could have done, then," she sighed.

"You could try growing a beard," he suggested, grinning. "That'd fox 'em." Lucinda fought back a laugh.

"I think I look quite enough like a boy as it is, thanks," she replied. "Though, I think people in the Otherworlds just see either a skirt or a pair of trousers."

"I think so too," Will agreed. "I'm sure you're fine. So um . . . why exactly *are* you dressed as a prince again?"

"Sara runs an agency for this sort of thing," Lucinda explained. "Her princes tend to run off and get married and become kings. And kings don't rescue people. They hang around having their kingdoms ransacked and their daughters kidnapped. So she hired me."

"That actually makes a lot of sense," he said. She turned to look at him, expecting a smile, but he was looking straight ahead of him with his lips pursed and his brow furrowed. "Master Tyrian said something about that. He's a king now . . . Tch, that Lir woman sure is crafty."

"Hang on." Lucinda didn't know all the rules that Otherworlders lived by, but being a prince was something she *was* familiar with. "Is he having problems because he's a *king*?" If Tyrian was a king, then he'd once been a prince. And princes did all kinds of things.

"You said it yourself, kings don't rescue people," Will said. "Kings who try tend to die in the process. It counts for pretty much anything important."

"Wait, but he's been doing important stuff," she pointed out. "Isn't he going to get in trouble for that?"

"At the moment I think he counts as a 'wandering king'," Will replied thoughtfully. "A king outside their country can do a bit of prince stuff on the side. They're a special exception. Brother Brightboots and all that. But he will be if he tries to do too much." Will looked worried, and there wasn't anything much she could say to reassure him. She didn't know enough about story karma to say anything one way or the other. She wasn't even sure if it was real, but he certainly seemed to think so. Perhaps it was time for a topic change.

"So, what are you doing in Fairyland?" she asked.

"I'm working as a fool," he replied, "for Master Tyrian, obviously. I'm on my gap year."

"That's . . . different," she replied. "You know, says me. So what do you do all day?" she asked, "Tell jokes and get hit by custard pies, or what?"

"I think you're thinking of clowns," he said, smiling. "Jesters are more like a sort of stand up comedian and fools are a bit different. I'm a bit of both."

"Go on?" she prompted.

"See, this is where it gets awkward," he answered. "You're going to think I'm weird." He rubbed his neck in what Lucinda recognised as displacement activity. He was thinking something he didn't want to say. He wasn't employed for his blood, was he? She felt sick at the thought.

"A fool is like, someone employed to be the king's friend. Nobles and royals choose ordinary people that seem like nice companions for them. Fools keep their master entertained, keep them company, talk to them . . . that sort of thing." Why he was reluctant became apparent.

"So, like a human pet?" she summarised. That was probably better than being employed as a blood bank. Probably.

"It's not quite as weird as it sounds," he explained. "You see, the fool is the only person who the king can connect with as another human being - or fairy, in Master Tyrian's case. The fool is outside the hierarchy. To everyone else Master Tyrian is interacting as a king. Who he talks to and favours and who he doesn't can get all political."

"I see." Lucinda could see how it might be tough if no matter who you were nice to, someone else got jealous or took offence.

"I mean don't get me wrong," Will continued, "sometimes I feel like he's *this* close,"-he made the obligatory gesture with finger and thumb-"to getting me a fluffy ball with a bell in it. But that's fairies for you. They kinda feel like that about us humans, you know? They don't mean anything bad by it. It's just their culture."

Finally, the two of them came to the train station. Will eyed the sign, obviously thinking the same thing Lucinda had earlier.

"Do you have any money?" she asked.

"Not on me," he replied. "My wallet is back at my host mother's house. It's not like I needed Earth money in Sheva. And I'm not entirely certain they'd like me to get on a train with this thing." He indicated the sword, which he had strapped across his back in a makeshift scabbard. She had to admit it didn't look too friendly. The light glinted off the black blade and its gilded runes in a eerie fashion as they made their way along the deserted street and under the railway bridge.

"I don't suppose you could phone your parents?" she tried, feeling awful for suggesting it.

"I could, but I don't want to," he admitted. "They don't like that I went to Fairyland, and if I tell them there's a war, I'll not be allowed to go back. I know it sounds dumb, but I won't leave Master Tyrian alone to win this war. I'm too worried about him to sit at home and do nothing." Lucinda understood that all too well. She wished they'd let her go and look for

Erlina. Her own parents would stop her from going to work if they knew what she was up to.

"Speaking of parents, mine don't know about all this Otherworld stuff. And I'd like to keep it that way." Will nodded.

"Understood," he replied. "My mother knows all about the Otherworlds. That's kinda the problem. She knows all about fairies and she used to tell me that Fairyland was a terrible place full of monsters and things."

"Yeah?" Lucinda slowed down a little as she thought about the implications of this.

"It was a really stupid thing to say to a small boy," he said. "She might know about fairies, but human psychology isn't her strong point." Lucinda had to agree. She'd been told she was going to be rescuing princesses and fighting dragons and she'd been all over her job. She hadn't quite thought Sara had meant for real, of course. But she knew in her heart of hearts that if she *had* known it was for real, it wouldn't have made much of a difference. Humanity was largely dull. At least monsters were interesting.

Lucinda could see a light on in the living room. Luckily, it was Friday. She wasn't going to get told off for being out late on a school night. There was a plethora of other things she was going to get yelled at for, and one of them was going to be for bringing a strange boy home and asking if he could stay the night. She found herself wishing he was a fairy. He could have made himself invisible and get into her room without having to bother her parents, then. On the other hand, having an invisible boy around the house would be pretty traumatic. Will was from Earth though, so at least he knew how to behave himself. So she hoped.

Lucinda stared balefully at the door, running the impending conversation through her head and trying to work out the likely pitfalls. But as she reached for the doorknob, the door opened to reveal her mother wearing that special 'concerned anger' expression she always had when Lucinda came home late.

"*Lucinda Martin!*" she thundered. "What time do you call this?"

"I did say I'd be back late today," Lucinda explained with as much meekness as she could manage. "My boss had a very important ceremony that she invited me to." Motherly outrage fought motherly pride and, backed up by remembered facts, lost, at least temporarily. But she had to find *something* to be cross about;

"And you went in *that*?" Her mother indicated her prince outfit. "Couldn't you have gone in something *nice*?"

"I had to go in this," Lucinda explained patiently. "My boss insisted. Um, speaking of work-" Her mother had already spotted Will, and she could see that the only reason she wasn't getting the full force of Hurricane Mum was that she appeared to have brought a friend over. Friends were a magical buffer against tellings off, particularly since she'd moved from her old town. "This is Will," she introduced him. "He's a friend from work. There was kind of a situation and he's left his wallet somewhere and the trains aren't running," she babbled, "so I said I'd ask if he could crash on the couch tonight?" she finished, putting on what she hoped were puppy dog eyes.

"I'm really sorry to trouble you ma'am," Will said. He touched his forelock respectfully. "It's been one thing after another the past few days, I'm afraid. I left my wallet where I changed into my clothes for the event and normally I could manage something, but it's so late and all."

"Maria, can you yell at Lulu inside?" came her father's voice from down the hall. "It's blowing a right draft in here with the door keep being open."

"Well, come in, anyway," Lucinda's mother beckoned them both in and shut the door. "I'm sure we can figure something out. Would you like a cup of tea or anything?"

"Yes please," Will answered.

"I'll sort everything," Lucinda said, waving her mother away. There was a hurried, muted conversation from the living room in which the words 'as long as he sleeps on the couch' were included. Satisfied that they could retreat to her room and talk in private, she made them tea and nodded to the door, indicating that Will should move. Will followed her out and she stopped by the living room door briefly so her dad could see who he was letting into the house and that Will could greet him.

"Hello, I'm sorry for the trouble," Will apologised to him.

"You're from Lulu's work, I see," her Dad remarked. Will looked like a beige-favouring swordsman, particularly as he still had Tyrian's sword strapped to his back. "But you're not local then? You sound a bit foreign." Lucinda cringed, but Will merely laughed.

"My mother is foreign, yes," he answered. "My dad is British though. They live in Stratford-Upon-Avon. I commute, that's how I got stranded."

"Oh I see," Mr. Martin nodded. "Bit of a trip home for you then. You're welcome to the couch, but I will be using it for a bit longer! I'm sure Lulu can keep you entertained for a while though, she stays up late on weekends." The two of them having been suitably polite and getting actual permission for Will to stay, they went upstairs.

"Dad probably won't stay up too much longer, he has work tomorrow," she explained, putting the mugs down on her bedside table. Will shuffled inside and she shut the door so that her parents wouldn't overhear anything inconvenient. He looked around her room, taking in the models, manga-filled bookshelf and anime posters.

"So you like Japan, then," he observed. Lucinda tensed up. What if Will thought she was childish?

"Just a bit," she replied tentatively.

"Cool," he replied. "I've got some of these myself," he continued, studying her bookshelf. "I did a working holiday program thing in Japan last year and I brought a lot of stuff back. My mother complained about it. I can't read Japanese very well yet, so they're mostly decorative right now. But I argued that I'll never get better if I don't have something to practice on." Lucinda breathed out. She hadn't realised she'd been holding her breath until she stopped doing it. She gestured vaguely at the bed.

"You can sit down, if you like," she offered, sitting down on the end nearest the pillow and picking up her drink. She wanted to ask him about Japan, but something made her afraid of looking stupid. So she decided to stick to a nice, safe topic on which they were on even ground. Like magical, alien, civil war, for example. "So, what will you do with the sword?"

"I dunno," Will replied, picking up his own mug and sitting on the end of the bed. "I can't just leave it any old where, he might want it back and if it's somewhere too obvious, well, we can't have the Wilders finding it." There was a knock on the door causing them both to jump.

"Lulu, I'm off to bed." It was her Dad's voice. "Your friend can have the couch whenever he likes. There's a sleeping bag in the airing cupboard."

"Thanks Dad," she called back.

"I think a good night's sleep would be the best plan right now." Will stifled a yawn. "The sword isn't going anywhere tonight for sure." Lucinda agreed.

She got him some blankets and the two of them said goodnight.

"Did you see that? There's another one now!"
"I wonder what she'll make of that."
"I still think she should come herself."
"Look, we've been through this. It would get awkward. So just shut up and get on with it."

The bickering voices. She'd all but forgotten about them. It was just a dream, after all. Lucinda 'awoke' to find herself in the same place as last time, a pond surrounded by all kinds of flowers, trees and bushes.

"Oh, she's noticed us again," came a female voice from the tree.

"Shh!" came a harsh, male voice from the bushes.

"Look, you can please yourselves, I'm just going to go ahead and ask," came another voice. Lucinda looked up to see a black bird, some sort of crow, sat in one of the trees. There was a long, thin creature like a cross between a weasel and a leopard, with a lemur's tail thrown in for good measure. There was also what appeared to be a small, red kangaroo peering out from another bush.

"No, no, no!" came the shrill voice from the bushes again. "Have some caution!"

"Oh, to the four winds with caution!" the black bird snapped. "I don't intend to be flying around playing spy for weeks." All the visible animals looked right at her.

"Er . . . can I help you?" Lucinda asked, feeling terribly strange. She was pretty sure that she wasn't awake. This must be a dream. She distinctly remembered coming back to Earth, and animals didn't talk there.

"Talking is not a remarkable feat my dear, it's what use you put the words to," the lemur-leopard-weasel remarked. Lucinda shuddered.

"Apparently you also read minds," she replied weakly.

"No, we just have a lamentable amount of experience with humans and their limited view of the world." There was a brown blur, and a tiny, brown bird emerged from the bushes, perching on the edge of one the leaves.

"What are you?" she asked them. "Is this a dream?" Something felt . . . wrong. This wasn't what it appeared to be somehow. She felt strange, as if she were drugged. She would have liked to get up and move, to feel in control, but her whole body was just a vague fuzzy sensation.

"Well might you ask!" replied the tiny bird. "I am Wren, King of the Birds!"

"Only because you cheated," chattered the crow-like bird.

"Should we tell the girl who we are?" came a mild, male voice. It was the kangaroo this time.

"One must build up bonds of trust if one is to work with others," came the solemn tones of the weasel-leopard. "Let us introduce ourselves, that the child does not grow weary." 'The child', was it? So she was dealing with something that though she was inferior. Were they fairies in disguise? Could fairies control dreams?

"I am what is known as a spotted linsang," the leopard-weasel introduced herself. "You may address me as Li, should you so choose. I shall be spokesman, that we may speed this up."

"I am a red wallaby." The small kangaroo gave a small bow. "I have no wish that you should call me anything."

"I am a jackdaw, a bird of some magical talent!" announced the black bird. "My name is Jack, like the nimble man or the giant slayer! I live in stories too, my girl. Don't think you can trick me."

"So tell me," Li began, "did you steal the green pendant?" Lucinda felt almost sick, and that was even through the fuzziness of the dream. The probability that they were fairies sent to hunt down the pendant had just gone up. How could she defend herself in a dream? Nothing in her prince training had covered this. At least she had words.

"I didn't steal the green pendant!" Lucinda protested "It was stolen *from* me!"

"It's not yours!" The little wren fluffed up his feathers in a huff. "It's not yours, so what were you doing with it?"

"I was given it by someone, they asked me to keep it safe!" she protested. What would happen if these animals attacked her in a dream? What if she *died*?

"Who gave it to you?" Li asked her, in a calm tone.

"Doesn't matter!" the wren protested. "It wasn't theirs to give!"

"Be quiet, King," the linsang warned. "You shan't get a straight answer from the girl if you bait her." So the sensible sounding one wanted a straight answer. Was it a trap? If Tyrian's enemies really had sent these dream creatures, they might kill her. She knew fairies couldn't move around too freely on Earth though; she'd have to try and use that as a trump card. She decided to go for honesty.

"It was given to me by Tyrian von Stollenheim," she replied. The animals set off chattering. The linsang hissed at them all.

"The fairy king gave it to you, you say?" She stared at Lucinda thoughtfully.

"Yes," Lucinda replied. "He wanted me to keep it safe, and I lost it." She was feeling increasingly ill and now the hot knife of shame sliced through her as well. It took all her effort to add, "You won't find it without me." There was a derisive laugh from the wren.

"Find it without you?" he chattered. "We already have it, you fool!"

Lucinda woke with a start. Feeling sickly, she lurched out of bed and to the bathroom. She was trembling all over. The dream was already fading. It could be her conscience playing tricks on her. She *did* feel awful about the pendant, and it wouldn't be the first time she'd had a dream about something she felt guilty for. After all, why should some random animals know who Tyrian was? She drank a few mouthfuls of water until she felt a little better and went back to bed. She lay awake, tossing and turning. She wished Erlina was here. Erlina could have explained that there were no such fairies that could tamper with dreams, or cast something to make her feel better or done some kind of protective charm, perhaps. As it was, she would have to settle for plain old science-based medicine.

She crept downstairs and into the kitchen. There was someone in there, looking through the drawers. She froze in the doorway, and saw the figure turn, holding a knife-

"Does this have iron in it, do you think?" it whispered. "I'd have turned the light on, but I didn't want to wake anybody. And I *really* didn't want to explain what I want iron for." Lucinda wasn't in the right frame of mind for this, but her prince work had taught her to repress the urge to panic. She flipped on the light switch. The 'intruder' was Will and he was holding a bread knife. "Are you all right? You don't look so good."

"I just found someone wielding a knife in my kitchen in the middle of the night." Lucinda breathed out. "I'm surprised I don't look worse." She went over to the medicine cabinet and rifled through it until she found the medicine she was looking for.

"I'm actually kind of glad that you're up," Will admitted, sliding onto a chair and resting his head on his arms. "I had a weird dream and I woke up feeling like I was being watched, and being in a strange house and everything . . ." Lucinda looked around at him. He was still clutching the bread knife. His face was pale.

"You did?" she replied, her own abated worries rising again. "What did you want that knife for?"

"I'm pretty sure it has iron in it," he explained. "Fairies are afraid of iron. You have no idea how glad I am that it's *you* I'm explaining this to and not your mom." Lucinda ran a glass of water as she considered whether she really wanted to hear this explanation. Will was *frightened*.

"You think there are fairies after us?" she whispered, suddenly worried that they might be overheard. "But we're on Earth!"

"Fairies come through Earth all the time," he whispered back. "I mean, they just pass through and maybe mess with people on the way, sometimes they take things . . . but that dream . . . well, it was *pretending* it was a dream, but it was real, I'm sure of it." Lucinda started;

"Did some talking animals come and ask you if you'd stolen the pendant?" she blurted out.

"You had the same dream?" he asked, his face grim. "They asked me about the sword, but that proves it. Something is watching us, and it got into our heads. I don't like that. Things trying to eat me from the outside I can handle, but things trying it from the inside is a terrifying thought." Lucinda was seized by a powerful desire to be elsewhere.

"Let's get out of here," she muttered. "I don't care what time of night it is, I want to be somewhere else." She shuddered. "I won't be going back to sleep. I'll get changed back into my prince clothes and we'll go back to the office. Maybe Sara and the others are back."

"What should I do with the sword?" Will asked. "Master Tyrian asked me to keep it on Earth somewhere, but . . ."

"We'll take it with us," she replied firmly. "If something knows it's here, I don't want it coming in and getting my parents involved."

The two of them got their things together, left Lucinda's parents a note explaining that she had headed off to work early, and set off back to the office.

"You must search for her," Day answered. And she gave Nature's child a pendant. "This will guide you. Use it to look for Nature, and when you find her, bring her back."

Day and Night continued to perform Nature's duties. In time, they saw how much Nature had been burdened.

Just as all seemed lost, the eldest child returned with her mother. The siblings fell upon her and apologised.

"Truly sister, yours was the greatest task," Night proclaimed.

"Please, will you not resume your duties?" Day pleaded.

Chapter 6:

Into The Desert

Having gleaned all they could from the largely sand-filled scrying that Sara had performed under the instruction of Rosie, the party set out into the desert. Scrying, where a witch or other magic user looked into a mirror upon which water was continuously poured while the mirror showed them visions of whatever they were looking for, was an imprecise magical art. They'd been able to tell Erlina was in there somewhere, but little else. The fact that the desert looked more or less the same for miles on end hadn't helped at all. But Sara was familiar with it, and she thought she knew where to head.

Tyrian trudged through the sand after the new queen feeling surprisingly happy. Erlina had made some good friends in her absence. It was too bad she hadn't realised just how good. Running off into the desert was bad enough, but it would be even worse if she reached Fairyland first. He doubted she had the sense right now to get to his palace in safety. She must have taken her cloak at least, or they would have caught up with her already. Changelings like Erlina were a sub-species of fairy; a hybrid between a true fairy and some other magical creature, such as a yokai or a djinni. Their magic was weaker as a result, and they used their cloaks to augment it. The cloaks had several spells contained within them, including a signature transformation spell – hers allowed her to become a swan. He just hoped it would get her through the desert unharmed.

It didn't seem to be presenting Sara with any problems. This woman must have been *born* a queen. He was envious. He was having to *learn* how to be a warrior monarch, whereas it seemed to be hot-wired into her brain. He'd done plenty of heroics in his time, but they weren't the same. They weren't *leadership*. When you saved a damsel in distress from a dragon or discovered an ancient treasure you didn't have to worry about how *everyone* felt about it. No-one harangued you about how you shouldn't harass the dragon for being a dragon or told you that the treasure didn't belong to you just because you'd found it. But suddenly you were wearing a different crown, and every little thing you did *mattered*. He couldn't even *talk* to one noble without insulting another. He wasn't a *person* any more, he was a political advantage. A king's words were favour, and royal favour was something to be hoarded and jealously guarded. Gaia forbid he forget to invite Lord Thingummy's wife's second cousin-in-law to a courtly gathering. He'd stopped having them altogether. Thank goodness for his fools and his remaining family. And now he'd found Erlina, only to lose her again.

"Do you suppose she got far?" Tyrian asked Sara as she walked along ahead of him. There was still no sign of anyone or anything on the horizon.

"I was going to ask you the same thing," she replied. "My knowledge of the desert is fine, but my knowledge of fairy durability is not. She's been a capable employee all year, but I never asked her to trek through the desert at night with no supplies. And she was unwell until a month or so ago."

"She can last at least a day, I'm sure," he answered. "We're good at more than invisibility."

"I don't suppose she'll be using invisibility now?" Sara asked.

"Unless she's become *completely* irrational, I doubt it," Tyrian responded. "She's not an idiot. There's no point being invisible where there's no-one to see you in the first place."

"Forgive me, but striding off into the desert alone was pretty idiotic," Sara replied.

"I have to agree with you there," he conceded. ". . . Can I ask you something?" He made an effort to catch up and match her stride, unused as he was to walking through sand.

"You can ask whatever you like, but you might not get an answer," she replied.

"Why are you helping me?" he asked. "You don't like me. For several reasons, I believe. And they don't even appear to be anything to do with the fact that I'm a fairy."

"Casual national racism is no concern of mine," Sara waved a hand airily. "In my line of work I have to deal with all kinds of species." Something seemed off about that.

"But you hate vampires?" he said.

"That's a personal grudge," she replied matter-of-factly. "It's completely different." There was silence for a while before she added, "You think of yourself as a fairy, don't you? Why not a vampire?"

"I *am* a fairy. Besides, 'fairy' is a culture as well as a species," he answered. "I suppose 'vampire' might also be a culture, but I don't understand any of that human vampire business, it seems entirely unnecessary."

"I see . . ."

"Just think of me as a fairy," Tyrian said, "Even my name that you so despise is just a label. You never know, you might even start to like me."

"You're barking up the wrong tree there, Mr. Fairy," Sara replied. Oh? Was that a flicker of a smile? He was going to run with that.

"Like girls, do you?" he grinned.

"No," she replied, slight shock in her voice. It almost sounded like she'd tried not to laugh.

"There's nothing wrong with liking girls, Your Majesty," he carried on jovially. "I like girls just fine. I've taken quite a shine to you."

"Would you like to die in a sandy grave, King of the Fairies?" she threatened, but he could tell her heart wasn't in it.

It was some time before they reached any kind of landmark. They came to an oasis, similar to the one the coronation had been held at. Freya went over to inspect the water.

"Hmm," she mused, as she studied something at the water's edge. "There are fresh footprints here. Small. They look like they are Lina's. They go that way-" Freya pointed.

"We shall do the same," Sara said. "After we rest a little."

"Shouldn't we press on?" Tyrian asked Sara, as she sat down on a rock.

"Ten minutes to rest our legs won't do us any harm," Sara replied. "We're already going to be tired because it's late, we don't need to be tired from physical exhaustion as well. Get a drink, have some rations and have a sit down." Tyrian grudgingly agreed.

"You know, I'm not sure if I've actually thanked you for this yet," Tyrian said, as he settled down on a smooth boulder. "But thank you. Thank you for this, and for looking after Erlina all this time. I'm very grateful."

"You shouldn't thank me," Sara replied. "It's nothing to do with you. I'm not about to let my employees die in the desert even if it is their own stupid fault."

"You're a terrible liar, aren't you?" Tyrian remarked. "By which I mean you lie all the time, not that you're no good at it. You haven't meant hardly anything you've said to me since we met."

"And you've meant every word," she replied. "You shouldn't wear your heart on your sleeve like that. Did it never occur to you that I could use your feelings against you?"

"So you think I should just hide them all the time, like you do?" he asked.

"Yes," Sara replied. "I'm a cold, heartless woman. No-one will ever manipulate me with love or gratitude or sadness. They won't even try. My people will never have to suffer because of my personal feelings, because *clearly* I don't have any."

"Oh yes, clearly," Tyrian muttered, shaking his head and smiling. " . . . Thank you for the advice. I appreciate it." She gave him that stern look of hers;

"What did I *just* say?"

When they set off again, Tyrian wished that Sara hadn't mentioned how late it was. He wasn't too tired to keep going, not by a long shot. But he could feel the beginnings of fatigue and he didn't like it. At least he knew they were on the right track now. They trudged on for a good while longer before they came upon another landmark. A colossal, stone archway made of carved sandstone stood before them. It marked the border between Sheva and Fairyland. There was plenty more desert and how anyone was supposed to tell at any other point on the border, he had no idea. But the thing was huge. People would be drawn to it, just like they had been. The three of them approached the arch with some caution. On this side, it was carved with the Shevan symbol of the phoenix.

"Halt!" came a pair of female voices.

"Oh, what now?" Tyrian complained.

"Who goes there?" one of the unseen women demanded. Tyrian shaded his eyes as he looked up to the top of the arch. There was a silhouette of something like a centaur, half-horse and half man. But it wasn't a half-horse that leapt down from the archway. A dark-skinned woman with braided black hair and the body of a lion stood proud before them.

"We guard the borders," the sphinx said. "No-one shall pass one way or another without our permission." It was now the wee hours of the morning, and Tyrian wasn't putting up with this.

"I happen to be the king, ladies," he pointed out as another sphinx jumped down to join her companion. "I don't need your permission to get into my own country. Stand aside."

"It makes little difference to us." The first one shrugged. "Besides, what proof do you have?"

"If you don't recognise me, I don't have any," Tyrian replied in an irritated tone. "I refused to have the coins re-minted until my parents are confirmed dead, so my mother is still on our currency."

"The girl who came through didn't even think of that," the second one sounded impressed. "She claimed she was royalty too."

"You sound a lot more convincing," the first one agreed.

"So Erlina came through here," he guessed. "I don't suppose that means you'll let us through?" The sphinxes giggled.

"Of course not, silly!" The first one replied, putting her hands on her hips. "Anyone can claim they're royalty. But that doesn't mean you can't pass. You just have to pass something else first."

"A little test," the second one added. "Answer our riddle and you can go through."

"Is the answer 'man'?" Tyrian said, before they could ask. Everyone knew the sphinx's riddle by now. The traditional one went 'What walks on four legs in the morning, two in the afternoon and three in the evening?' and the answer was man because as a baby, people crawled on all fours, as an adult walked on two legs and as an old person walked with a stick, thus walking on three legs.

"Too bad!" the first one laughed. "We don't use that riddle any more."

"Everyone knows it and we *know* everyone knows it," the second one said. "But lucky for us guarding stuff in the middle of the desert gives us plenty of time to think of new ones."

"It's kind of a species-wide hobby," the first one continued. "Don't think it's going to be easy."

"I've got a riddle for you," Freya threatened. "How do you get frostbite in the desert?" The sphinxes considered this.

"Ooh, that's a good one!" The first clapped her hands together. "Go on then, how?" Freya stepped forward, whilst making to remove her jacket. Tyrian held an arm out to stop her.

"Now then, you can't solve everything with frost, my good woman," Tyrian answered. "It's against the rules, you know." Freya gave him a look that said it had worked fine so far.

" . . . He has a point," Sara agreed reluctantly.

"We accept your challenge, ladies," he said, making a bow. "Go ahead." The two sphinx women beamed.

"Okay, then!" the first one said before they asked together;

"What has a spine and a tail but no head?" They stood side by side, patiently waiting for the answer.

"That's an easy one, I should think," Tyrian replied. "Unless the answer is something very silly, like a headless chicken, we can't be talking about any animal."

"Hee hee, that would be a naughty answer to set, now wouldn't it?" the first sphinx said.

"So I'm on the right track, then." He paused to think over his answer before saying finally, "I believe the answer is 'a book'. A storybook, to be exact. A storybook would contain one or more 'tales' and all books have a spine." The sphinx clapped politely.

"That's right!" the second one said. "Very well, you may pass." The three of them went to move towards the arch, but the sphinxes barred Freya and Sara from moving forward.

"Is there a problem?" Sara complained. "We answered your riddle. Let us pass." The first sphinx made a tutting noise and wagged her finger at the elf.

"'We'?" she repeated. "The alleged king here answered his riddle, but you two still have to answer your own." Sara sighed.

"Very well then," she conceded. "But we're in a hurry."

"What came first, the chicken or the egg?" the two of them asked together.

"Is this a trick question?" Sara asked, giving the pair an extremely sceptical look.

"It's a riddle," the first sphinx replied.

"Is there a riddle that *isn't* a trick question?" the second one added. Sara tilted her head to one side.

"That isn't a new riddle, and for the life of me I can't understand why people think it unsolvable," Sara complained. "A lot of things lay eggs. I should think many of them were around long before chickens were. Next time, why don't you try asking 'Which came first, the insect or the egg?' That should stump people."

"Well done!" The two of them clapped politely.

"And thanks, that's a great tip!" The second one beamed.

"Just one more now," the first one smiled warmly at Freya. Freya returned her warmth with a cold glare. Tyrian understood her irritation, but these were the rules. You couldn't just use violence on everything, it wasn't fair. Okay, so there were times when a well-placed punch instead of say, a card game, would do wonders, but that wasn't the point. Bullying your way through life was in the realm of What Bad Guys Do, and would only lead to a sticky end.

"You know, if I can't answer your riddle," the snow woman said, sticking out her chin, "then you'll find out the answer to mine." The two sphinx women studied her expression, then looked at each other, and back again.

"W-we can't just bend the rules you know?" the first one said. "It's not fair." The pair of them looked at one another again before appearing to come to a decision. The second one said slowly and solemnly;

"What walks on four legs in the morning, two legs in the afternoon and three legs in the evening?" *Now* Freya smiled.

"I believe the answer to that is 'man'," she replied.

"Very good ma'am!" the first one replied, clapping.

"You may pass," the second one said, before the pair of them bowed out of the way. As the three of them walked off, there was some hurried muttering, and one of them came cantering up calling;

"Ah, ma'am, if we may detain you a just a teeny tiny moment longer?" Freya stopped, turning her head slightly to listen. "Your riddle truly is an excellent one," the sphinx praised her. "Could you please tell us the answer?"

"You want to know how do you get frostbite in the desert?" Freya removed a glove and waved her hand, sending a wave of cold air across the dunes. "You annoy a snow woman," she answered smugly. The two sphinxes drew closer together, sharing a look before turning back to Freya with grins spreading across their faces.

"That's a *really* good one!" the first one squeaked happily.

"Yeah, no-one will ever get that!" the second added with glee. As the two of them waved the little group off, Tyrian reflected that despite his misgivings, sometimes a well-placed threat could *avoid* a lot of violence.

As they walked through the archway, the scenery changed abruptly. They were no longer in the desert, but in a vine-filled jungle. The plants were growing so tightly together that the path looked like a tunnel. Massive trees supported dense, vivid green foliage, creepers and vines. The air was thick with the smell of leaf mould, damp earth and flowers.

"What just happened?" Sara looked around and back at the archway. From this side, it was covered in climbing plants and hidden behind trees.

"It's called magic," Tyrian answered, grinning. "Maybe you've heard of it?" He saw Sara's expression and put on a straight face. "It used to be hard to get into Fairyland, you know. You couldn't just walk in. This magic tunnel is a relic of that age."

"I believe that Fairyland is surrounded by desert, sea and mountains," Sara pointed out. "It was never possible to 'just walk in'."

"Even so, we put all manner of barriers and things in place, to keep uninvited guests out," he replied. "I mean, we did like to travel a lot and we took plenty of people in ourselves-"

"Kidnapped them, you mean?" Sara said.

"Well, sometimes," he admitted awkwardly. "But we made plenty openings to other places, is my point. With traps to prevent anyone just stumbling in."

"This tunnel is an ancient Otherworld door?" the elf guessed.

"Yes, from when we hadn't perfected making our own doors," he said. "There were a few. I just hope this isn't the one with the six inch thorn bushes and underground tunnel filled with rivers of blood." Freya raised an eyebrow;

"Rivers of blood?" she repeated.

"We *really* didn't want people to get in," he said, shrugging.

The three of them walked through the tunnel of trees for some time. Apart from the chirp of insects and the occasional rustle of leaves, it was quiet and peaceful.

"Well, this is most irregular," Tyrian complained. "It's too quiet."

"It does seem so," Freya agreed.

"Normally when you come across ancient tunnels you get things flying out at you and crumbly floors and lots of other things generally making your life difficult." Tyrian folded his arms and scowled at the scenery. "And there's been no obstacles at all." Neither of the women bothered to ask why that was bad. Stories just worked that way. If you did something or went somewhere that was bound to get you in trouble and nothing happened, *that* was when you should be worried.

"I would certainly have expected some better defences than this," Sara said. She looked around suspiciously. They walked on for a little longer. Still nothing.

There was a squeak from behind them. They whipped around, expecting trouble. Instead they found Erlina.

"How did you . . ?" she began. Her eyes were red. She'd been crying again. Thankfully, she looked more relieved than upset. But only at seeing him. She turned to Sara.

"If looks could kill," Sara remarked.

"Says you, Your Majesty," Tyrian muttered to himself.

"Why did you follow me?" Erlina demanded of the elf. "You don't care about me or my situation, so just leave me alone!" Tyrian drew himself up to his full height. The dignity of his country was at stake. Perhaps he *would* try some of Sara's tactics, if it would calm the situation more quickly.

"Erlina, think for a moment." He stuck a thumb towards Sara. "If she doesn't care why did she just trek across the desert with someone she hates on principle until the small hours of the morning? We're all very tired so please don't be difficult." He waited while this sunk in. Her face reddened and she looked down at the floor. Success! Perhaps pretending you believed something you didn't had its advantages after all. Erlina looked up with a confused expression.

" . . . Why does she hate you again?" she asked. "Did you do something?" Perhaps not, then.

"I believe it's to do with these." He tapped one of his fangs.

"Oh yes. That," she replied vaguely. She paused for a moment before adding, "She doesn't seem to hate vampires half as much since-"

"Just how did you end up behind us, Erlina?" Sara cut her off. "You came through the gate before we did, you must have." Erlina looked around.

"It is rather baffling," she replied simply. "I expect it's some kind of spell." Sara ran a hand through her fringe.

"I could have told you that," she replied, irritated. "What kind of spell is it? How do we navigate past it?"

"I believe the answer is what it always is," Tyrian replied for her. "Magic. Lina, we'll search for the exit together. Use your cloak and go back the way you came, I'll go the other way." Changelings, with the aid of their signature cloaks, had the ability to shift into other forms, such as birds, seals or even mist. "Look for any irregularity in the walls," he instructed. "Keep in mind it may not be visual."

"You aren't just going to leave us in a fairy tunnel, are you?" Freya asked. She folded her arms.

"I understand your concern, but we can look for the exit a lot faster than you," he explained. "We shan't be long."

"What if fairies come while you're gone?" Sara asked.

"This tunnel is ancient, and thus, unused," he explained. "There are far more convenient ways in. Frankly, I'd say the most likely person to come along here would be Aunt Tannie, and that would be just splendid, seeing as she could end the war in a heartbeat."

"I suppose we have little choice," Sara conceded. She settled herself down on the floor. Freya did the same.

He made a signal to Erlina. She wrapped her cloak tightly around herself. There was a brief blur in the air, and where she had been stood was a young swan, still tinged with the grey feathers of a cygnet. As a regular fairy and indeed as a vampire, Tyrian didn't need a cloak. He cast his own spell, and bounded away on black paws as a wolf. He looked to the left and right as he sped along, trying to see or sense the exit. Fairies had a sense for magic, but it wasn't particularly strong. Magic users developed it too. Magic could be felt most strongly on Earth, where the natural level was low. It was easy to feel then. Trying to sense magic in Fairyland however, was like trying to pick out a particular scent after tipping an aromatherapy lab on a midden. It also helped if you knew what sort of feeling you were looking for, which he didn't. If you were trying to find the lavender bottle, it would help a great deal to know what lavender smelled like in the first place.

He ran on. He was tired and that was worrying. It could just be the lack of sleep, but he was starting to get a little cranky, and that was usually a sign that he was getting thirsty. Back home at the palace that wouldn't be an issue, but none of the present company were suitable blood donors. It wasn't acceptable to bite children because it could stunt their growth and they simply didn't have as much blood as adults. The snow woman would freeze his face off. Sara was actually the best candidate, and that was just how bad things would be if he wore himself down.

He caught up with Erlina; she was fairy-shaped again, and staring at a gap between two trees. He changed back himself and studied the gap.

"I can feel . . . a draught." Erlina seemed to be struggling for words. "It's hard to explain. On Earth, the air is so dry and horrible, and it's like the opposite of that." She screwed up her face as she tried to think of a more suitable explanation.

"No, I understand." He closed his eyes and held a hand between the trees. It didn't help much. He tried putting his face closer. That helped. The air seemed fresher, somehow. Cleaner. It might not have had anything to do with magic whatsoever. If he was going to install a tunnel like this in the middle of the blasted desert, he would have put in some air conditioning. "I'll see if it's safe. If it turns out to be an Otherworld door, I might not be able to get back. If that happens, apologise to Her Majesty for me." If you left ladies alone somewhere when you had specifically promised them you wouldn't and you were an ordinary person, then it was an unfortunate circumstance and you were a jerk. If you were a king and you left a queen alone somewhere when you had specifically promised her you wouldn't, it was a major political incident and you might even start a war. The title 'king' really did have a lot of annoyances. If he was a prince, he could have pranced off and left her on purpose even and faced no more than her sneaking into his palace in disguise and showing him up, but now that he was a king, oh no that was *completely* different. The whole kingdom might collapse. Not that it wasn't anyway, so perhaps it wouldn't matter.

The doorway wasn't an Otherworld door at all, luckily. It led out into a grove of silver trees with golden leaves. Apples sparkled amongst them like rubies. There was a high probability they really were. He pushed his way through the leaves and ignored the fruit. This was a 'stupid person trap', designed to trick any non-fairies who got this far into eating something deadly. There was a fountain in the middle of the orchard. He ignored that too. He walked a little farther on and stopped, shading his eyes against the glare of the newly risen sun. Clearly visible in the distance, gleaming like fire thanks to the sunrise, was the crystal palace of the Light Realm. He'd better go back, then. This was occupied territory, less dangerous than the Wild Realm certainly, but it wouldn't do to just wander about in the open. He returned to the tunnel.

"Right then!" he announced. "I've found a way out and it isn't guarded, at least so it seems. We can make it back to the palace from here. So without further ado," he said, clapping his hands together, "let's get some sleep!" The other three wore blank expressions, but they were the bleary-eyed visages of the sleep-deprived, and proved his point for him. "We're all very tired and I'm not trying to sneak through occupied territory when I'm half asleep," he explained. "I don't think anyone will bother us here, but just in case I'll set up an alarm spell." Too tired to argue, they all curled up in the moss by the path's side and slept.

Seeing that she need not bother with the clay creatures any longer, and thus her burden was lessened, Nature agreed. Day and Night proclaimed that Nature was to be the most celebrated among them.

The child, having found her mother finally asked;

"Mother, how shall I rule?"

"However you see fit," Nature replied.

Nature returned to her duties, but she is still the one with the most burdensome tasks, and sometimes she grows weary and neglects her duties. Sometimes she gets angry and lashes out, for she cares not for we creatures of the clay. But still we call her wonderful and beautiful, for she is the greatest of Gaia's children!

Chapter 7:

A deal

It was 5am and the streets were quiet. The moon was still visible in the sky, but it was fading fast, as minute by minute it got lighter. Lucinda and Will climbed up the creaky fire escape and opened the door to find the office silent and deserted.

"I guess that means they aren't back yet." Lucinda bit her lip. Sighing, she sat herself down by the desk to wait. She wanted to talk to someone who understood magic, preferably Rosie. But *all* her mentors were either in the desert or asleep in Sheva, which she had no desire to return to right now. There was the possibility that enemy fairies were lurking there unseen. They had Tyrian's sword still, and they were alone. If something attacked them they were done for. Lucinda was mostly despatched to fight beasts which were none too smart; something intelligent and magic-wielding was well beyond her abilities. Will seemed to know a lot about those kinds of things, though. He still had the knife he'd taken from the kitchen.

"Why did you want to know if that knife had iron in it again?" she asked. "Does it matter?"

"An old superstition says that fairies are afraid of iron," he explained. "They used to say that to stop a fairy stealing your child, you should put an iron poker over the cot. People used to put up horseshoes to ward fairies off, too."

"Does it work?" Lucinda asked. "Are they afraid?" "Some of them are," he replied. "They think it absorbs magic, and they believe that magic is the same as life force, so they treat iron like poison. They blame Earth being full of technology, and thus iron, for the decrease of magic there." He managed to smile. "Some of them run away if you show them a video camera or a television."

"Not all of them though, right?" Lucinda replied. "Erlina was never scared of any of that stuff. A bit weirded out by it I think, but not afraid."

"It depends where they were brought up," Will explained. "The Light Realm is on the verge of being the sort that wear flowers apparently, the Wild Realm is full of die-hard traditionals and the Dark Realm is somewhere in-between. That's where most of the refugees have settled." He sighed. "That's what caused the war, more or less." Lucinda looked nervously at her watch. Princes not usually wearing watches, she didn't normally wear it to work, but she wanted to know how much time was passing. She felt a little better to be inside the office which had withstood Sara's enemies for years, but she was unhappy that they were still alone. To pass the time while she waited, she may as well ask about this war she'd been dragged into;

"*What* caused it?" she asked.

"Well, that's the excuse that Lir used anyway," he replied. "The traditional fairies think that Fairyland is letting in too many foreign species. There were people complaining about it anyway - you get that in every country, trust me - but then this rumour got around that other species somehow destroy magical environments and it all kicked off. They're saying that Fairyland is going to be corrupted, since humans can come in and study without being invited, and there's big populations now of things like yokai and loads of demi-fairies."

"Yokai?" Lucinda was sure she'd heard the term before, but she didn't know what it meant.

"It's a Japanese word meaning something like demon," he explained. "Things like yuki onna fall into the category. They're native to Japan, although some other species fall under 'yokai' classification in the Otherworlds too. Like kelpies. It basically covers anything that has an animal form and a human one," he continued. "They can still live on Earth, but as their habitat gets destroyed they either adapt, move or die." Lucinda frowned. Erlina certainly hadn't been able to live on Earth for more than a few months without getting sick. She hadn't known the cause, only that she felt uncomfortable, like the air was prickly and dry. It would make sense to move somewhere else if you felt ill living where you were. "It was the same with other species; harpies, centaurs, naga. Human populations kept growing and when they encroached on the territories of magical species they clashed. So the magical peoples moved to Fairyland, where they were accepted. Their behaviour made it hard for things like elves and humans to put up with them you see, so they were driven out of other places." Lucinda nodded. She remembered the bad reaction Erlina had got in a town called Polvan. The townspeople had wanted to lock Erlina up because she was a fairy, and they were having trouble with the local mermaids at the time, too. It was after that that Erlina had got sick, and she'd had to go to Rosie's, where she'd learned about mana deprivation. Then she'd had to go alone to another victim of the condition . . . she sat bolt upright. Of course! She had wanted to speak to Rosie because she'd studied witchcraft and might be able to tell her what was going on. However, Rosie wasn't the only witch around.

"I know where I can find a witch!"

"Sorry?" Will asked.

"We can't go to Sheva, so I can't ask Rosie about those dreams," she explained. "But I know someone else who knows magic. I just hope she'll actually help me this time."

"So where are we going?" Will asked, as they made their way through the Blue Forest.

"I don't suppose you've ever heard of Contessa Von Stollenheim?" Lucinda replied.

"I've met her, actually," Will replied. "She comes to visit Master Tyrian sometimes."

"Oh, right," Lucinda replied.

"She's like, four hundred and seventy years old and she's been related to the Fairyland royalty for about two hundred of those," Will carried on. "It was her youngest daughter Cordelia that married into the Dark royal family, about four generations ago-"

"You're a walking Otherworld encyclopaedia, aren't you?" Lucinda's mouth engaged without consulting her brain.

"Heh, pretty much," Will admitted. "It's a good idea to know about countries you're travelling to, so you don't cause offence. Especially when fairies tend to curse you or kill you for doing that. Then there's things like deadly magic orchards and stuff. I mean when even the *fruit* is out to get you, you have to be careful, you know?"

"If it's so dangerous, why did you insist on coming?" Lucinda was utterly fascinated. She wished he'd been around when she'd started working at Rent-A-Legend. Someone like Will to explain this stuff to her would have been a great help.

"I like to travel." He shrugged. "I knew about the Otherworlds from when I was a kid and my Mom used to tell me all the old stories. I couldn't get enough of them. Plus, it's kinda a personal thing. My family tree starts to look even weirder than Master

Tyrian's if you go back far enough. There's even some centaur in there."

"No vampires, though, right?" Lucinda asked, smiling.

"Now there's something I'm sure you know already," Will said, holding up a finger. "The children of vampires are always vampires. I read that witch's research too."

"Yeah, I learned that talking to Johann and Rosie about it," Lucinda replied.

"It's funny, really," Will mused. "Master Tyrian told me about that research, that all true vampires were originally witches or sorcerers that got too powerful. You'd think they'd teach their children everything they know, but they seem to leave it at how to turn into a bat and talk in a funny accent."

"But they don't forget the magic they've learned," Lucinda pointed out. "That's why I think Contessa can help us. She might not act like it any more, but she *is* a witch."

"Good plan," Will responded. "Maybe she can help us hide the sword, too."

"Hey . . . if fairies don't like iron," Lucinda began, "What's that sword made of?"

"Legend says it's made of adamantite," he answered. "It's a legendary mineral with magical properties. I think all three treasures are made of it. There's an inscription written on it in Ancient Fairy, but I can't tell what it says. Hardly anyone speaks Fairy any more, you see. They still use it on official documents, but it's like Latin on Earth. Usually only scholars or really old fairies can read it. I tried to learn it actually, but the materials are so scarce-"

The two of them carried on along the path, with Lucinda listening intently to Will's cultural information, most of which she couldn't believe she'd never heard of or thought to ask about before.

Finally, they came to the edge of the forest. She had a plan, and she hoped it would work. She was on a sort of quest after all, so they'd *probably* help her out.

"I don't suppose anyone would kindly help me get to Contessa's mansion?" she said out loud.

"I don't suppose anyone would?" Will replied, confused.

He looked round in puzzlement, and something behind him caught his attention. He stared into the trees and then ducked down like a hunter.

"Uh, don't take offence at this," he whispered, his tone urgent, "but are you a virgin?"

"*Excuse me?*" Lucinda felt her face turn red. She was about to ask what the heck he thought he was asking out of nowhere, when he turned, grabbed her hand and dragged her towards the nearest tree.

"It might be a good idea to get out of the way anyway-" He checked around the bulk of the trunk to look at whatever had agitated him. "Quick, they're coming this way!" Will grabbed the nearest branch he could and got one foot on the tree while holding out his other hand for her to take. Lucinda, having never been attacked by anything in the forest before, risked a quick glance around the tree to see what had him so upset. A pair of unicorns were pushing their way through the foliage towards her.

"Maiden, we are here to assist thee!" one announced in a slightly high-pitched, female voice as she emerged from the forest.

"You answered me after all!" Lucinda said, beaming. "I was worried you wouldn't, since I'm not technically on a quest. That is all right, isn't it? You'll still help?"

"Of course, maiden," the filly answered her. "We unicorns live a long time, to help you, why, 'tis but the blink of an eye and a pleasant diversion." Will remained frozen in position on the side of the tree. The other unicorn emerged from the bushes.

"What ails thee maiden?" he asked her, his voice surprisingly deep for a sparkly, deer-horse hybrid.

"I'd like you to take me and my friend to the mansion on the plains if you would," she asked them. She indicated Will, who had his mouth open. He flinched as they looked over, and he was gripping the branch so hard that his knuckles were white. He looked at her as if she'd just sold him out to a pair of murderers. They stared at him and the colt flared his nostrils and snorted.

"We don't hold with-" he started. The filly interrupted him.

"I don't see that it should matter," she argued. "He is with the maiden."

"But tradition says-" he protested.

"He seems like a nice boy." The filly studied Will as he loosened his grip on the tree finally. "Come here, boy. We shall not harm thee." Will hesitated for a moment, before climbing down the tree and standing meekly before the two unicorns. The colt shook his head about, plainly in disagreement, but he stayed where he was. The filly regarded Will critically for a few moments before declaring, "I shall carry you, fear not. My companion shall carry the maiden, since he is being difficult." The colt mumbled something about tradition and females, but then he turned to Lucinda and knelt down, offering her his back.

"Thank you," Lucinda took hold of the unicorn's silky mane.

"Yes, thank you very much," Will said earnestly. "I appreciate you bending the rules for me, I know it's hard. If I can make it up to you in some way, please let me know."

"Good deeds are their own reward," the filly replied simply. The four of them set out across the plains.

When they were dropped off at Contessa's 'cottage' – a huge, three storey, white-washed, thatched mansion – the sun was well risen and the morning dew was starting to evaporate.

Lucinda thanked the unicorns again, as did Will, and they went on their way, the filly giving them many backward glances as she went. Will had a huge smile on his face.

"I can't believe I just rode a unicorn." He did a little jig. "I think I can die happy."

"Let's hope you don't any time soon though," Lucinda said. "I'm just glad we're at Contessa's. I hope she'll help us." They knocked on the door with the heavy, brass knocker, the only outward sign of what lay within. This was, despite its outward appearance, the abode of a vampire. The door creaked open. There didn't appear to be anyone there. Lucinda strolled confidently through the door, followed by Will.

Contessa descended the stairs wearing a silk nightgown. The elegant effect was spoiled somewhat by the fluffy bath robe she was wearing over the top. Obviously she'd been caught unawares. Vampires weren't meant to even *own* fluffy bath robes, let alone wear them. Her face wasn't too silky-looking, either.

"Ah, Johann's friend," she said. "Go through zen, make yourself at home." She waved a hand towards the drawing room. They walked in before her and seated themselves on the chaise longue. The ashes of last night's fire were still smouldering in the grate. She picked up a few logs and threw them on the fire before making a sweeping motion with her hand. The fire blazed up around the logs, throwing out a sudden wave of heat. "So," she addressed Lucinda, "vhich one of my relatives is acting up now?"

Lucinda explained her strange dreams, as did Will. The woman listened intently, occasionally stopping to ask them for extra information. When they finished she sat back in her chair and thought.

"So you vant a charm or talisman to protect you from spirits," she concluded. "And your house, too. Zis may be a little difficult. A charm to keep avay *all* spirits is very difficult."

"You can't do it?" Lucinda asked, disappointed.

"I never said zat," Contessa replied. "I can make some charms for you, that vill keep out anything zat does not belong in your house. Ironically perhaps, it is not unlike vhat people use to keep vampires out. I vill also make charms for you to vear, that vay, you vill be protected vhen outside as vell."

"Thank you very much," Lucinda began, feeling relieved. The feeling didn't last very long. Contessa held up a hand to stop her.

"Do not thank me yet," she replied, her face still serious. "I'm afraid I require payment for my services." Lucinda's heart missed a beat. She felt an overpowering urge to clamp her hand to her neck.

"There's nothing else you'll take for payment, is there?" Lucinda asked her, skipping the obvious question.

"I'm sure you know zat I require blood to live, and besides zat, being a student of the Silver Vitch as you are, I'm sure you're avare of her research concerning vampires and magic," Contessa said. "Charms like zese do not come cheap, magic-vise. So unless I vant to put myself in danger, I must ask blood of you. I'm sure you understand." Lucinda *did* understand, but it didn't make this any easier. She liked her blood where it was. But her parents might be in danger. This was no time to flinch at memories of vampire-induced trauma. She suppressed a shudder. There was no help for it-

"I'll do it," Will volunteered, holding up his hand and nodding at Contessa. "I don't mind." Lucinda looked sideways at Will. Contessa gave him a wan smile.

"Oh? Are you sure I von't get you in trouble with my grandson?" she asked.

"I'm not his property, Your Ladyship," he replied simply. "And it's not like it's a big deal." Shocked at Will's flippant attitude to his own body, Lucinda opened her mouth to protest, but she quickly shut it again. They didn't have much choice right now. If they saw her expression, they ignored it.

"Very vell, it is settled." Contessa shook Will's hand. "You are in a hurry, yes? I shall set to making the charms right avay."

Lucinda returned home with the charms in a little bag. She had to set them up in each corner of the house. The charms were made of twigs, bound together with some kind of dried plant stems and thin, multicoloured ribbons. They were shaped like pointy ovals. She managed to secret them about the house without her parents noticing. She was sure she'd be forbidden to do it if they saw the charms. Parents. Try to protect them from evil spirits, and they give you a lecture on how that doesn't go with the décor and how you aren't bringing that occult rubbish in here, thank you. Will had stayed behind at Contessa's place. He had to go through with the 'payment' after all, and he still needed somewhere to hide the sword.

After fixing up the final charm in a corner of her bedroom, Lucinda collapsed on her bed, exhausted. She was a little afraid to go to sleep, but she did have to see if they worked. And the sooner they got tested, the better. She didn't bother to get changed, she merely lay there until she drifted off.

Lucinda awoke from a thankfully dreamless sleep. The charms were probably working then. She had no proof either way; only time would tell. They'd *better* work. With a guilty twinge, she wondered how Will was doing. Get on with life as normal, that would be best. True, her normal life included things like dragons and fairies but they had the decency to bother her in ways she could deal with. At least she wasn't required at work today. Sara was supposed to be setting everything up as new ruler and that was something best left to genuine royalty that been preparing for it all their lives, not to some teenager who'd been given a sword and a cape and told to get on with it.

It was already early afternoon. She'd slept most of the morning. She booted up her laptop and almost immediately her messenger dinged. It was 'Pens', her best friend from her home town.

'Hey, shouldn't you be at work?' he asked. 'Won't Sara be mad?' Pens didn't know much about Lucinda's actual work. He *did* know about her boss's temperament, though.

'I have the weekend off,' she typed back.

'Tch. You could have said,' he typed. 'I have the day off too, I would have come over.' Tired as she was, that was disappointing. She'd not seen Pens since their trip to America. Granted, it wasn't that long ago, but it certainly seemed like it.

'You could still,' she typed back. 'I didn't plan on doing anything today.' There was a pause that was a bit too long before he replied;

'I made other plans, Cinders, sorry.' Lucinda pouted at the screen.

'I can't join in on these plans then?' she typed back. 'I could come and visit you instead, maybe.' What possible plans could her best friend have that couldn't accommodate her too?

'I kinda have a date,' came the reply. 'You gotta admit, that would be awkward.' She stared at the screen. She hesitated before typing back;

'That really would be awkward.' For several reasons. 'That's too bad,' she typed. Then she thought about it and quickly added, 'About us not being able to hang out, I mean. I'll let you know in advance next time!'

'Yeah, don't worry about it,' he typed back. 'Let me know next time you have a free day.'

'Will do,' she replied. Will. She wondered for the second time how he was doing. It almost seemed silly now, in the light of day, that she'd been so worried. And *he* was the one who'd paid the price for the talismans. She'd have to make up for it somehow. She was supposed to be a prince, she wasn't supposed to get all jumpy and end up having other people bleed for her. That wasn't right. She talked for a while with Pens until her mother called from downstairs.

"Lulu! Are you up?"

"I'm up!" she shouted back.

"There's a friend here to see you," came her mother's reply. A friend? No-one ever called by from school. It must be Will. Maybe he got sorted out and found his way back to her house. She was still in her prince clothes. Not much point in getting changed, really. She hastily brushed her hair and came downstairs. Her visitor wasn't Will at all. It was Shu.

"Hey!" Shu gave her a cheery wave. "I was passing and I thought I'd drop by." Lucinda was genuinely surprised. Sara had once said, 'I know where you live'. Apparently she wasn't the only one. Her mother left them alone and Lucinda invited Shu into the kitchen.

"So, is something wrong?" Lucinda asked after offering her a drink and the usual niceties.

"Does something have to be wrong? Besides, I wanted to ask you the same thing." Shu was resting her elbows on the table, both hands cupping her face. "You were cosying up to the new girl and I got worried that you were lonely. So I thought I'd come and see you."

"Oh." Lucinda blinked. She had no idea that Shu actually liked her enough to be concerned about her behaviour. "No, it's nothing like that. I just know what it's like to be the new girl, is all." 'And I thought she took my stuff,' Lucinda added in her head. She still had no leads on the pendant. If it wasn't Rina, maybe it really did walk off its own. It was a magical artefact, after all. "Thank you though. It's nice to know someone at school notices what I do."

"Anyone would notice you wearing that," Shu said, indicating her costume. "I'm not making you late for work am I?"

"Nah," Lucinda replied. "I don't have work today, I just fell asleep in my costume." Shu didn't need to know *when* she'd fallen asleep in it, after all.

"Heh, they work you hard, eh?" Shu smiled. "Still, I bet it's a fun job. It'd be cool if they had an opening. You should take me with you, sometime." Shu was not very subtle when it came to hints, then. Lucinda made a mental note not to talk about work around Shu too often, in case she kept this up. Or at least to make it sound less interesting. Which would be difficult, because apart from the fact that it was hard to make being a prince sound dull, all she really talked about was work, in a roundabout, I-don't-really-fight-dragons sort of way.

"So how did you know where my house was anyway?" she asked, changing the subject. She really was puzzled by that. She was quite determined that some of her classmates should never, ever, know where she lived.

"I saw you in the window," Shu replied, shrugging. "I mean, as I was walking past a couple of times. It's not like I stare into your windows or anything."

"Ha ha, I'm sure you don't!" Lucinda laughed. Shu grinned at her over her glass of lemonade.

"Yeah, only creepy vampires do that," she said. "And there sure aren't any round here, right?"

"Heh, course not," Lucinda replied. Tyrian was more irritating than creepy, and in any case he'd only been passing through. There was a long pause before Shu replied;

"So, like, you wanna go to the cinema or hang out or something?" she asked. "Seriously, you can't just work or be cooped up in your house." Lucinda might have replied 'Yes I can' if she wasn't feeling so touched by Shu's concern. It would be a welcome distraction and break from the events of the past few days.

"Sure. Just let me get changed." Lucinda went back upstairs to change and typed a hasty goodbye to Pens, who mocked her for once again wanting him to come over but then having a friend immediately turn up. She pulled a face at him out of habit. Then she checked herself in the mirror briefly and went back downstairs.

The two of them had a wonderfully uneventful day. They wandered around the shops, went for some fast food and now they were on their way to the cinema. Lucinda realised that she hadn't had a normal day in quite some time, not even when she was in America. It was actually refreshing, doing average teenage things. She would have been surprised at herself for thinking that, a year ago. This had been the life she didn't want. She suspected she wouldn't be enjoying it so much if it was like this *every* weekend, but for now, she was happy to bask in normality. She found herself wondering what Will did on his days off in Fairyland. Maybe he could do with a normal day on Earth for once, too. She should try and find him tomorrow. She had to check that he was all right at the very least. But those were Otherworld thoughts, and they weren't allowed today. Today, for once, Earth wasn't such a bad place . . .

Chapter 8:

Ransom

Tyrian and the others arrived at the Dark Palace without mishap. Erlina stopped short at the doors, turning to stare at the Light Palace turrets, glittering in the distance.

"I'm sorry I was so difficult," she apologised. "It's just that, mother . . ."

"It's all right Lina," Tyrian told her, giving her a one armed hug. "We're all back safe, that's what matters."

"His Majesty has returned!" came a cry as they crossed the threshold. The shout was echoed along the battlements. He wasn't long through the doors before he met with Aurelia. He smiled warmly at her, but she didn't return it.

"One of Lir's men brought this just now," she said. She held out a scroll, which he took. As he unrolled it, a few curls of blonde hair fell to the ground. It read;

'Since scrying and other location spells have failed,
I am forced to resort to less honourable means.
Return my treasure and I will return yours.
Meet me at the Temple of Gaia in three days.
You will have until sundown.
If you do not comply I will be cutting off more
than just hair.

Morgana Lir'

Gritting his teeth, Tyrian ripped the note in half.

"If that woman has hurt Will, I swear I'll rip her
throat out," he growled. "Someone get me a mirror!"

"You're going to call her?" Aurelia asked. "You
don't think you can reason with her, surely?"

"No, sadly," he replied. "But firstly, I have to see
if she really does have Will, and secondly I have to
explain the situation. Thirdly, I want to tell her
exactly what I am going to do to her if she touches a
single hair on his head-" Aurelia's eyes flicked to the
blonde curls on the floor. "It's just an expression!" he
added crossly, seeing hers.

"Master Tyrian . . ." she began. "She's going to
laugh in your face. Don't give her the satisfaction."

"I know," he sighed. "But still, I must call her,"
Tyrian continued, pacing up and down and rubbing
his temples. "This is an attempt to avoid a prolonged
fight and bloodshed that would cripple the country. It
would be almost praiseworthy if the wretched woman

wasn't the cause of everything in the first place. If she's willing to avoid a fight, perhaps we can come to an understanding. I have to at least try."

The mirror was brought, and Titania's mirror was called. A footman answered it.

"Bring me Will at once," Tyrian demanded.

"Her Majesty has sent orders not to oblige you," the man answered.

"Her *Ladyship*," Tyrian corrected him, "can come and overturn her orders herself, then." Much as it irritated him, Lir genuinely held the authority while Titania was away, but he wasn't having the soldiers forget she was regent. If Titania returned, authority would revert back to her; it was no wonder Lir was so desperate to get her hands on the three treasures.

"Very well, Your Highness," the man replied. Tyrian scowled at the empty room displayed as the man left. Apparently he wasn't allowed to forget he was a regent, either. But his situation was different. His parents were missing, and despite the best efforts of his nobles and advisers, he refused to have a coronation. A coronation meant accepting his parents' deaths, and he couldn't bring himself to do it.

"I really didn't want to do this you know." Lir slid into view. She had Will by the shoulder.

"Master Tyrian, I'm so sorry!" Will started. "Earth didn't seem safe, so we went to Lady Contessa's-"

"You'll speak when you're spoken to, human!" Lir snapped at him, giving his shoulder a shake.

"Will has nothing to do with this, leave him be," Tyrian said.

"He has *everything* to do with this!" Lir shouted. "A foreigner, coming here uninvited, polluting our country, our magic. *We* stay put, the other species should do the same! And if they *won't-*"

"If you hurt him, I swear-" Tyrian threatened.

"Oh, *what* do you swear?" Lir laughed. "Let's hear it. What are you going to do? Kill me?"

"The thought had crossed my mind," he said, glowering into the mirror.

"You don't have the guts," she replied. "That's what's wrong with you. You and the rest of the royal family. You've all gone soft. Letting all these foreigners in, believing all these sob stories about their homes disappearing. What about *our* homes? You're *weak*."

"It is not weak to be kind, Lir," he replied.

"Is it kind to neglect your duties because of selfish pleasures?" Lir accused him. "You spend all your time with this boy. Meanwhile, you ignore the nobles who support you, and throw banquets for the commoners, you refuse to marry-"

"I'll resume the court, and I'll marry," Tyrian fumed, "when I am damn well ready and not before! What business is it of yours? I didn't *ask* for my parents to disappear!"

"It's poor government and it's a blatant disregard of your royal and sacred duty to produce an heir!" Lir snapped. "Don't you *care* if Gaia's bloodline dies out? Don't *any* of you care?"

"What on Gaia are you talking about?" Tyrian asked her.

"Titania is a drunken old maid, that little changeling brat is illegitimate and *you* refuse to marry!" Lir stormed. "The royal family is a *disgrace* to Gaia's name!" Lir's tone changed, and her next words were almost a sob, "Don't you *care* if our magic

disappears?"

"That's not-" Tyrian began, frowning.

"How *dare* you!" Erlina exploded behind him. "I am *not* illegitimate, my mother is Maia, Queen of the Light Realm!"

"And your *father*, changeling girl?" Lir's sneer returned. "Your cloak is proof of your impurity. Back in the old days, you'd have been switched out for a human pet, to stop the impurity passing on!"

"My father is a demi-fairy of some sort, I was told..." Erlina mumbled. Looking back up, she continued defiantly, "Changeling or not, my mother is the queen. My legitimacy is beyond refute."

"Ha, well so should mine be," Lir scoffed. "I have just as much royal blood as either of you! I'm pure fairy too, but I'm going to have to fight for my royal status. That *stupid* law."

"That 'stupid law' was made to stop us ever having another Reign of Hel and well you know it," Tyrian growled. "It was made to keep bitter, jealous people like *you* as far away from power as possible."

"Enough!" Lir shouted. She grabbed Will by the hair. "Whether you believe in my royal lineage or not, it makes no difference. Law or no law, when I have the three treasures you will *have* to accept me. Bring me the pendant, or your little friend here dies."

"But I don't have it!" Tyrian protested.

"Then you'd better remedy that situation, hadn't you?" Lir said, in a sickeningly sweet tone.

"Lir, you do realise . . ." Tyrian said, changing tack, "if Titania . . . Look, why expose yourself to bad karma like this?"

"Bad karma happens to other species!" She shook her head. "This is why I have to stop this! This corruption of our story karma, we'll end up just like Earth, where half these creatures came from! Why don't you understand?"

"Why don't *you* understand Lir?" Tyrian replied. "All I've ever seen story karma do is take away my loved ones and drive my family to despair! I *don't care* if it disappears!"

"Listen lady," Aurelia spoke up, shoving Tyrian aside. "I didn't *want* to come here. I got *stuck* here when story karma took me away from my parents when I was *seven*! I corrupted *nothing*. I've lived here for forty-three years now and I've done as much for this country as any native," she continued. "And Will is just some Earth kid who wanted some fun! I suppose you're going to tell me fun is bad for magic now? You might be able to fool the masses into thinking you're not on a self-righteous quest for power fuelled by speciesist propaganda but we're not buying it. And,"-she leaned closer to the mirror and snarled- "Master Tyrian might hesitate to bump you off, but *I* won't. You got that?" Lir fell silent for a long moment.

"Another pet foreigner, I see," she said quietly. "Cats and their aggressive displays."

"It's not a display, woman." Aurelia flexed her fingers. "I heard how you nearly got your head chopped off by that elf queen. I wouldn't have given you a second chance to back down-"

"I can't imagine you're a threat, but I didn't get this far by being careless," Lir interrupted. "So allow me to up the stakes a little. Tyrian. If you or any of your little cronies *do* have the guts to kill me, know this," -she leaned forward into the mirror-"blondie here isn't my only hostage. I had to keep them out of the way until my ascension to power was complete, you see. It's such a pity, they were the only competent ones amongst you all." Tyrian's blood froze. Surely she couldn't mean . . ? "If you kill me, you'll never see your parents again. Oh, and I'd check on that human grandmother of yours, too. She took quite a beating." She dropped the covering cloth over the mirror and it went blank.

"*LIR!!*" he screamed. She didn't answer. He balled up a fist and drew his arm back. Aurelia caught his wrist.

"*Don't,*" she told him. "I want to smash something too, but she isn't worth it."

"Aurelia, what do I do?" he entreated. "I don't have the pendant, and Lucy doesn't even know for sure where it is." He buried his face in his hands. "If I *do* give it to her, and she returns Will and my parents, how can I face them? 'Sorry but while you were gone, I handed over the country to a mad woman'? What if she's bluffing?"

"We'll work something out, Master Tyrian," Aurelia soothed him. "We should check on Lady Contessa. Perhaps she can help us locate the pendant."

"I'll go there at once," he replied. "Erlina, you stay here. I'll call some guards-"

"No!" Erlina refused, stamping her foot. "Did you hear what that boy said? He said Earth didn't seem safe! I have to get back to Lucinda!"

"Stay here," he replied. "I don't want to lose anyone else."

"Neither do I!" Erlina protested.

"Why do the people I love the most refuse to let me keep them from harm?" he addressed to the world at large, making an expansive shrug.

"I might ask you the same question!" Erlina retorted. "It's all right for *you* to go alone but not me? Don't talk such nonsense. Besides, once you have checked on Contessa you shall have to find Lucinda, and I expect you do not know the fastest doors back, the area or where she lives. You do not have time to argue with me." Tyrian groaned inwardly. Erlina was right. He needed a guide, especially if they were going to try scrying, and he needed all the time he could get.

"Very well," he agreed reluctantly.

His concerns about the missing pendant and what could be wrong on Earth vanished as soon as he came within view of his grandmother's mansion. The door was hanging off its hinges and half the thatch was burned off. There were gashes in the floor all around the building where spells had rebounded off the barriers. Contessa had several anti-vampire hunter spells on her mansion, but they clearly hadn't worked well enough. They hadn't been designed to stand against fairies, after all. He sprinted into the still smouldering house, followed by Erlina.

"Grandma!" he shouted. The inside of the house had suffered much the same fate as the outside, though the spells had kept the place from setting ablaze. The hallway was a mess; the furniture was knocked over or blown apart and several previously valuable objects were now worthless shards of porcelain and dust littering the floor.

Dust. *No.*

"Grandma! Grandma!!" He ran from room to room. No-one downstairs. He tore off up the stairs with his heart pounding.

Please. *Please* let there be a body.

Finally, in the third bedroom he found his grandmother, collapsed halfway between the fireplace and the doorway, her hand stretched out as if she'd been crawling towards the door. He breathed a sigh of relief. He knelt beside her and felt his hand hit a rod on the floor. Raising his hand to look at it, he saw it was an iron poker; he gasped and flinched away, but his grandmother's hand clamped around his wrist. She pulled his hand towards her and bit down hard. He ignored the pain. Having banished the fear that his grandmother had been reduced to a pile of dust downstairs was worth it.

"Grandma, I'm so sorry you got dragged into this," he apologised.

"I couldn't protect him," she answered. "There were too many of them, and he wasn't the only one I had to shield. My servants made it out through the secret passages, but they were gunning for him . . . I told them not to come back until I sent for them."

"It's not your fault," he said. "I'm relieved you're all right." He fell on her with a hug as tight as he dared. She returned it weakly. She was too exhausted to even do the accent. His grandmother had been learning English for over one hundred and fifty years, yet she still insisted on sounding like she'd just moved out of the old country, even around her family. 'It vould not do to slip' as she'd explained to him once. How close had she come to running out of magic? He suppressed a shudder as he felt the dust of more ornaments grind under his knee.

"Grandmother, I . . ." he trailed off. "I wanted you to help me locate something, but you're in no condition. I needed a scrying spell."

"I can do it," Erlina volunteered. Tyrian blinked.

"*You* know a scrying spell?" he asked. "Why do you know a scrying spell? *I* don't know a scrying spell!" Royals didn't really need to know such spells. They had servants to find things for them. That was one of the many things servants were *for*.

"Rosie taught me," Erlina explained. "She used to use them to look for ingredients, but since she can't use magic any more she taught me. I tried to teach Lucinda too, but she was useless."

Erlina used the same method he saw Sara use back in the desert. She muttered an incantation, then poured water on the mirror while she gazed at it. He couldn't see anything. The mirror was blank under the water.

"What can you see?" Tyrian asked.

"Nothing," she replied. She squinted and continued to look.

"Still nothing?" he said after a few minutes.

"Ugh, yes." Erlina looked away, rubbing her eyes. "It's no good. I think there is a barrier on it."

"Lir's note did say scrying had failed . . ." he responded. "A barrier. That can't be good. Perhaps this is why Earth didn't seem safe." What was he going to do? Lucinda may not be able to get the pendant back by human means, and magical means were apparently out of the question. And that was if this Rina girl was even the culprit. He couldn't leave Will with that woman . . . he just couldn't.

"Maybe I should just offer her the crown, without the proof of the pendant . . ." Tyrian trailed off. Lir would have the Dark Realm, but Will would be safe. Wretched story karma, forcing him into such decisions. He could lose Will and prolong the war, probably losing it anyway, since she could always repeat her little trick until he broke, or he could hand over the pendant or his kingdom and the entire country would hate him for being weak, even though that was exactly what any of them would have done.

"*No,*" Erlina replied firmly.

"No?" Tyrian looked back up at her, surprised.

"No," Erlina repeated. "The three treasures are merely symbols. It doesn't matter if she has them or not. But you will *not* hand over your authority, Tyr." Tyrian blinked.

"It doesn't . . . matter . . ?" he repeated. The three treasures were merely symbols? That was right. *The three treasures were merely symbols.* That gave him an idea, but would it work? It was a long shot. He still had to find the pendant, first. That was important. It would never work if he didn't pull off the deal. "Erlina, you're right. Let's get to Earth, quickly." After making sure her servants were on their way, the two of them left Contessa in their care and set off.

Along the way, Erlina became strangely quiet. Eventually though, she spoke up;

"Do you suppose she is angry with me?" she asked.

"Who?" he asked back.

"Lucinda," she replied.

"Would you be angry with you?" Tyrian asked her.

"Yes, I certainly would," Erlina replied.

"Well, she isn't you," Tyrian answered. "So I wouldn't worry."

* * * * *

Lucinda walked out of the cinema, tossing the remains of her popcorn in a bin as she did so. It had been a fun film, if a bit silly. It had taken her mind off things, at least until a plot hole that the Otherworlds would have made sense of reminded her of them and she'd thought about Will, and what *he* was doing to take his mind off everything. She brushed the thought aside and strolled out of building, giggling about some of the sillier plot points with Shu.

"Oh my God, when that guy went rambling on about his motivation, I could have slapped him," Shu snorted. "I mean come on, your enemies are right there, just kill them already!" Lucinda felt compelled to disagree;

"That's just how things go though, right? I mean, it's bad manners to interrupt a villain doing a monologue and you have to give the good guys a chance to escape, I guess?" Shu grinned.

"To Hel with bad manners," she retorted. "I wouldn't, I don't care if it's the rules." She nudged Lucinda. "That's what's so great about Earth, right?" Lucinda giggled;

"I don't know about that-" She stopped. Shu had missed a step, as if she'd stumbled over a brick. "You okay?"

"Yeah fine, just, er . . ." She was looking across the car park in front of the cinema. Following her gaze, Lucinda saw Tyrian trying to walk towards them nonchalantly. At speed. While trying to give the many parked cars a wide berth. It was giving him some trouble. No wonder Shu was distracted. He was trailed by Erlina.

"Lucy!" he called, giving her a wave. "There you are. I was looking for you." That idiot, what did he think he was doing approaching her when she was with Shu? With Erlina no less! He'd remembered to disguise his teeth as well as his ears this time, but he was unfortunately wearing obviously Otherworldly clothes, so the disguise was pretty pointless.

\

"Oh, hi," Lucinda said, trying to keep a straight face. "I wasn't expecting to see you here." She shot a glance at Erlina, but she wouldn't meet her gaze. "This is Shu, a friend of mine from school." She hoped they would get the hint. Erlina at least had learned long ago not to broadcast the fact that she was a fairy. Tyrian however, was a bit of a wild card in that area. He glanced at Shu and frowned, before looking back at Lucinda;

"I'm sorry to pull you away from your friend," he said, "but we have an emergency."

"Um." Lucinda looked from Shu to Tyrian. Shu was wearing an expression much like his.
"What's wrong?"

"It's Will," he said, giving her a pleading look. "I must talk with you elsewhere, could we go to your house?"

"Yeah, sure," Lucinda agreed. "Shu, I'm really sorry. Thanks for hanging out with me today. Let's do this again sometime." She went to walk away with Tyrian but Shu grabbed her wrist.

"Lucinda, do you know these people?" she asked.

"Yeah, they're friends of mine from work," Lucinda replied.

"This is going to sound weird," Shu said, "but are you sure about that?"

"Yes," Lucinda replied. Tyrian stared at Shu.

"You're the girl who said she didn't know where Lucinda was," he observed. "Apparently you did. I'm not sure what you think we're going to do with her, but I really must speak with her alone."

"Oh no, I don't think so," Shu replied.

"I *really* don't have time for this," Tyrian responded crossly.

"Shu, it's fine really!" Lucinda tried to reassure her. "Um, it's a work emergency, I'll have to go or Sara will be really mad!" She laughed nervously and broke away. Shu tried to grab her, but she ran off across the car park. She shouted over her shoulder, "I'll see you later, okay? I'm really sorry!" Great. She'd finally managed to have a nice day with a normal friend and now that had all just gone up in smoke. Shu had looked like she was going to slap her. She ran off towards the nearby supermarket so they could lose her. Ducking in one side of the entrance hall and emerging on the other, she led them around the back of the huge building where she hoped they wouldn't be followed or seen. Tyrian cast something, and his disguise faded.

"Invisibility spell," he explained.

"Go on then," she sighed. "What's happened now?"

"Will has been kidnapped," Tyrian replied solemnly.

"But . . . but he was with Contessa!" Lucinda protested.

"She couldn't fight off a fairy battalion by herself," he said. "We have three days," he added, handing her a scroll. She unrolled it and stared in dismay at the words. This was *her* fault. She shouldn't have let Will deal with the payment, she shouldn't have left him at Contessa's and she certainly shouldn't have lost that *stupid* pendant.

"'Scrying and other location spells' it says here," she read aloud. "We could have used spells to find the damn thing?"

"Not exactly," Tyrian told her. "The spell is only any use if it shows you a location you're familiar with. We'd hoped it was somewhere around here and Erlina would recognise something but we ran into an unexpected problem."

"Which was?" Lucinda asked, with a sinking feeling.

"The pendant seems to have a barrier around it," Erlina said. There was a long moment of silence as the three of them considered the implications.

"Did Lir put a barrier on it?" Lucinda asked.

"That wouldn't make any sense," Tyrian said. "She carried it with her, it was only by chance that I was able to steal it away. It would only impede her attempts to recover it. Someone else must have cast the barrier."

"Does that mean a witch has it?" Lucinda asked.

"I suppose that is a possibility," Tyrian replied. "Did you find out anything from that girl you suspected?"

"What, Rina?" she asked. "Yeah, I asked her, but she didn't seem to have taken it."

"'Didn't seem to have'?" Tyian repeated. "Are you *certain* she didn't?"

"Well, no, not 100%, look, she's really difficult to talk to and she acts so angry all the time," Lucinda said. "Besides, she's not a witch."

"Are you sure?" Tyrian asked. "Crotchety, difficult, secretive, a loner. Typical witch traits." Lucinda had to admit that the same things could be said about Rosie.

"Can witches even live on Earth?" she asked.

"Oh yes," Tyrian replied. "Miss Rosie can't because she's been damaged by over-use of magic, but a witch with no over-exposure would be able to live here just fine, as long as she didn't overstretch herself. So I understand, anyway." Erlina nodded agreement.

"Rosie told me I would have been able to live here for a much longer time if I hadn't been forced to use my magic constantly," she said. "You have to be overexposed to magic first before you suffer from being underexposed, she says. Fairies are already overexposed, but humans are not."

"And there are still people on Earth with fairy connections," Tyrian said. "Will is such a human. His great grandmother was a changeling, you know. Stronger connections may yet exist, despite our avoidance of Earth these days."

"I'm still not sure," Lucinda said. "Why didn't she just take it from you directly?"

"I suppose if doesn't take it and then steals it, she doesn't have to give it back," Tyrian theorised. "And it's infinitely useful for an Otherworld traveller. Much like Erlina was impossible to find with her world hopping, so would it be, even without a barrier."

"How the heck are we going to find it?" Lucinda lamented.

"I was hoping you could tell me . . ." Tyrian trailed off. "Listen, is there somewhere we can talk where I won't have to burn through my magic like this?"

"I guess we'd better go back to my house," Lucinda replied. "We'll have to take the bus. I might just about have enough change, but I don't know-"

"Oh no, I'm not getting in one of your iron contraptions!" Tyrian refused.

"Don't be a baby, Tyr," Erlina complained at him. "I took buses and things plenty of times and I was just fine."

"Oh yes, *completely* fine," Tyrian replied, flicking the white streak in Erlina's fringe.

"Then how do you suggest we get to my house?" Lucinda asked him.

"Like this!" Tyrian gave his arms a shake, before sweeping Lucinda up off the floor. She shrieked. They started to rise off the ground.

"Hey, what are you-" Lucinda started. "We can't *fly*, it's cold up there and there's not enough oxygen! People will see us!"

"We're not going to fly up very high so you won't get cold or suffocate, and we're invisible remember?" Tyrian explained.

"Well, yes, but-" Lucinda faltered, as they rose further off the ground.

"But I'd like to remind you that we are perfectly audible, so you might want to keep your voice down." He tilted his head to the corner of the supermarket, where Shu was standing. She appeared to be looking for them. Lucinda grabbed onto Tyrian as best she could.

"You win," she mumbled. "Let's get out of here."

The flight back home might have been fun in different circumstances. The weather was decent, and Tyrian had been right, she wasn't cold at all and she could breathe fine. But all she could think about was Will. It was *her* fault the pendant had been lost and it was *her* who had left him with Contessa. If he died-

"Where does this Rina live?" Tyrian asked her all of a sudden.

"I don't know," Lucinda replied. "She's new here. I'm still not convinced it's her."

"Neither am I, but we have no other leads," Tyrian said. "We had best at least try to confront her before considering other plans of action."

"We should land," Erlina prompted. "I see the park below."

"Maybe I can look something up on the internet, I don't know," Lucinda said, as Tyrian put her down. "I don't suppose you can scry for Rina?"

"I have to be able to visualise my target," Erlina explained. "You can't do magic and Tyr only saw her the once. More's the pity."

"Magic is not like your technology where you can just push a button and get it to do what you want I'm afraid," Tyrian added. Lucinda wrote off the last comment as coming from someone who didn't understand technology. Nevertheless, she had one last ditch attempt to find Rina.

"I've got an idea, but it's a long shot," Lucinda said. "Let's go."

Up in Lucinda's room, Lucinda opened up her laptop and typed in her school's website address. Erlina was leaning over her shoulder, but Tyrian was sat on her bed what he must think was a safe distance away from the possibly poisonous technology. She clicked on the 'staff' section. She just hoped the website was up to date.

"Lucinda, whatever are you looking for?" Erlina asked her.

"Rina said her mother is a teacher," Lucinda replied. "They just moved here. If I find out her mother's name, I might be able to find her in the phone book." She looked through the names, copy-pasting ones she didn't know into her word processor, ignoring the male ones. She had a vague memory of the teacher introducing Rina by her family name her first day back. It began with a W and ended in an R. She looked at the list of names. Only two women fit the criteria. One was Mrs. A. Walker and the other was a Miss. H. Warner. Miss Warner worked in the geography department, Mrs. Walker in English. Come to think of it, she'd been in the English department when Rina had hit her in the face with that door. Telling the fairies to stay put, she went to fetch the phone book and her mobile.

Returning, she opened the book to the residential numbers section and flicked to W. It took her a few minutes to find 'Walker'. She groaned and planted her face onto the open pages.

"There's a hundred Walkers in here!" she moaned.

"What exactly are you trying to do?" Tyrian asked her.

"I thought if I could find Rina's phone number, I could find out her address, maybe phone her and see if she was in," Lucinda explained. "But I can't phone a hundred people, I haven't got enough credit and I can't use the house phone, my parents will want to know why."

"How were you going to find her address again?" Tyrian asked.

"The addresses are in here," Lucinda replied. "Oh wait . . . the addresses are in here! That's it!" If Rina walked to school through the park, she must live somewhere close by. Lucinda could eliminate a lot of the Walkers that didn't live in town. She grabbed a pencil and started at the top of the list, crossing out anyone who didn't live nearby. That narrowed it down to about ten people. Now was the bit she was dreading. She was going to have to phone a lot of strangers. If Rina got angry again with her mother listening, that might make things difficult for her at school if she took it the wrong way. All that was nothing compared to being held hostage by fairies, she reminded herself. She steeled herself and rang the first number.

"Hello?" came a man's voice.

"H-hello," Lucinda replied. "Can I speak to Rina please?"

"Rina?" the man replied. "I think you've got the wrong number, there's no Rina here."

"Oh, I'm sorry," Lucinda apologised. "I must have wrote it down wrong." She ended the call and sighed. It was only to be expected that the first call would be a dud. She typed in the second number and pressed call . . .

There was only one number left and one of the Walkers had given her a lengthy telling off thinking she was telemarketer. What if Rina's family weren't in the phone book yet? What if she'd remembered the name wrong? If magic didn't work and technology didn't work, however would they find the pendant? She typed in the last number and pressed call. It started to ring. She waited. It carried on ringing. She bit her lip. What if no-one answered? She couldn't keep ringing and ringing and then use the 'sorry, wrong number excuse'.

"Hello?" came a breathless voice. "Sorry, I was upstairs!"

"Is Rina in, please?" Lucinda asked. Please. Please be in.

"No," the woman answered.

"Sorry, I-" Lucinda started to answer.

"She's gone to the park," the woman carried on. "She's only gone to walk the dog, she shouldn't be long." Lucinda nearly collapsed.

"Thank you!" Lucinda replied gratefully. "I'll see if I can find her!"

"Um, I can get her to call you back?" the woman said. "Who is this?"

"Oh, no please don't worry, it's nothing," Lucinda said quickly. "I'll phone back later if I don't see her! Thank you, bye!" She hung up before the woman could ask anything else and stood up. "She's at the park!" she said. "Let's go!"

The three of them rushed to the park. Erlina used her cloak to disguise herself as a swan and Tyrian made himself invisible again.

"Look for a girl with mid-length brown hair, a bit longer than mine, she's about the same height as me and she's walking a dog!" Lucinda instructed.
While Erlina flew above, Lucinda and Tyrian searched on foot. There was a honk from above and Lucinda looked up to see Erlina circling before flying

off towards the gates. Lucinda took off after her, looking up and then back down. She spied Rina, heading out of the park.

"Rina!" she called out. The girl turned and blinked.

"Yeah?" she said, before realising who it was. "Oh good, it's my stalker."

"Um, yeah sorry," Lucinda began, catching up with her and huffing. "So this is awkward. But please, have you seen the green stone? It's really, really important."

"I thought I told you, no," Rina replied. "Do you have a memory like a sieve?"

"Look, seriously, you don't know how much trouble I'm in if I don't get it back-" Lucinda tried.

"Why do you keep asking me?" Rina asked, putting her free hand on her hip. "Wait, you don't think *I* took it?"

"It's just that you're the only other person who saw it, and-" Lucinda tried to explain.

"You really *want* me to have taken it, don't you?" Rina replied, studying Lucinda's face. "Is this because I didn't want to be super special best friends right away, or what? Don't be so pathetic!"

"I'm not being pathetic!" Lucinda shouted. "I *need* it back, a friend of mine is in trouble-"

"Then call the police and leave me alone!" Rina yelled back, turning on her heel. "If you or that weirdo come near me again, *I'll* call them!"

"If she's a witch Lucy, then she's doing a very good impression of being an ordinary Earthling girl," came a solemn voice near Lucinda's ear as Rina stormed away. Tyrian dropped his invisibility spell. He lurched towards a nearby park bench and collapsed onto it, burying his head in his hands. "What am I going to do . . ?"

"I'm so sorry," Lucinda apologised. "This is all my fault."

"No, no, it's mine," he said, digging his fingers into his temples. "Everyone knows how I feel about him, I should never have let him out of my sight. Queen Saharaleia was right. Perhaps kings shouldn't have feelings . . ."

"Isn't there *any* spell that-" Lucinda started to ask. There was a furious flapping and they both looked up to see Erlina, still swan formed, being mobbed by a crow. Erlina was bigger, but she was ungainly, and the smaller, more agile bird had the upper hand.

"Erlina!" Lucinda shouted, looking away from Tyrian and stumbling back out onto the path where she could see the sky better.

"Lucy," came a strangled call from Tyrian. "I believe we have found our witch." Lucinda turned to see Tyrian with his hands in the air. Someone had a knife pressed to his throat.

"Lucinda, run!" his assailant shouted.

"*Shu?*" Lucinda gaped at her.

"I'll explain later, just run!" she shouted. Lucinda just goggled.

"*You* took the pendant?" she said, aghast. "Why? What could you possibly-"

"Return the pendant to me at once!" Tyrian demanded. "You've no idea what's at stake!"

"You're in no position to make demands, Your Majesty!" Shu replied. "Lucinda, why are you still here?! Jack can't keep the other one busy forever, just *go!*" Things had just gotten a lot simpler and yet a lot more complicated at the same time. Lucinda didn't know if she should kiss Shu or slap her. She settled for using sarcasm;

"Can't I introduce my friends to each other without someone pulling a knife?"

"You're *seriously* telling me you're friends with the King of the Fairies?" Shu asked.

"You're seriously telling me you *know who he is?*" Lucinda countered. "I can't *believe* this. I just want you to know that I've fought things that have more heads than legs, my best friend is currently a swan and I *flew* here not so long ago, and *I can't believe this.*"

"I can explain-" Shu started. "See, I didn't *mean* to steal the pendant," Shu told them. "I saw it on the floor, and the resemblance to one of the legendary treasures was uncanny, so I picked it up. I couldn't ask to borrow it, because what would I say? I was going to return it after break, but I was shocked to find out it was the real thing, so I couldn't give it back until I knew what was going on exactly."

"Go on," Lucinda prompted, folding her arms.

"Well, the first thing I had to do was to see if you actually knew what you'd gotten yourself into," Shu said, "I asked you a couple times if you'd take me to your work, but you refused. I know you like cosplay and stuff so I thought maybe you didn't have anything to do with the Otherworlds after all and you'd come across it unknowingly. I was curious before, but I couldn't just outright ask you about it, it's against the rules, and anyway, if I was wrong, you'd think I was crazy!"

"I refused because I thought you thought I just worked somewhere kind of normal and I thought Sara wouldn't appreciate it if I brought people," Lucinda explained back. "Oh and the crazy thing, too."

"Yes, yes, everything would be so much easier if only we talked to each other," Tyrian complained. "Could we please do this without me at knife point? It's unnecessary. I'm a king and Lucy here is a prince, it's the standard 'get foreign princes to do what you aren't allowed to do yourself because you'll die' thing. I'm not trying to kidnap her or enchant her. And please call off your jackdaw."

"You're a *prince?*" Shu asked Lucinda, lowering the dagger a little.

"My boss keeps running out of real ones." Lucinda shrugged.

"That explains the outfit. All right," Shu admitted. She lowered the dagger and jumped back. "Jack, lay off." The jackdaw flew down and landed in a tree, cawing triumphantly. Erlina flew down into the trees nearby, presumably to change back. That was a relief, but Lucinda was going to have to say something or explode;

"Do you have *any idea* how much trouble you've caused?"

"I'm really sorry, I thought I was protecting you," Shu said. "There's a war on."

"We noticed," said Tyrian and Lucinda together.

"I thought Wilders would come looking for it, but then *you* showed up." She indicated Tyrian. "It's not yours and you were looking for Lucinda, so I panicked. I had no idea if I should give it back or what, so I gave it to my grandma for safekeeping and asked my totem to go investigate. Then I was caught totally off guard when he actually found you, and I heard you scream and I couldn't find you, then I rushed back here and I thought he was mad at you for losing it, and-" Lucinda had worked in the Otherworlds long enough to catch on quickly;

"Is your totem, by any chance, a bunch of talking dream animals?" she asked. "And I am *definitely* slapping you for that one! I thought I was gonna die in my sleep!"

"I'm kinda sorry, but I'm also not sorry," Shu replied. "Most of us commoners don't even know what this war is about, there's just been a lot of kicking off about foreigners and the royals are all squabbling over power. Everyone says we're heading for another Reign of Hel and we're all scared!"

"I promise you, I won't allow that," Tyrian tried to reassure her. "Now *please*, return the pendant to me! A dear friend of mine is in dire trouble-"

"It's *not yours!*" Shu protested. "It belongs to Queen Titania!"

"I know damn well who it belongs to, but if I don't hand it over to Lir she's going to kill Will!" he pleaded. The two of them glared at each other. "Look, if I wanted to get it just for power, why would I be here with the heir of the Light Realm, whose mother is also held captive and her not trying to stab me or anything? Lir is the one getting grabby, not us."

"Are you really the missing princess?" Shu asked Erlina sceptically.

"Will you believe me if I say yes?" Erlina said. Shu gave her a critical look.

"Um, I can verify that, kinda," Lucinda said, putting her hand up. "Unless there's more than one princess in Fairyland, anyway. Erlina is most definitely a fairy princess. Trust me on that. I've known her for nearly a year." Shu looked from Lucinda to Erlina and back. She tutted.

"Let's say I believe you, for now," she said, finally putting her knife away. "You're going to have to go through one more firewall first." She pulled out her mobile phone and dialled a number. "Hi, it's me. So, I have a situation." There was a pause. "Yeah . . . No, I didn't . . . The king *and* the princess allegedly . . . Can you contact Grandma and tell her to open the door for me? Thanks."

They followed Shu through the town. Eventually, she waved them into an alleyway and followed them in. Then she shut her eyes. After a moment she said;

"Lao Li says we're clear, but we have to wait for a little bit."

"Lao Li?" Lucinda asked.

"One of my spirit guides," Shu explained. "She's a linsang. You've met."

"The sensible one," Lucinda replied. "Yeah." She wasn't quite sure that she had forgiven Shu for everything yet, but she'd deal with that later.

"This is where I came in the first time," Tyrian remarked, looking around. "I recognise the rubbish." He wrinkled his nose. They waited in an awkward silence for what seemed like forever.

Suddenly, a door opened in the air. A black haired, fairy woman motioned for them to step through.

"Quickly!" she said. "While no-one sees us!" Once they were through, the door closed and they were led through a barren area around a lake, then into a forest.

"Thanks Grandma," Shu said.

"This lady is your *grandma*?" Lucinda remarked. Lucinda was trying hard not to stare. She looked as if she were only twenty-something! "You're part fairy then?"

"The way I was referring to fairies as 'we' ought to have tipped you off," Shu replied. "My mother is a halfling. That's a half-fairy, half-human."

"Shu dear, we have to get out of the open," the fairy woman told them. "Explain yourself later, we should hurry."

They followed the fairy woman across a barren waste and into the forest. The air was humid, and various brightly coloured insects were buzzing about. Lucinda didn't think much of normal insects, never mind magical ones. She jumped when something touched her hand, but it was only Erlina. Giving the fairy a relieved smile, she took it. Erlina squeezed her hand pretty hard.

They stopped at a house, standing alone in a clearing, but they didn't go in. The fairy woman stood up straight, directly before the door.

"Your Majesty, Your Highness," she addressed Tyrian and Erlina in turn, bowing as she did so. "My granddaughter here gave me Gaia's pendant for safekeeping, and I will return it to you. On one condition."

"And what is this condition?" Tyrian asked.

"Stop this war," Shu's grandmother pleaded. "We don't want royals squabbling again and ruining the country. We don't want another Hel."

"I will try," Tyrian told her. "I've *been* trying." Without saying a word, the woman vanished into the house. Everyone waited. She reappeared, holding the pendant. Before handing it over, she added solemnly;

"Do more than try. We are counting on you. We are afraid, and as our king, it is your duty to quell that fear."

"I know," he said, secreting the pendant in a pocket. "Your faith shall not be misplaced. I will return to the palace to form a battle plan immediately." He turned to Lucinda. "Lucy, please take Erlina with you back to Queen Sara and the others. Please inform her I will be making a visit to her office tomorrow morning, Fairyland time."

"Is that a good idea?" Lucinda asked him. "Whenever you give me charge of anyone or anything, it goes missing. Also Sara. What do you want to talk to her about?"

"Erlina was safe with you all once, she shall be again," he said. "Besides which, if I don't send her with you, she will sneak out after you anyway. As for Sara, I will tell her myself tomorrow."

"Okay," Lucinda agreed. She'd been working with Sara long enough to know that these things required secrecy, so she left it at that.

"Excuse me," Shu piped up. "If you don't object, I'd like to help. I know my attempts to help so far have not been great, but I can be an asset."

"Lucinda?" Tyrian asked. "You're the one who knows the lady."

"I'm still pretty mad about basically everything," Lucinda answered. "But I understand why you did it. I'm pretty sure the enemy won't try to protect me and I think we need all the help we can get."

"Very well," Tyrian agreed. "If you truly want to end this war, I will accept your help. As Lucinda said, we need all we can get."

Leaving Tyrian to return to the palace, Lucinda and the others walked back to the door, Shu's spirits checking it was safe. Now that everyone had finished yelling at each other, it was time for some proper answers.

"So are you a witch?" Lucinda asked. "I never would have guessed. I thought you were just a normal teenager."

"That's because I'm better at this whole secret identity thing than you!" Shu laughed. "I'm a shaman. It's kind of like a witch for spirits and humans alike. I mediate between the two and try to solve problems."

"Spirits and humans?" Lucinda asked, noting the sudden switch from Shu's identity as a fairy.

"Fairies don't really need a shaman, since they can often talk to spirits directly or indirectly, but we do act like priests for them at festivals and stuff sometimes," Shu replied. Lucinda had other questions on the subject, but they could wait until later.

"What was all that about a reign of Hell?" Lucinda asked. "Please tell me you don't mean the place with all the fire."

"No," Shu replied. "Hel was an ancient queen of Fairyland."

"She was second in line to the throne, and she was not content with the title of princess," Erlina said. "She killed her older sister, and imprisoned her parents, threatening to kill them too. She gathered all three treasures and declared herself supreme ruler. She claimed to have communed with Gaia at the temple and received great power."

"All sounds like fairly standard royal behaviour," Lucinda remarked.

"The next bit wasn't so standard," Shu said. "She demanded a tribute from every village."

"Some stories say she demanded this every year, some say every seven years," Erlina added.

"Fairies don't use printing presses or paper, they still hand write stuff on vellum if they need anything written down, so our history is pretty muddled up," Shu explained. "No-one even knows what she looked like. Some say she had black hair, some say white, some say it was half black, half white which sounds to me like they're mixing her up with the Norse goddess Hel. But what she was definitely, was bloodthirsty. Figuratively and literally."

"So by 'tributes' you mean . . ?" Lucinda asked, knowing the answer.

"Yeah, she wanted those people for their blood," Shu answered. "They were sent to the temple for some awful ritual. No-one ever came back, so the terrified people started taking humans for the purpose. They say all the laws that were designed to keep humans from leaving were so that we could keep them for Hel. Dark times." Lucinda shuddered.

"Was she a vampire?" she asked. "Tyrian's not related to her, is she?"

"Dunno," Shu replied, shrugging. "'Vampire' isn't a word that really meant anything to us until a hundred years ago or so. Fairies um, kind of eat people and stuff anyway, so it would have made little difference."

"And Hel's line is extinct," Erlina said. "Eventually, the people got fed up of her tyranny and rebelled. After a terrible civil war, she was captured and executed. I expect that is why people are so frightened. I can understand why you hid the pendant."

"I see . . ." Lucinda replied. No wonder Shu hadn't wanted to give it back once she found out it was real. She could have been aiding a tyrant.

"Her parents were long dead by then, so they took on an illegitimate heir instead," Shu continued. "It was one of those 'long lost heir returns to save the kingdom' deals. He was the son of the old king by some mistress or other." Erlina snorted.

"What?" Lucinda asked.

"That woman," Erlina muttered. "Back at the palace, she called me illegitimate. The nerve of her." Shu laughed.

"This is that advisor of Queen Titania's isn't it?" she said. "People have been gossiping about her for years. She's just jealous because she doesn't count and you do. That's the whole reason we have that law."

"What law?" Lucinda asked.

"Fairyland's monarchy is a bit . . . odd," Shu began, "compared to how other monarchies work, I mean. Women inherit first before men, and though children of male royals with mistresses aren't considered legitimate, the children of any queen or princess are, regardless of father or marital status."

"That's weird," Lucinda replied. "How come?"

"You see, Fairyland has a culture of, um, 'free love' and quite frankly, a lot of people could claim to be an heir to the throne. So to avoid disputes, they made it so that only women can have legitimate heirs unless there's marriage involved. If the queen or princess gets pregnant, there's no doubting it's her kid, but with men . . ."

"Makes sense, I guess . . ." Lucinda trailed off. "Wait, so you're saying this Lir woman is the daughter of some royal?"

"She's sort of the unofficial official next in line to the Dark Realm throne," Shu replied. "Apparently she's descended from King Arawn, King Tyrian's great, great grandfather. His wife was human, er, a human vampire anyway, so she died and he was still in his prime and he got worried that something would happen to his son and there'd be no heir, so he took a mistress."

"I'm *really* glad I'm not actually royalty," Lucinda muttered. "'Prince' is just my job description."

"Speaking of which," Shu began, changing the subject, "I'm finally going to get to see your workplace, huh?"

"Yeah, but I'd best go with just Erlina today," Lucinda replied. "My boss is a bit difficult. A lot difficult, actually. And she doesn't like uninvited people. I'll tell her you're coming tomorrow and explain everything first, okay?"

"Okay," Shu agreed. "See you tomorrow then."

Chapter 9:

Waking Gaia

Back at the palace, Tyrian rallied his troops and explained the situation. The note hadn't said 'come alone' thank goodness. He had to deal with Lir honourably, because that's What Good Guys Do. From the note, it *sounded* like Lir would be honourable too, but would she? Despite sounding like she'd swallowed the Big Book Of Villain Dialogue, she didn't seem to have gone completely off the deep end. She could have killed Maia, but Maia was alive. If she had been killed, they'd have been told, loudly and proudly, to damage their morale. There were rules, but it depended on how bad you wanted to be. Lir ought to be on the terrible end of the scale, laughing manically and tying up heroes above tanks of sharks, but here she was saying she'd tried to do things

differently . . . but of course, this was his most hated of all things, politics. It was all about playing the good guy while being the bad guy. Or being the good guy and looking like the bad guy. Lir was an advisor and had been keeping the Wild Realm together while

Titania was away. Titania had been away a long time and they weren't called 'Wilders' for nothing. No wonder she'd started spouting villain nonsense. He wasn't taking any chances, though. Saying you'd let the hostage go and then killing them anyway was a known villain pattern. At least he was more confident about his 'handing over the pendant' plan now. He actually had the thing, for a start. But Shu's grandmother had given him more than just the pendant. She'd given him hope.

"Why are you calling Lir again?" Aurelia asked him, as he strode into his chambers.

"I want to show her I have it, and I want to arrange a little something," he answered her. "I have a plan, but I need her co-operation."

"You need her *co-operation?*" Aurelia said.

"I want to arrange a little spectacle," he replied. "Let's see if she's willing." Tyrian called up Titania's mirror. Once again, it was answered by a footman. "Get me Lady Lir immediately."

"Her Majesty has said she is not open to negotiation," the man answered stiffly.

"Her Ladyship can tell me herself then," he replied, flashing the pendant. The guard started. His eyes darted off-mirror. Then he rushed away. A few minutes later, Lir arrived.

"Show me," she demanded, her eyes suspicious. He held up the pendant. "So it wasn't a trick. Well now. Seems my little stunt got results." She smiled.

"I'd like to move the handover to tomorrow evening," he said. "I don't want to leave Will in your hands any longer than I must."

"Better results than I thought." Lir's smile became a smirk. "Why not sooner? I'm happy to hand your little friend over immediately."

"Much as I wish I could," he replied, "I cannot. I have a condition for handing over the pendant. I wish to make it official, in front of the whole country."

"I see," Lir mused. "That way neither of us can pull anything. I'd say I can't believe you're willing to risk country-wide humiliation for your little human, but I can. I agree."

"Tomorrow evening we will make the trade," Tyrian said. "That allows us to make a royal proclamation in the morning, to announce it. That should be ample time."

"At the temple of Gaia, as per my note," Lir stipulated. "Agreed?"

"Agreed." Tyrian nodded.

"Tomorrow evening then," Lir said. The mirror cut off. Tyrian breathed out. His openness about his emotions had actually helped this time. He would have liked to speak with Will, but he was afraid Lir would catch wind of his plan if he tried to reassure him.

"Aurelia, I need to write the announcement for tomorrow," he said, turning to her. "And . . . I need to make a battle plan. I need a back up in case things do not go smoothly."

"I knew you weren't going to just hand it over, Master Tyrian," Aurelia said, smiling. Her expression changed, and she gave him a stern look. "You're still not going to call Parliament, are you?"

"There's no time," he replied. "Besides, if my plan fails, it won't matter if the nobles support me or not..."

* * * * *

Lucinda and the others made their way back out of Fairyland and onto Rent-A-Legend. Just before they parted ways, Shu hesitated. Lucinda thought she might ask to come and see Sara after all, but;

"I really am sorry, you know," Shu apologised. "I didn't mean to freak you out. I thought you'd think it was just a dream. I wish I could've asked you directly, but we're not allowed to openly interact with Earthlings."

"I was never told, but I kind of guessed," Lucinda replied. "You don't just stumble on a magical door to lands full of griffins and fairies and stuff and go around telling everyone, even if you can prove it. I mean, you just don't."

"Ha ha, the Otherworlds are rubbing off on you!" Shu replied.

"Yeah, they do that," Lucinda said. "I'll warn Sara I'm bringing a new person and hopefully she won't pull a dagger or order anyone to get the heck out."

"Sounds like a real dragon," Shu replied.

"An elf, actually," Lucinda said.

"Ah," Shu responded. "See you tomorrow then."

With Shu seen off home, Lucinda and Erlina went through the door and straight into Sheva. They were treated graciously and led into one of Sara's rooms. It was filled with hanging silks and the floor was strewn with colourful rugs. There was a large window at one end, open to the sky, except for a fine mesh cloth to keep out insects. Sara was lying on a couch near the window, relaxing. It was the first time Lucinda had ever seen her at rest. She almost felt bad bringing up the war next door, but it had to be done.

"You're bringing who to my office tomorrow?" Sara asked her, after Lucinda had explained the situation.

"Shu," Lucinda replied. "She's a friend from my school, but it turns out she's also a shaman and part fairy. Oh, and Tyrian wants to meet you tomorrow morning, Fairyland time. It looks like he has a plan to deal with this Lir woman but he wouldn't say."

"No, I expect he wouldn't," Sara replied. "Good."

"Good?" Lucinda repeated.

"I was worried he didn't have a plan, and we'd have to deal with Lir ourselves," Sara replied. "Though the desert has always protected us from outright invasion by fairies, it doesn't mean we didn't suffer raids and things like everyone else. No doubt he's waiting until a mere half a day before this trade is supposed to be made to maintain secrecy and avoid it being leaked. I will wait and see what he has to say tomorrow. And yes, bring this friend. She may be a valuable addition to the company. I'll trust your judgement."

Morning in Fairyland was a few hours earlier than morning in England, but Lucinda arrived wide awake, if a little rough around the edges. It was hard to sleep when you had a battle planning to attend in the morning, especially one that was partly your fault for losing people's stuff and getting their friends kidnapped.

"I'm going to exchange the pendant for Will tonight at the temple of Gaia in the centre of Fairyland," Tyrian explained. "Most of the country has been invited to watch to prevent foul play on either side. I'd like to beg your aid, if I may."

"As I stated, my official position as Queen of Sheva is that we will not get involved," Sara replied. "The political consequences for us both are far too great. If elves were called in to help you, well, I'm sure I don't have to remind you that our species are not exactly on friendly terms."

"Please," Tyrian started. "I know you don't-"

"As head of Rent-A-Legend however," she continued, holding up a hand to stop him, "my position is different. Maybe I do still dislike vampires," she said, scowling, "but what I *really* hate are *throne usurpers*. Now." She put her hands on her hips, and her expression softened. "What do you need?"

"I have a plan, but whether it works or it doesn't, Lir is not going to be pleased with me," he explained. "She may retaliate and I don't want Will to be in the line of fire. I need to get him off that temple and to a safe place. I understand that your office is such a place."

"It is." Sara nodded.

"That isn't all," Tyrian continued. "Will is not the only hostage Lir has. Erlina's mother Maia is being held under guard in the Light Palace." Sara looked startled.

"You don't think she'd hurt Maia do you?" She bit her lip. "A fellow fairy?"

"I honestly don't know," Tyrian replied. "She appears to be playing by the rules, for all that she's on the point of breaking out into maniacal laughter."

"We should get her out just in case," Sara said. "I propose a simultaneous rescue. We get Maia out as the trade is taking place. I know that divides our forces, but if we got her out beforehand, they may catch wind of your plan."

"That sounds sensible," he replied. " . . . Thank you. I appreciate your co-operation, even if there are those amongst my people who would not."

"You shouldn't thank me," Sara said, giving him that look of hers. "I'm not doing it for you."

"Nevertheless," he said, smiling at her, "I'm grateful."

"I think it would be best if we kept involved people to those who can blend into Fairyland society," Sara continued, ignoring him. "I will send Freya for Will. She's a one woman tank. As for Maia," she said, "Erlina, I think you, Lucinda and the new girl . . . what was your name again?"

"Shu, ma'am," Shu replied.

"You three get into the palace and get Maia out," she instructed. "Bring her back here. Lucinda, get some potions from Rosie."

"I thought you said only people who look like Fairyland residents will be able to help?" Lucinda asked.

"Out in the fray, where practically the entire country has gathered, yes," Sara explained. "Since you'll be sneaking in and sneaking out, I hardly see that it matters, and in any case, you're with the Crown Princess. Pretend you're her servants if you get caught."

"Can do!" Shu pulled off a salute.

"Thank you, Sara," Erlina said solemnly.

"I suggest we spend the remaining time available to us planning escape routes and stocking up on potions," Sara said. "Let's get to work."

Lucinda and Shu both spent the afternoon helping Rosie make potions. Erlina was busy at the office, working out the best routes in and out of Fairyland.

Once everyone was stocked up and the appropriate outfits procured, all they could do was wait.

"Sara, shouldn't Gerda come with us or something?" Lucinda asked.

"No," Sara asked. "She's too conspicuous. You two will pass for handmaidens, she won't. And I still need someone here to man the desk and open doors. Just in case the worst comes to the worst, take some iron with you."

"Culturally insensitive much?" Shu remarked.

"I'd rather you be culturally insensitive than dead," Sara replied. "I'm betting that woman's followers are traditionalists, so iron is a last resort to ward them off."

Lucinda couldn't wear her sword as she was dressed as a handmaiden, so Rosie lent her and Shu a few of her knives. In addition to containing iron, they were sharp and pointy which would deter anyone. The two girls were both wearing basic peasant dresses and hooded cloaks. Tyrian had insisted the girls wore cloaks to try and hide the fact that they were humans. Fairies were experts at invisibility and disguise spells, so any magical attempts to hide their humanity were pointless. A simple cloak had worked for Will, so Tyrian hoped it would work for them.

Erlina led the way to the Fairyland door in the Blue Forest, which came out in the Light Realm. Shu's grandmother had sneaked across to open it from the other side. They stepped out into an open, airy woodland, carpeted with pale green moss and tiny purple flowers. It was like walking on a colourful sponge. Golden birds flitted from tree to tree, warbling to each other.

"Unless it is an emergency, do not speak unless spoken to," Erlina instructed them as she led them towards the palace. "Remember, you are handmaidens. That goes double for pulling out that iron you have. Unless we are discovered, leave it be."

"Understood," Shu replied, saluting.

"Right," Lucinda said.

The castle loomed in the distance. It was made of white marble; the walls were inlaid with glass and gold, and it gleamed in the sun. Erlina led them to the back, through some stables and into the kitchens.

"We're a bit exposed, aren't we?" Lucinda whispered.

"The servants still have to work, whether the castle is occupied or not," Erlina whispered back. "I thought they would not notice a few more people milling about. We will go through the kitchens. Act like you belong. Do not look around or as if you have nowhere to be."

"You sound like you've done this before," Lucinda remarked.

"Princesses are often well practised at sneaking in and out of their castles," Erlina replied. "Now hush."

The three of them walked straight through the kitchens and up some stairs. There were little windows in the marble on one side, but blank wood on the other.

"Is this a secret passage?" Lucinda asked quietly.

"Lucinda, once we are in the palace proper I must ask you to stick to the 'no talking' rule," Erlina scolded her. "No, it is not. It is better. It's a servants' passage. It allows the staff to go about their work without being seen in the halls. No-one will think it odd there is someone in here."

"We're bound to run into guards somewhere though," Shu said. "Want me to check where they are?"

"If you would." Erlina nodded.

"Hang on a minute then," Shu replied. She stopped dead, and sat cross-legged on the floor. She closed her eyes. It was several minutes before she opened them again. "Lao Li says there's guards outside the gates and guards on the walls which we've managed to bypass," she reported. "The real problem is the guards on the Queen's chamber. She's being kept in there."

"I see . . ." Erlina replied. They continued up the stairs and out into the corridor. Erlina had to lift a whole section of wall away. They left it leaning on the wall and carried on. To Lucinda's alarm, Erlina was making no attempt to hide herself whatsoever. She strode right up the corridor and up to the two guards outside Maia's bedroom. "I want to see my mother!" she demanded.

"Go and see her then?" One of the guards suggested. Erlina made to step past the guard. "Woah there, what do you think you're you're doing?"

"I told you, I want to see my mother," Erlina repeated. "She is in there, I believe." Erlina indicated the locked door. The guards shared a look.

"Are you saying you're the missing princess?" one of them asked.

"I am clearly not missing, but I am certainly Princess Erlina and you will let me pass immediately or there will be consequences," Erlina said, crossing her arms. "I have been travelling and have just now returned. Stand aside."

"Just one moment princess," the guard and his companion shuffled over to one side. They had a hurried conversation. One of them opened the door and looked in, looked back at Erlina and back in again.

"Certainly looks like the queen's daughter," the other guard said.

"Very well, go through," the other said. "Leave your attendants here."

"I will do no such thing!" Erlina retorted. "What do you think they will do? They're only humans." She pulled down their hoods. Lucinda tried to keep a straight face, but her horror must have still been visible;

"Heh, they look tamed enough," he remarked.

"I do not want to leave them alone, someone may steal them," she continued. "I'm quite attached to them, and besides, I do not want to go to the trouble of getting new ones."

"Very well, take them through," the guard conceded.

"Our apologies, princess," the other said, waving them through. Once they had crossed the threshold however, he added, "because you're going to be in there for some time." With a nasty grin he slammed the door, and there was the sound of a key in the lock.

"What are we going to do?" Lucinda whispered.

"I'm not sure, be quiet and let me think," Erlina replied. Lucinda looked around the room for potential escape routes. They were in a lavish bedroom, the biggest Lucinda had ever seen, all shiny oaken furniture and expensive draperies. The walls were decorated with swirls of gold inlay, much like the outside of the palace. A huge portrait opposite the four poster bed might have concealed a secret passage, but the walls here didn't look thick enough. The only other way out was the window. Seated by it was a fairy woman. She stood up, staring, rendered speechless. There was no mistaking her identity. She had pale, green eyes and long blonde hair that cascaded in soft waves almost to the floor, and was wearing a long green dress decorated with gold brocade. Even if they hadn't expected to find Erlina's mother in here, the resemblance was clear.

"Lina, it really is you!" She ran across the room and fell on Erlina, hugging her and kissing her forehead over and over. Breaking away she said,

"You shouldn't have come back. There's a war, sweetheart."

"I know, mother," Erlina replied, hugging her back. "I was expecting a heavier guard. Why have you not escaped?"

"Where would I go?" she replied. "My Realm is occupied, and without me, the people would have no-one to rally around. I couldn't leave. Lir seems to know that. I'm afraid this is all up to Tyr. He should be all right. He's a prince, after all."

"He's a king now, mother, remember?" Erlina replied, pursing her lips.

"Oh dear," Maia responded.

"At least he is not going into battle." Erlina clasped her mother's hand. Erlina dropped her voice. "We must leave. Tyr has a plan, but Lir will use you as a hostage if you stay here."

"But where will I go? What of our people?"

"Your Majesty," Shu cut in, "as a member of your people, um, sort of, I assure you that they'd rather you be out of the country and safe, rather than remain as a means for the enemy to dictate what happens to it. Please come with us."

"You ladies appear to be humans?" Maia asked.

"Species and race are of little consequence, Your Majesty," Shu replied, shrugging. "We're all fairies at heart. We wish Lir and her followers would understand that."

"I understand," Maia said, standing up. "Let's go."

"How are we going to get out, though?" Lucinda asked.

The door opened and the two guards stepped inside.

"Ladies," the first one began, "this door is not soundproof. Perhaps you have mistaken us for human guards who have all the intelligence of a mud brick, but we are not."

"We've called for reinforcements," the second one added. "You're going nowhere." Lucinda looked over to Erlina;

"Would you agree that this is an emergency?" she asked.

"I do believe this qualifies," Erlina replied. Lucinda and Shu both pulled out their knives.

"It's actually a good job you're not human," Lucinda said, advancing on them. "These have iron in them. We checked." The guards recoiled.

"You dare bring *iron* into Fairyland?!" the first one screeched.

"Sure do, now who wants to be first to find out if it really is poisonous?" Shu threatened. The guards practically fought to get out of the doorway. Shu and Lucinda kept them at bay while Erlina and her mother got out into the corridor. When they had a clear run at it, Lucinda and Shu took off after them.

* * * * *

Tyrian walked slowly up to the steps of the temple, heart pounding. He looked down at the pendant clasped in his hand. Erlina was right. It could find doors, yes. But it was only a symbol. It wasn't weakness to trade a mere symbol for a loved one.

The temple was a stout pyramid, made of weathered blocks of dark grey stone. There was a small altar at the top, surrounded by four pillars carved with leaves. They supported a large, triangular stone roof. The area around the temple was thronged with people; Fairyland natives and expats alike. There was a ring of guards around the base, keeping the citizens back. They moved to let him pass, then closed behind him. As he climbed the steps, he turned to look nervously behind him and saw Freya push her way to the front of the crowd.

When he reached the top, Lir was waiting for him by the altar, along with three of her guards. Two were stood behind her, the sword and the staff lying on the floor in front of them, in a V shape. He thought it odd, but his thoughts did not linger on them - the third guard was holding Will. He was pale and he had bags under his bloodshot eyes. Tyrian clutched the pendant so hard, his knuckles whitened.

"Master Tyrian," he spoke up as Tyrian got close enough. His voice cracked. "Don't do it. I really wish I could tell you to do it, I'm terrified, but the people won't like it and you have no guarantee she'll do as she says."

"Will, even if I could bear to leave you at the mercy of that woman even one second longer,"

Tyrian replied, "whoever heard of anyone *not* handing over a precious artefact for a loved one?"

"Oath breaking is for human scum, boy," Lir said, gliding across the temple. "We fairies keep our promises. And *I* promise *you* Tyrian, the next time you refer to me as 'that woman' I'll have your tongue cut out."

"Lir, you must know," he said, holding out the stone, "there will be consequences for your actions."

"How terribly humanised you are," she replied, shaking her head. She turned to address the crowd. "Did you hear that?" she asked them, in an almost sing-song voice. "Tyrian says there will be *consequences.*" Turning back she bellowed, "We are *fairies!* We *are* the consequences!" She snatched up the stone and held it aloft in triumph. "Gaia put us here to keep the other species in check, and if they've forgotten that, then I will just have to remind them!" She snapped her fingers and the third guard released Will, pushing him roughly towards Tyrian, who scooped him up into a hug, planting kisses on his forehead.

"There," Lir continued smugly. "You have your little human back, and I have the kingdom. Was it worth it? It just shows how weak a king you really are. I've taken over just in time."

"Is that right, Lir?" Tyrian replied. "Because you know, I really don't think so."

"Excuse me?" Lir snapped, her expression hardening.

"I traded you the pendant for Will," Tyrian explained. "No-one said anything about the kingdom."

"I have the three treasures!" Lir protested. "The proof of rulership!"

"Hel had the three treasures, too," Tyrian pointed out. "Her rule was ended, and not because they were pried from her grasp, but because her head and her body parted ways."

"*Why you-*" Lir advanced on him. "The legend says-"

"You see, one thing you learn at a very early age when you're a vampire," he continued, backing away towards the stairs, "is that if people don't like getting bitten they'll come after you with pointy sticks and chop your head off. And vampires aren't the only ones vulnerable to the peasant's axe. Kings and queens throughout the ages have lost their heads to it, for all their noble blood."

"What's your point?" Lir asked. "The legends say whoever has the treasures is the ruler! The people see I have them! They see the proof!"

"Indeed, they've seen quite a bit," Tyrian agreed. "We made sure they did. We wanted them to see what manner of rulers we are."

"And so they did!" Lir declared. "They saw you're pathetic!" Tyrian turned to address the crowd;

"Citizens of Fairyland!" he began. "Lir holds the sword, staff and pendant of legend, the proof of rulership handed down from Gaia. Legend says they unlock power, but I say that is a falsehood."

"Master Tyrian, what are you doing?" Will whispered.

"Hush," he whispered back, before shouting, "Once upon a time, there was a queen named Hel. Second in line to the throne, she murdered her own sister, incarcerated her own parents and demanded fear and tribute from her own subjects with that power, as well as giving us a reputation that still echoes in fairy stories today." He paused, to let this sink in. Then he continued, "Lir says I'm weak. Perhaps she's right. I traded the pendant for Will. It's common knowledge that he's precious to me. I'd have gladly traded all three treasures for him if I'd had them. He's a helpless human boy and under my care. It was my duty to rescue him from peril. Now, let me ask you this,"-he drew a deep breath-"would you rather have a ruler who will lose face and give up trinkets and emblems to protect their loved ones, or would you rather have one who will strip you of what is precious to you, to exploit your weaknesses so that she may become strong? Is that the sort of queen you want? I say the power comes not from the treasures, but from the people! Will *you* give *her* power?" There was a muttering amongst the assembled fairies;

"If that was *my* human . . ."

"What if she starts demanding tithes?"

"All the other races already hate us . . ."

"Lir says we're a proud people," Tyrian shouted, "and I *agree!* Far too proud to bow to such despicable tactics! Are we going to let such a thing pass?"

"No!" the crowd responded.

"Do you want another Reign of Hel?" he shouted.

"No!" the crowd screamed back.

"Do you *care* who has the 'proof'?" he asked them.

"*No!*" the crowd bellowed.

"*Who's your king?*" he roared.

"*You are!*" The crowd erupted, with angry fairies rushing forward to tackle Lir's guards, with the dissenters getting knocked off their feet in the rush. Tyrian turned to see Lir advancing on him again, her face contorted with fury. Hugging Will to him with one arm, he used his free hand to hurl a spell at her. Knocked off her feet, she tried to call her guards, but they had their hands full trying to keep the crowd under control. Some fairies were climbing up the sides, attacking the circle of guards around the bottom and doing their best to knock them down. They fought back with fireballs and transformation spells which got rebounded onto the temple and knocked great chunks out of the stone. She clambered to her feet.

"Stop, stop, you're damaging the temple!" Lir cried in horror. Not daring to move any closer to her with Will at his side, Tyrian hung back, attempting to shield him from the debris. Lir shot him a look of pure hatred, but instead of moving towards him, she fell to the floor, slamming the pendant down; at first he thought she was trying to break it, but then he saw that the artefacts had not been carelessly abandoned on the floor as he'd first supposed, but slotted into depressions in the floor. The floor began to tremble, and a large square of rock right under Lir started to drop out of sight.

"Apparently they aren't just symbols, after all," Tyrian muttered. Still clinging on to Will, he stared at the deepening hole before him. He wasn't risking Will's life by recklessly plunging after her, but he couldn't let her get away either.

"Tyrian!" came a shout from the stairs. The crowd practically melted away. The air temperature had dropped dramatically, and there was also a woman threatening everyone with a black, stone dagger.

"Let me past, damn you!" Sara commanded as she warded off ally and foe alike. She was wearing a purple tunic with white and gold patterned edges, similar to traditional fairy attire. "Freya, take the boy. I'll give His Majesty a hand with the usurper." The snow woman started to put her fur cloak back on.

"I thought you said it would look bad if I got help from an elf?" Tyrian whispered to her.

"What elf?" she said. "I don't see any elves. I'm a *fairy*. Twinkle, twinkle, damn those elves, etcetera." Dying a little inside, both from the casual speciesism and the hilarity, he pointed to the hole.

"She went down there," he said. Freya scooped up Will, ready to carry him away.

"What are you still doing up here then?" Sara asked him. "Get in there." Tyrian planted a kiss on Will's temple.

"If I don't come back, blame Queen Sara," he told him. "This lady will protect you until I come and get you." He nodded to Freya. "Please take care of him." She nodded back, and then set off like a juggernaut down the temple steps.

"Go on then," Sara prompted. "I heard your little speech from down there. Who's their king?"

"King or not, there's no sense in being incautious," he complained. Walking to the edge of the hole, he peered inside, on the lookout for any errant spells. There was a faint glow, but it appeared to be coming from some runes inscribed into the passage. When nothing tried to blast his head off, he reached inside and felt around. "It's just a stone tunnel. I suppose we'll have to climb down. You, guards!"

"*What?*" snapped a guard who was busy trying to fight off an enraged changeling girl half his size.

"Calm this crowd down! Clear a path and bring me some rope!"

"I don't answer to-" the guard started.

"What part of 'I am your king' do you not understand?" Tyrian demanded. "Clear a path and bring me some rope, I said! Citizens!" he shouted. "I appreciate your support, but a riot is no longer helpful! Please calm down and remove any dissenters and indeed most of yourselves from the area! Things may yet be dangerous!"

"That's more like it," Sara said.

* * * * *

Lucinda and Shu made for the servants' entrance but Erlina ran onwards down the corridor, suddenly ducking into a room. Once inside, she and her mother swung a massive painting to one side and pushed at the wall. It slid open. They hurried inside and the portrait swung back. They slid the wall back into place and moved on.

"Hopefully they'll think we took the servants' way out again," Erlina whispered. "Let's go."
They emerged at the side of the castle. There were trees here, no doubt planted to cover what was genuinely a secret passage.

"Where are we going?" Maia asked.

"To Rent-A-Legend," Erlina replied. "I've been working there for the past year. We will be safe there."

"Is it far?" Maia asked.

"Just a little further," Erlina replied. "There is a door to the Blue Forest, if we can get there we're safe." They continued along under the trees, but the further they got from the palace, the more they thinned out, and Lucinda began to feel exposed. The springy moss might be fun to walk on, but it wouldn't help if they had to make a quick getaway. A jackdaw flew above them cawing loudly. Shu stopped dead, and looked up. The jackdaw circled once and then flew away.

"They know where we are," she warned them. "They're heading this way, we have to hurry!"

"We must take to the road then," Erlina replied. "I'm afraid we have little choice but to go out into the open." They moved onto the road. Walking as quickly as they could, they made better progress, but Shu was jumpy.

"How far is it?" Shu asked. "They'll be here any minute!"

"It's just beyond that bend-" Erlina began. There was the blast of a horn, and the sound of hoof beats.

"What should we do?" Lucinda asked. "We can't lead them to the door!"

"We can defend ourselves easier through the door than out in the open like this at least," Shu suggested. "I think we should go for it!" They ran, but the fairy soldiers charged ahead and cut them off.

"Not so fast," the leader said. They stopped and bunched together. "We understand you have iron, but our horses do not fear it. It will do you no good." Lucinda swore. They definitely couldn't intimidate the soldiers while they were on horseback. However;

"That's why we brought these!" Lucinda grabbed the first potion vial in her cloak and hurled it at the nearest guard. He swore and fell of his horse sideways. Shu sent another potion sailing at the guard behind him, and Erlina and her mother sent spells flying. Another guard fell, one clutched at a leg, another an arm-

"Enough, apprehend them already!" came a shout from the back. The guards launched spells and the women ducked. Lucinda felt her arm go numb. She tried to grab the knife with her other hand, but she fell. Erlina caught her and tried to support her, deflecting another spell. Shu collapsed too, and Maia backed towards them-

* * * * *

The crowd dispersed and some climbing equipment brought, along with a few reinforcements, Tyrian prepared to climb down into the temple. Legend said that Gaia slept beneath it, and that it had been built to keep out the noise of the world so that she wouldn't be disturbed. Perhaps they were afraid that if she woke up, she wouldn't like what she saw.

"Any idea what's down there?" Sara asked him.

"No," Tyrian replied. "Legend says our mother goddess, but I don't believe that for a second."

"Oh?" Sara raised an eyebrow. "Why not?"

"Legend also says I'm descended from her and if I was a god, I wouldn't have let all this nonsense happen in the first place."

"Gods seem to like nonsense," Sara replied.

"Further proof I'm not one, then," he said, testing the rope was secure.

"Yeah, no, you don't like nonsense *at all*," Aurelia teased, as she shone a lantern down the hole. "I suggest we get down there. Whatever Lir is doing, the longer she's free to do it, the worse it'll be. I'll go first."

"I'm the king and I'll go first," Tyrian argued. "I already put one of my fools in danger-"

"I'm not your fool any more," Aurelia said, punching him in the arm. "I'm your bodyguard, and it's my *job* to go first."

"Could we please not injure one another before we get down there?" Sara complained. "I'm sure Lir is more than willing to do that for us."

"Yeah, yeah." Aurelia gripped the rope and started to climb down. "Um, hey. Someone is staying up here to help in case we get stuck or something, right?"

"Freya will be back once she's got that boy somewhere safe," Sara reassured her.

The three of them climbed down the passage, the way lit by a faint, green glow coming from the walls. It was a square hole, dug right into the mountain by the looks of it. Runes had been carved into the stone the whole way down the shaft. After a while the stone changed from dark grey to black, and warm air came up from below. What was down here? It looked like the three treasures were keys to a lock, meaning that only the royal family could get down here, and only by the consent of all three reigning monarchs. But what was here that needed keeping under lock and key? What could *fairies* possibly want to lock away? Maybe Gaia really was down here . . .

The shaft seemed to go on forever, but it finally came out into a wide cavern, carved with more runes. Most of the cave was flat and empty but the dim, green light illuminated several pillars in the centre, arranged in a rectangle. There was a shallow, rectangular pool in the middle of them, with a statue of Gaia on a pedestal at the far end. She had her head held high and her arms outstretched. Lir had placed the staff and the sword in her hands. She was standing in the pool at the base of the statue, running her hands along the bottom and under the water. She was holding the pendant in one hand. It was glowing faintly. Engrossed in her task, she hadn't noticed them.

"It must be here, it must be." Lir's muttering was carried clearly across the cavern. "Where is it?" Ready to use the pillars for cover and walking as quietly as possible across the hall, they saw her stop and gaze up at the statue. She gasped, and ran up to it. As she went to climb up it, she glanced around and spotted them. In a panic, she aimed a spell at them, causing a line of fire to block their way. She clambered up the statue, slipping on the stone and her wet dress. There was a click that resounded around the hall as Lir pressed the pendant into the statue's neck. As they ran around the fire to get to Lir, the statue began to tremble and there was a rumbling sound. Lir lost her footing, and fell out of sight.

"Where did she go?!" Tyrian shouted, his words echoing through the hall. The three of them ran to the pool, but it had vanished. What little water there had been was pouring into a hole as the floor of the pool slid back, to reveal a tiny square room underneath, with a black, stone throne sitting a little way away from the end with the Gaia statue. Lir had fallen onto it. Reaching out, she clutched onto the throne and stroked it.

"I found it, I really found it!" she exclaimed. "Hel's throne! It's real!"

"I'm not from Earth," Sara warned, "and I know it's a different one, but nothing with 'Hell' in the name is *ever* good."

"I don't suppose you know what it does, Master Tyrian?" Aurelia asked him.

"No, but I'm willing to bet we won't like it," he replied.

"Ha!" Lir scoffed. "That's what you get for abandoning your heritage. If we still spoke Fairy instead of English, everyone would have read all about in the ancient scrolls. This is where Hel communed with Gaia! And I shall do the same."

"If we could commune with Gaia, we would have been doing so for millennia," Tyrian protested. "This place has been sealed up, I don't need an ancient scroll to tell me that. I suggest that you desist from whatever you're doing right now. This has bad story karma written all over it."

"Bad story karma is something that happens to other species," Lir replied. "That's human talk. I'll soon put an end to that, when I'm queen." Lir sat herself on the throne, wiggling about to get comfortable.

"You heard the speech," Tyrian said. "And you heard the reaction. The people won't accept you as queen."

"If they won't accept me willingly, then I'll just have to force them. It's for their own good," Lir replied, glaring up at them. "Now be quiet, I will ask Gaia what she thinks of all this."

"And just how is a bit of rock meant to force us?" Aurelia asked her.

"Hel's Throne is so named because legends say that she sat upon it and received the power of Gaia," Tyrian explained. "I didn't think it was an actual thing, I thought it was one of those 'the gods said I get to be leader' legends."

"You'll see," Lir sneered. "Gaia gave Hel great magic here. If Hel was worthy, then so am I."

"You really think that monster was worthy of *anything*?" Tyrian asked, disgusted.

"I do not," Lir replied. "Ultimately, she hurt her people by letting her power get the best of her. It shall not happen to me."

"Lir, nothing good ever comes of saying these things, get out of there at once!" Tyrian demanded.

"More human talk!" Lir shouted. "Once I speak to Gaia, she will give me the power to restore the country, and the people will remember they are better than those clay creatures. The world can return to how it was meant to be-" While Lir rambled on about fairy supremacy, Tyrian rubbed his eyes. Was his vision blurry? Lir seemed to be out of focus.

"Should I just drag her out of there?" Sara asked. "I'm really not in the mood to listen to pretentious monologues about how fairies are better than everyone else."

"You!" Lir stood up and pointed an accusatory finger at Sara. "You're that elf, you stopped me at Sheva! What a liar, I heard you announce you wouldn't get your country involved! You elves shall be next after I fix our magic!" Tyrian squinted. It wasn't just Lir, the throne was blurry too. And it wasn't his imagination. Lir's hair was turning grey.

"Master Tyrian, I second the 'drag her out' suggestion," Aurelia said. "She's obviously got a bad case of villain, I'll be happy to slap it out of her-"

"*Don't move-!*" he commanded, as the two women went to jump over the side. "Run back and fetch the rope, quickly!" Sara gave him an odd look, but Aurelia immediately obeyed. "Lir get out of there! You are standing on a mana vent!"

"I see, so that's why she built it here," Lir said, unconcerned. "What better place to speak with Gaia?" Sara gasped.

"Get out of there, you idiot woman!" she yelled. "The magic is poisoning you!"

"Stupid elf!" Lir retorted. "Magic doesn't poison fairies! It doesn't poison anything! Magic is life!"

"*Then why is your hair turning white?*" Tyrian demanded. Lir looked down at herself. She ran her fingers through her rapidly paling hair.

"This is just . . . the power of Gaia," she mumbled. "It must be. Magic doesn't . . . poison . . . The witch's research said . . . only humans . . ." She gasped and clutched at her throat. Staggering sideways, she leaned on the wall for support. Aurelia got back with some rope and threw it down into the hole.

"Climb up and be quick about it, because if you faint I'm not coming in there after you!" Aurelia shouted to her. "I've lived with vampires for forty-odd years and I know a blood swoon when I see one!" Looking up with frightened eyes, Lir obeyed. Her hair was now white as snow, and she trembled as she struggled to climb up the rope. She clambered over the side and Tyrian rushed to assist her. He saw Sara run over to the Gaia statue, and prise the staff out the statue's hand. Lir shook him off and ran to stop her.

"Don't you dare take those!" she screamed. "Those are mine, do you hear me?!"

"Do you want me to close the poison spewing room or not?!" Sara yelled back, as she plucked the sword from the statue's other hand. The stone floor of the pool began to close. As Sara hoisted herself up to pluck the pendant from the statue's neck, Lir caught up with her and grabbed her leg. The two women slipped, and the pendant fell out of Sara's hand, bounced off the pedestal and into the throne room. Sara clung to the statue struggling to regain her balance, but Lir jumped down after the stone.

"Are you mad?!" Tyrian screamed, running to the side of the pool. "Take my hand, quickly!" He leaned as far over the side as he could. Lir stood up, and clasping the pendant to her breast as if it were a child, she ran over to him and reached up. The gap left by the closing floor was getting ever smaller.

"Couldn't lose it," she muttered, as she strained to reach him. "Our precious heritage-" Tyrian reached down as far as he could. He almost lost his grip; he felt Aurelia grab his waist.

"If you *die* for that woman, Master Tyrian, I'll never forgive you!" she screamed in his ear. He managed to grab Lir's wrist. He pulled with all his might and he flew backwards, landing on Aurelia. He stared in horror at his hand. He had a fistful of dust. Darting back, he was just in time to see Lir, her skin and hair a blinding white, staring forlornly at the dropped pendant before she collapsed into a swirling cloud. The pool floor closed with a thunk.

"No . . ." he whispered, staring at the blank stone.

"I'm *sorry*, Master Tyrian," Aurelia consoled him.

"No!" he slammed his fists down on the pool's edge.

"We'd better get out of here *now*," Sara said. "I don't want that to happen to any of us."

The three of them ran to the stone platform that had taken Lir down here.

"We'll have to climb up," Aurelia said. "I wish I could climb faster. Apart from the excess mana, traditionally, temples like this collapse or explode when you're leaving them."

"Don't give the damn thing ideas," Sara warned. "Your Majesty, can you use some kind of levitation or kick starting spell on this platform?" Tyrian nodded. They seated themselves and he started to raise the platform back up to the temple summit.

* * * * *

Maia tried to shield the three girls as the guards advanced.

"*Cease and desist immediately!*" demanded a furious female voice from behind them. The guards looked around in a panic. "Stand aside fools!"

A brown, curly-haired, fairy woman dressed in green trousers and a short, white shirt strode forward as the guards parted, a human boy and a green-skinned woman in tow.

"Tannie?" Maia started.

"Honestly, I go away for what, six or seven years and you turn on the other Realms?" she admonished the soldiers, actually clipping the nearest around the ear. "What is this country coming to? Be a bunch of dears and throw yourselves in prison for a bit."

"Y-your Majesty?" the leader stuttered. "You're back?" There was a stunned silence as they took in her attire. Her top was tied in a knot at the front and she was wearing a red bandanna. It was most unqueenlike.

"Do I need to chop some heads off or what?" she tutted. "I believe I gave an order."

"Y-yes Your Majesty!" The guard saluted with his working hand and turned his horse around. The remaining guards followed him. Titania kicked one of the stricken guards.

"Get up and undo these spells, you," she said. The guard tried to move but couldn't. Titania sighed. "Very well, let's see if we can't find you a witch. There's bound to be one around somewhere, the place is always full of students." Erlina gazed warily at the newcomer. Maia heaved a sigh of relief. She rushed over and kissed the older fairy on both cheeks.

"Tannie, it's been so long!" she said. "Please don't disappear again for a very, very long time, okay?"

"Oh honey, you know I can't promise you that," Titania said. "Wild Queen over here. Called that for a reason. Lina sweetie, is that you? Look how big you've grown!"

"Witch, please," Lucinda interjected from the floor, clutching her arm. "Now, please. Rosie lives close enough, if we go through the door."

"Of course dear," Titania said, patting her on the arm. "I'll let Maia take you, I have a war to stop or whatever." She flounced off, taking her companions with her. When she was gone Lucinda asked as she was helped upright;

"*That's* the missing queen?"

"I guess so," Shu answered, staggering to her feet.

"So she disappears for seven years, comes back and goes 'LOL did you guys have a war?'" Lucinda summarised.

"I believe she just did, yeah," Shu replied.

"Okay, so I can kind of see why Lir rebelled . . ."

* * * * *

The stone floor ascended in silence. Tyrian stared blankly at the floor, glad that he had a spell to concentrate on. When they reached the top, he let the women disembark and then sank to the floor on the solid part of the temple. Aurelia touched him gently on the shoulder.

"It's over now, Master Tyrian," she said. "It's over."

"I d-didn't want . . ." he stuttered. "What have I done?" He tried to blot out the image of her, a white statue, her face frozen in horror.

"Shh," Aurelia soothed, hugging him. "It wasn't your fault, and it's over." Sara grabbed him by the arm and dragged him to his feet.

"Move," she ordered. "Now. Mourn if you must, but move while you do it." She led him down the steps, faster than his leaden feet wanted to go. They met Erlina halfway up.

"Is it over? Freya sent me to check on you," she explained. "Tyr, whatever's the matter?" She took his hand and squeezed. He merely shook his head.

"Lina, good timing," Sara said. "Lina, where is the door you took to the Blue Forest when you first ran away?"

"It's not too far, just a little way into the Light Realm," she said. "Lucinda and the others are there now."

"Take us there immediately," Sara commanded. "We need to see Rosalind."

He followed Sara through the door, into the forest where he'd found Erlina. She was leading the way. As soon as the cottage was in sight, Erlina ran to the door and wrenched it open.

"Rosie!" she called, without going in. "Sara says Tyr needs looking at!" The witch appeared at the door and came right over.

"What now?" she complained. She looked askance at Sara. "Are you *escorting* an injured *Stollenheim* Your Majesty?"

"*I* didn't injure him if that's what you're implying," Sara replied. "Listen, that mana sickness you have, overexposure to magic, he might have it. Can you look at him?"

"A *fairy* with *over*exposure?" Rosie sounded alarmed. "I can't imagine a fairy would suffer from it."

"We didn't have to imagine it," Sara replied firmly. "We saw Lir turn to ash before our very eyes. He was hanging over the pit that did that to her, it was over some sort of mana vent, we think. He looks fine, but I didn't want to take any chances." The witch studied his face, turning it this way and that, then she stroked back his hair, combing it through her fingers.

"You look all right," the witch told him. "But just to be safe, stay here for observation for a little while. It may be a few hours, it may be a day or two."
Maia emerged from the cottage, a bemused look on her face.

"I thought I heard . . ." she trailed off, catching sight of Sara. "It can't be . . . Khalira? No, of course not, that's impossible," she mumbled. "Little Sara?"

"Queen Maia, I'm so glad to see you're safe," Sara responded, bowing.

"Oh, don't be so stiff!" Maia ran to the elf, hugging her and kissing her on both cheeks. "I haven't seen you for years! Oh, you shouldn't have got dragged into this mess!"

"You know my mother?" Erlina asked, blinking.

"I told you when we met, she and my mother used to take tea together," Sara replied. "She was my mother's dearest friend." Tyrian merely stared. "I told you I wasn't doing this for you." She shrugged.

Tyrian was asked to lie down in Rosie's spare room. She gave him a mug of what he recognised as tea. It seemed to be the default British response to *everything*.

"I was expecting medicine," he said, as he sat up to take the cup from her.

"Tea first, medicine later," Rosie replied. "I don't know what to give you. This mana vent. You were hanging over it?"

"Not exactly," he said, looking down. "I . . . I was trying to reach Lir . . . I failed . . . She . . . her hair was turning grey, and we got her out but she jumped back in and . . . it went white . . . she went completely white and . . . crumbled . . . " Rosie shuddered.

"I'm sorry," she said. "But I had to ask you. So tell me, when did you last drink blood?"

"About . . . a week and a half ago, perhaps two," he answered.

"How often do you normally have to drink?" Rosie asked.

"I'd say every two weeks, sometimes I can manage three," he replied. "But three is pushing it."

"Are you thirsty now?" she asked.

"No," he replied.

"Do you remember being thirsty before today?" she continued.

"Yes," he said, sitting up. "I got stuck on Earth, and I had to use a lot of magic to get about, and I was getting thirsty but there was nothing I could do about it, not to mention Grandma Connie bit me. With one thing and another, blood was the last thing on my mind."

"I see . . ." Rosie mused. "I think perhaps your mana level being low coupled with only scant exposure to the vent means you've escaped damage. Unfortunately, fairy physiology is different to humans, and we still don't know how to tell early mana damage in humans without the tell tale changes in hair and eye colour."

"Meaning?" he asked. Rosie shrugged.

"You're a vampire anyway, so any damage done to you would be masked by your already visible symptoms, i.e.: fangs and blood requirements. I suppose all we can do is wait and see. If I had to guess, I'd say any damage done would merely result in you needing blood more often."

"So . . ?" he prompted.

"You ought to be fine," she answered.

"Good," he replied. " . . . May I get some sleep? And if you have it, could I have a potion for that? It would be much appreciated." Rosie brought him the potion as he had asked, and left him alone.

When he awoke, it was dark, and someone was asleep on his legs. Struggling upright, and rubbing away his fatigue, he saw it was Will. Disturbed by the movement, Will woke up too. He practically launched himself at Tyrian, hugging him tight.

"Master Tyrian, you're awake!" he said. "They said you might be ill, so I didn't want to wake you. Do you need anything?" Tyrian hugged him back.

"Will, I promise I will never force you away from me again," he blurted out. "I'm so sorry, I-"

"I should have stayed on Earth like you wanted me to," Will cut him off. "It was my fault."

"You wouldn't be my fool if you did as you were told," Tyrian replied, laughing. "That's what fools are for." He planted a kiss on Will's forehead. Will kissed him back.

"You know full well that's nonsense, but that's what *you're* for," his jester said, grinning. "Um, speaking of what fools are for . . . if you're better, you need to return to Fairyland," Will told him. "The princess, Her Majesty Queen Maia and the others are holding down the fort, but there's still some unrest and it'll only get worse the longer you're away. Um, and Aurelia says if you don't call Parliament, she's going call it for you."

"Very well," Tyrian said, swinging his legs off the bed. "Bed rest never suited me anyway."

The fears of the people that they had lost yet another ruler quelled, and the Light Guard and Dark Army having taken into custody any dangerous dissenters, Tyrian ought to have been able to relax. But it was impossible. How could he sit still, how could he be calm, when he knew his parents were out there somewhere, trapped?

He returned to the temple of Gaia. Standing on the dais, he stared resentfully at the stone depressions in the now immovable elevator. He'd had it sealed. It was no wonder his ancestors had built a new temple to seal that thing off. But with Lir gone, and the pendant lost, he had no means of finding his parents.

Seeing her die had been scarring enough, but his failure to rescue her was also the loss of his one lead on his parents' whereabouts.

Only the desperate prayed here. Perhaps it was time to pray.

Getting down on his knees, he put his hands on the floor in front of him, and touched his head to the ground. He had no idea if that was right, but Gaia was in the ground, and so he should speak into it.

"If you're there, I'm sorry to wake you," he mumbled, feeling foolish. "I've lost my parents. I love them dearly, even though with my mother I'm sure it didn't seem like it. I'm sorry we weren't able to stop this war and all these awful things from happening, and I'm sure you're very disappointed. But they *tried* to stop it, and story karma doesn't seem to have dealt with them fairly for it. Please . . . help me find them."
He stayed still for a few moments, before sitting up and sighing. Gaia was asleep, if she was there at all. Perhaps the Gaia in the legend was merely the mana spring that had killed Lir. Was story karma even real? It wasn't justice, what had happened to his parents.

"He's up here Your Majesty," came Will's voice. "Master Tyrian?" Standing up, he called back;
"What is it Will?"
"Tyrian!" came a familiar voice. "I'm back sweetie, did you miss me?" Titania came skipping up the steps.

"A-Aunt Tannie?" he said. She was trailed by Will and another human boy he didn't know.

"I hear Morgana has been causing a ruckus," she said, embracing him. "It's such a pity. I suppose I'll just have to have her executed," she said, pouting.

"It's too late for that, Aunt Tannie . . ." he said.

"I see," she replied. "Oh well. She was getting a bit Grand Vizier-y. It's too bad, I was going to hand the crown to her if I didn't have any kids. I suppose I should have told her." She tutted. "Too late now. I guess I ought to get married or something, then. Have kids or whatever. Probably." She gave him a kiss on the temple before wandering off down the stairs. Tyrian and Will both stared after her.

"I can kinda see why Lir rebelled," Will remarked quietly.

"Oh, that's right, silly me! I nearly forgot!" she said, skipping back up the stairs. She dragged the other human boy with her. She held out a scroll, and pushed the young man forwards. "Look what I found!" she exclaimed, unrolling it. "And I brought this boy back with me. He isn't very happy about it, but he'll get over it."

"Aunt Tannie!" Tyrian scolded. "I'm surprised at you! You can't keep humans against their will, I thought you were better than that!"

"Oh yes dear, but," Titania continued. "Neens and Connall are missing yes? This boy is vital to getting them back, although it's not going to be easy."

"Young man, I apologise for my aunt," he said laying a hand on the boy's shoulder. "I see you're injured and you've had a hard time, but please, anything you can do to help me get my parents back will be greatly appreciated and rewarded."

After hearing what his aunt had to say, and making arrangements for the boy's employment, Tyrian sent him off with Will to find a place to stay. He lingered on the temple dais, until he was sure he was alone. Kneeling on the ground once more, he whispered;

"Thank you."

Standing up, he headed back towards the palace in the best mood he'd been in for weeks, months perhaps even years. He had Parliament to call, but the petty power struggles of the nobles would be nothing after all this.

Besides which . . . he had some parents to find.

THE END

Made in the USA
Charleston, SC
14 January 2017